ARROW'S EDGE MC

# EDGE
# OF
# TRUST

ARROW'S EDGE MC

## FREYA BARKER

Freya Barker writes a mean romance, I tell you! A REAL romance, with real characters and real conflict.

I've said it before and I'll say it again and again, Freya Barker is one of the BEST storytellers out there.

God, Freya Barker gets me every time I read one of her books. She's a master at creating a beautiful story you lose yourself in the moment you start reading.

Freya Barker has woven a delicate balance of honest emotions and well-formed characters into a tale as unique as it is gripping.

Such a truly beautiful story! The writing is gorgeous, the scenery is beautiful...

From Dust by Freya Barker is one of those special books. One of those whose plotline and characters remain with you for days after you finished it.

No amount of words could describe how this story made me feel, I think this is one I will remember forever, absolutely freaking awesome is not even close to how I felt about it.

Still Air was insightful, eye-opening, and I paused numerous times to think about my relationships with my own children. Anytime a book can evoke a myriad of emotions while teaching life lessons you'll continue to carry with you, it's a 5-star read.

In my opinion, there is nothing better than a Freya Barker book. With her final installment in her Portland, ME series, Still Air, she does not disappoint. From start to finish I was completely captivated by Pam, Dino, and the entire Portland family.

The one thing you can always be sure of with Freya's writing is that it will pull on ALL of your emotions; it's expressive, meaningful, sarcastic, so very true to life, real, hard-hitting and heartbreaking at times and, as is the case with this series especially, the story is at points raw, painful and occasionally fugly BUT it is also sweet, hopeful, uplifting, humorous and heart-warming.

ISBN: 9781988733814

Cover Design: Freya Barker
Editing: Karen Hrdlicka
Proofing: Joanne Thompson
Cover Image: J. Ashley Converse Photography
Cover Model: Christopher David

FREYA BARKER

# CHAPTER
# ONE

*Emme*

"I'll need a couple of boxes of whatever drywall screws are right for that cement board."

Rick looks up from the computer screen.

"Are you sure you don't want any help?" he asks, wearing a dubious expression.

It's not the first time he's offered, and the answer hasn't changed.

"I'm good. Appreciate it, though. You'll be the first to know if I change my mind."

I've been a regular at Durango Building Supply since I bought my dream house.

Well, not exactly a dream house yet, but it will be once I'm done with it.

I worked my ass off to buy the single-level, three-bedroom house backing onto Animas Mountain. It's the perfect location at the outskirts of town, not too isolated and within easy reach of all amenities, but far enough from the hustle and bustle to feel like a quiet sanctuary. Built in

1972, the place has never been updated. It needs a lot of work, but I'm not afraid to get my hands dirty. In fact, it was part of the attraction since it means I can make changes to fit my needs perfectly.

What sold the place to me was the large separate garage with a high overhead door. The previous owner had been a truck driver, who built the oversized building to fit his rig. The space was perfect for my studio and big enough to house some of my larger pieces. It had been the first project I tackled when I moved here a couple of years ago. With the skylights I installed and the new concrete floor and white-washed walls, it provides a bright open space for me to work on my metal sculpting.

Next, I'd turned my attention to the house itself, knocking down walls and gutting the small kitchen to create a large open living space from the three smaller main rooms. That took a hell of a lot longer to complete but has been well worth the amount of work. I love the roomy feel with the light from the big window at the front, and the large sliding glass doors at the back providing a view of Animas Mountain.

My current focus is on the main bedroom and en suite bathroom. I ripped out the old tub, sink, and toilet, and changed the bathroom layout slightly, putting in a large walk-in shower instead. I'm not a fan of baths myself, and in the unlikely event I have guests who do like them, I'll keep the tub in the main bathroom on the other side of the hallway. That one, and the two other bedrooms, will be last on my list of projects.

Renovating is costly, which is why I'm doing it myself and in stages. I plan to grow old here, so I'm not in a real rush. Besides, I have my day job and my metalworks as well, so I can only do so much at a time anyway.

"Okay, so I have twelve sheets of cement board, two buckets of compound, a couple of boxes of screws, and your rolls of tape. What about tile?" Rick wants to know.

"I haven't decided what I want yet."

I don't tell him I'll have to wait until the client who commissioned custom-made stair rails pays up. My savings account will run dangerously low after I pay for this delivery.

"When can you deliver?" I ask.

"Let me see." He starts flipping through a desk calendar. "Next Wednesday?"

I'll be working, but I may be able to slip home during the afternoon lull to receive it.

"Can we pin it down to between two and five?"

Rick grins. "Anything for you. Why don't I give you a heads-up when we're on our way?"

By the time I climb into my ratty old truck, my wallet is painfully light. I need to go after the twelve grand John Stoltenberg owes me for the six, sculpted metal rail panels I made him. Funny how it always seems to be the ones with the most money who are slowest to pay. I worked on those panels for close to three months, and they've already been installed in the investment banker's new custom home.

I make a quick call to his office on my way back to work to remind him. His assistant promises me she'll personally make sure the money is transferred to my account.

I sure hope so.

———

Friday nights are busy at the Backyard Edge. Even more so with Sophia gone for two weeks.

Sophia is the restaurant's manager and has taken her

first vacation since the birth of the twins. She's married to Tse, one of the Arrow's Edge MC members, and has three kids; seventeen-year-old Ravi, and three-year-old twins, Ella and Wyatt. Tse's club owns the Backyard Edge.

The family is in Arizona, visiting Sophia's parents, and I'm covering for her while they're away, but it means added responsibilities I don't exactly consider fun. I'd much rather stick to tending bar. I can handle the occasional pain in the ass customer, but don't have Sophia's gentle touch and endless patience when it comes to dealing with staff.

Right now, that means figuring out what the fuck Fred is up to, marching around the restaurant with a plate of fried chicken and yelling at the customers. The guy was Sophia's last hire, and I'm still not sure what the hell to make of him. He's supposed to have many years of experience waiting tables and, according to Sophia, comes with high recommendations. I'm starting to wonder if those previous employers weren't simply eager to get rid of him when they gave him the high praise.

Fred is probably in his fifties, abrasive with both customers and the rest of us, and is plain weird. I'm the last person to judge by appearances—hell, with tattoos all over my body, I probably look like a freak to some—but this guy takes strange to a whole new level. Judging by his unnatural orange tan he takes beta-carotene supplements by the fistfuls, and I'm positive those ink-black sideburns and disturbingly bushy eyebrows were drawn on his face by a five-year-old gone rogue with a black Sharpie.

The man draws attention on a good day, but right now he appears to be having a meltdown over a plate of chicken no one seems to remember ordering.

"Fred!" I call out to get his attention when he heads

back to the loud bachelor party taking up three tables at the front of the restaurant.

These guys have been a rowdy bunch since they walked in two hours ago. They only placed their dinner orders twenty minutes ago, after repeated prompting on our part, but they've been drinking the whole time.

Most nights—especially on the weekends—one of the Arrow's Edge brothers will be sitting at the bar. The sight of a rough-looking biker is usually enough to deter any trouble. Of course, tonight would be the one night the stool at the bar stays empty, so I've been watching the group like a hawk, waiting for a sign things are getting out of hand.

*Fucking Fred.* The last thing I need is the trouble I can see coming a mile away.

I grab the leather slapjack and hustle out from behind the bar when I see Fred slam the plate down on the middle of the three tables. A piece of chicken bounces up, hitting one of the guys in the chest. He jumps to his feet and swings around on Fred, towering over the five-foot-six waiter.

I reach the table just as the offended party grabs Fred by the front of his turtleneck and hauls back his other fist.

"Enough!" I bark, forcefully shoving my waiter out of the line of fire.

Of course, that places me squarely in it and I try to duck out of the way, swinging the slapjack to ward off the approaching fist. His knuckles graze my cheekbone the instant before my weapon hits his arm.

*Shit.* That's going to leave a mark.

Judging from the guy's curses though, I'm not the only one who got hurt.

All over a goddamn plate of chicken.

---

*Honon*

I scrape the remains of dinner off the last of the plates and hand it to Shilah, who is loading the industrial-sized dishwasher.

"That it?" he asks.

I take a glance around the kitchen, normally Lisa's domain. She's married to Brick, one of my brothers, and looks after the clubhouse. She was feeling under the weather this afternoon, and Brick whisked her off to the cottage at the back of the compound where they live with their three grandkids. I assured her Shilah and I would take care of dinner and cleanup.

Our simple fare of meatloaf, potatoes, and coleslaw was nowhere near the quality of food Lisa usually dishes up, but it served its purpose. It filled the bellies of the four boys we currently have in our care, as well as the two prospects, and the four of us living at the clubhouse. A relatively quiet night compared to most.

"Yup." I turn to Shilah, one of our younger members. "You gonna head to the gym as well?"

One of the other brothers, Mika, left for The Edge boxing gym half an hour ago to get in a workout.

"Nah. Gonna watch some TV in my room."

"You okay?"

I narrow my eyes at him. He's been moping around for almost a week now.

"Fine," is his curt response.

"You've been miserable all fucking week," I point out

before venturing a guess. "You still seeing that hairdresser?"

He snaps a glance my way.

"No. That's done."

*Bingo.*

"What happened?"

Can't believe I just asked that. There's a reason I choose not to get involved with anyone. It's messy and feelings are bound to get hurt. Much easier just to avoid the hassle altogether. Makes for a more predictable existence. So I'm the last one anyone should come to for relationship advice, and I have no interest hearing about them.

Still, I just opened that door.

"She dumped me and I don't wanna talk about it," he grumbles, brushing past me and out the door.

I blow out a breath of relief. Dodged that bullet.

With one last look around the kitchen, I flick off the light and walk into the clubhouse where I see Nosh sitting by himself at the bar.

Nosh, the former club president before Ouray was voted in, is old as dirt. The man used to command authority, despite being deaf and communicating mostly through sign language, but these days he's barely a shell of his former self.

He ran this club with an iron fist back when Arrow's Edge was still running arms and drugs. Ouray was responsible for turning the club around since he took up the gavel. Changing the direction of the club to legitimate businesses and a focus on sheltering and mentoring young boys. Mostly street kids, runaways, or boys who threatened to fall through the cracks. We offer them what the world out there failed to provide them with; a roof over their heads and a future to strive for.

That's how a lot of us ended up here. Lost boys ourselves until Nosh and his late wife, Momma, took us in. He gave us structure and purpose, a brotherhood and a family.

Jesus, look at him now. Unable to do much by himself anymore, let alone look after anyone else. His body was already deteriorating, but in the last few years his mind has been going as well. It's our turn to look after him.

Yuma—his son, who lives with his wife and kids just down the road—has been trying to get him to agree to go into a home. Not because we can't take care of him, but because it may be less stressful for Nosh to be in a quieter and more predictable environment. The clubhouse is definitely not that.

But with the faint hold on reality the stubborn old goat still has, he adamantly refuses to be anywhere other than here; the clubhouse he created.

He is stooped over, the beer I left him with earlier—his one daily indulgence, despite doctor's orders—still half full. I put a gentle hand on his shoulder and lightly shake him awake.

"Come on, old man, let's get you ready for bed."

I wrap my arm around his waist and lead him through the sitting area, where a couple of the older kids are watching TV, to the back hallway. It's not even nine but Nosh doesn't complain. He's been going to bed earlier and earlier in the past couple of months.

In his room I flick on the TV which is already set to his favorite channel, Investigation Discovery. There's an episode of *Very Scary People* on, which he's probably seen five times before already. He loves these true crime shows, and doesn't seem to notice most of them are reruns.

I guide him into the small bathroom, leaving him to take

care of business. Then I wait until I hear the toilet flush before opening the door to help him out of his boots and jeans. His eyes snap up, glaring at me.

*"Who are you?"* he signs.

"Honon," I explain, spelling it out with my fingers. "Remember? I live next door."

I point to the wall separating our rooms.

His eyes narrow as he studies me, but I'm still not sure he knows who I am.

*"You need a fucking haircut."*

My hand automatically goes to the beard I haven't trimmed in God knows how long. The same for my hair, I can't remember the last time I've seen a barber. His words have me dart a quick and very rare glance in the bathroom mirror, and I'm almost surprised at the face looking back. I look like fucking Grizzly Adams. The only recognizable part of my face are the blue eyes staring back. The rest of it is covered in hair.

Christ, the old man is right; I badly need a haircut. Maybe it'll help him remember me.

Tomorrow.

Five minutes later, I have him undressed and under the covers. He's already dozing off again. His TV is set to automatically turn off after a couple of hours so I leave it going as I back out of the room.

I stand there for a moment, unsure what I'm going to do with the rest of my night, if anything. My days of partying are mostly behind me. It simply doesn't hold the same appeal it once did. There was a time we had parties in the clubhouse on an almost nightly basis, but with a lot of my brothers getting into serious relationships, those are far more rare now and mostly family affairs. Nothing like the wild nights we've had here in the past.

Before I have a chance to make up my mind, the phone in my pocket rings. It's the restaurant's number.

"What's up?"

Mack, one of the bartenders at the Backyard Edge, is on the other end.

"We've got some trouble here, you may wanna send someone over. Emme is getting into it with a bunch of yahoos."

Emme, the blond bartender with a tough attitude too big for a woman her size, and a big reason why I avoid the restaurant if I can.

Fucking great.

"Into it, how?" I snap, already heading for the front of the clubhouse.

"Into it, as in the guy is holding his arm like she broke it, and she'll wake up with a shiner tomorrow."

I jog the rest of the way to my bike.

# CHAPTER
# TWO

*Honon*

When I drive up to the restaurant, I notice a group of young guys hanging around toward the back of the parking lot. One guy in particular stands out, holding his arm cradled against his body.

Pulling the bike around the rear of the building to the smaller staff lot, I leave it parked near the back door and head inside. Raised voices can be heard coming from the small office across from the kitchen.

I'm about to poke my head in when the door flies open, hitting me in the chest, and a short, skinny guy comes barreling out. He glares at me and slips past me. Swinging my head around, I watch him disappear out the door I just came in through.

I could've sworn the guy was wearing a mask.

"Who the fuck was that?"

Emme's head snaps up when I walk in, and I grind my jaw at the sight of the red, puffy skin around her right eye.

"Jesus, you startled me." She puffs out a breath as she pushes up from the desk. "What are you doing here?"

"Mack," I respond by way of explanation. "And you didn't answer my question."

"That was Fred, Sophia's new waiter."

"Really? That guy? He fucking looks like Groucho Marx and Chucky had a baby. That can't be good for business."

Emme snorts, her eyes sparkling as she grins at me.

"Believe me, that's the least of his problems. His attitude stinks, he's unpleasant to the customers, and he doesn't hold up well under pressure."

"He definitely wasn't smiling on his way out the door. Did you just fire him or something?"

Emme rounds the desk and leans her butt against it, supporting herself with her hands on the edge. Despite her small stature, she looks every bit the part of a tough cookie. Worn jeans, a printed tank leaving her tattooed, finely sculpted arms exposed, and a stubborn tilt to her dainty chin. When she shakes her head no, I notice her wincing a little, drawing my attention back to the swelling on her face.

"We had a rowdy group and he didn't handle it well, so I had to step in. He didn't appreciate being sent home."

I point at her face.

"If he's in any way responsible for what happened to your face, he's a hazard and you shoulda canned his ass," I grumble.

"Easy for you to say," she returns defensively. "It's not like we have a ton of flex in the schedule with Sophia away, and it's the weekend. We're booked solid tomorrow night. I can't afford to lose a waiter now."

I see the tension on her face and decide not to push it, but my ass will be on a stool at the bar tomorrow night, keeping a close eye on the guy. One wrong move or comment and that clown is out on his ass.

"Let's go." I grab for her arm and haul her to her feet. "That eye needs ice or you won't be able to see out of it by tomorrow morning."

She doesn't protest when I lead her to the large kitchen across the hallway. Chris, the restaurant's chef, looks up when we walk in.

"I notice you didn't call the cops," I point out after I lift her to sit on one of the prep counters along the wall.

Chris silently hands me a bag of frozen vegetables wrapped in a towel and I press it to her face.

"There was no need. We handled it."

"The fucker should be charged with assault. He hit you."

She brushes my hand out of the way and takes over holding the towel pressed to her eye.

"And I may have broken his arm. He threatened to sue, I reminded him he threw the first punch and I had a restaurant full of witnesses. His buddies dragged him outside and that was the end of it."

I brace my arms on either side of her hips and lean in.

"If that was the end of it, then why are he and his buddies still hanging around outside?"

"You're kidding, right?"

She drops the ice pack to the counter and shoves me out of the way before hopping down, grabbing a cast iron pan off the shelf, and she rushes out of the kitchen. I follow her into the hallway.

"What the hell do you think you're doing?"

She looks over her shoulder at me as she yanks open the back door.

"Fred."

Realization hits me. The waiter. *Fuck.*

She's barely through the door when I manage to grab her by the shoulder and slow her down as I move past. I don't see anything out of place in the employee parking lot as I rush to the corner of the building. Aside from a couple of remaining vehicles, this side is quiet as well, the group of men I saw earlier no longer there. When I look behind me, I notice Emme heading in the opposite direction toward the alley running along the other side of the restaurant. She raises the cast iron pan over her shoulder as she disappears around the corner.

*Christ,* she's a pain in my ass.

My boots pound the pavement as I hoof it along the back of the building after her. Slipping into the alley I catch sight of her rushing toward a crumpled form lit by the single flood lamp halfway down.

"Call an ambulance," she calls out when I approach.

My phone is already in my hand when I hear a man's voice.

"No ambulance, I'm fine."

Like a jack-in-the-box, the waiter I saw rush out of the restaurant earlier sits up.

"You're hurt," Emme protests.

"I just had the wind knocked out of me. I'm fine," he repeats, trying to get to his feet.

I grab his arm to steady him.

"What happened?"

He looks up at me. Too busy staring at those eyebrows, I don't notice the mark on his jaw until he lifts his hand to his face.

"That idiot from the restaurant happened, that's what," he snaps. "When I walked out, he was messing around near my car. He spotted me, chased me down the alley, and if I hadn't tripped over that pothole, I would've gotten away too. He only got a few kicks in before his buddies pulled him away and took off. I was just catching my breath when I heard you approach and thought they'd come back, so I played dead."

"I think you should be checked out," Emme tells him.

He squints his eyes when he turns to her.

"Maybe I should," he suddenly agrees, changing his tune. "Who knows how badly I've been injured. I hope the restaurant has good insurance."

What a piece of work.

I can't say I'm surprised after he made a point to mention the pothole tripping him up, but Emme looks taken aback.

"What the hell for?" she exclaims.

The little weasel shrugs. "Like I said, if not for that pothole, I wouldn't have gotten hurt."

He pretends to stumble back until he hits the wall and slides back down to the ground.

"I'm suddenly not feeling so good."

It takes everything out of me not to plant my own boot in his face, but instead I pull my phone from my pocket.

*Fucking worm.*

————

*Emme*

I'm bone-tired and my face is throbbing when I finally lock the back door behind me a little before midnight.

Fred was hauled off in an ambulance quite a while ago

already, but the cops, who'd showed up as well, took their sweet time questioning everyone about the night's events. They left half an hour ago and I sent Mack—who was the last to remain—home right after that. Of course, I still had to get the orders in or we won't have fresh supplies for tomorrow. I'm late as it is, since our main suppliers require a minimum of twelve hours' notice, but Saturday morning deliveries are usually a bit later. I hope they'll be able to rush my order through, or else I'll have Chris flipping out when he comes in tomorrow.

I startle when I turn around to head to my truck and find Honon sitting sideways on his parked bike.

"I thought you'd left."

"And leave you by yourself?"

I square my shoulders.

"Wouldn't be the first time. I can get myself safely home, you know? I do it almost every other night."

He gets to his feet and hooks his thumb over his shoulder toward the last two vehicles parked side by side at the far edge of the lot. My pickup and Fred's car.

"Not tonight," he states. "Not in that."

It's then I notice Fred's vehicle has an odd slant to it and my truck is sitting awfully low to the ground.

"You've got to be fucking kidding me," I spit out, heading toward my Ranger.

All four of my tires flat, slashed to shit. Three of Fred's as well. Those bastards. Replacing four tires is going to cost a sweet penny. It'll deplete me until Stoltenberg comes through on his payment.

*Shit.*

I hear Honon's footsteps come up behind me.

"Not sure if it was just the one guy or all of them, and I'm guessing he would've done the same to all the vehicles parked back here. It was sheer luck on his part he happened upon your truck first."

I reach into my backpack and pull out my phone.

"That's vandalism. I need to call this in."

"The cops already know. I pointed it out to them earlier."

My back instantly goes up.

"You knew? Why the hell didn't you tell me?"

He shrugs it off. His expression is hard to decipher underneath all of that facial hair, but I'm pretty sure those clear eyes don't show even an ounce of remorse.

"You had your hands full. I took care of it."

Annoyed, I cross my arms over my chest and throw him a raised eyebrow.

"Took care of it?"

Other than a twitch of his bushy mustache, he shows no sign of reaction to my sharp tone.

"Brick's gonna haul your truck up to the compound first thing tomorrow and get new tires put on. You can catch a ride in with him. We'll make sure the truck is back here by the end of your shift."

Okay, that's kind of nice.

I drop my arms to my side, feeling a little embarrassed I got my back up so quickly. I'm not normally this easily riled, but there's something about Honon that has me off balance. Maybe because in contrast to most of his brothers, I have a difficult time reading him.

Feeling suddenly self-conscious, I squirm a bit under his quiet scrutiny.

"How am I getting home?" I ask with a slight edge.

He turns sideways and points at his bike.

"Heading up the mountain anyway. I'll give you a ride."

My inner child does an excited fist pump I'm trying not to show on the outside.

For years, I've looked at those bikes longingly. I've always wanted a chance to ride on one. It's not like I haven't been asked before, but those offers were few and far between and would involve some kind of expectation. Since I wasn't interested, I declined, not wanting to send the wrong message.

This time though, it's for purely practical purposes. I seriously doubt Honon suddenly developed some kind of interest in me, so I feel safe enough accepting his offer. Besides, like he said, he's going past my place anyway. The clubhouse is just five minutes up the road from me, he doesn't even have to go out of his way.

He flips up his seat and lifts out a helmet, handing it to me. It's one of those cool half-helmets that sit on top of your head like a bad haircut. It fits a bit too big on me and I fiddle blindly as I try to fasten the straps under my chin. Honon impatiently brushes my hands aside and does the job himself.

I hold my breath when I notice how close he suddenly is. About a foot taller than me, he has to bend low to be able to see what his fingers are doing. When his knuckles brush my jaw I gasp, feeling goosebumps breaking out all over my skin.

His eyes suddenly lift and lock on mine.

"Breathe, Emme," he rumbles, before dropping his hands and stepping away.

He casually swings his leg over the bike and pats the seat behind him.

"Ever been on a bike before?" he asks when I don't move from my spot.

"Nope."

"See this peg? It's a footrest. There's one on the other side too. Put your hands on my shoulders, your left foot on this one here and swing your leg over."

First, I slip both arms through the straps of my backpack, then I take in a deep breath and do as he instructed.

I bite my lips to keep from grinning like an idiot when I hit the seat and he starts up the engine, the deep rumble vibrating through my body. I can't seem to stop my ass from sliding forward a little, no matter how hard I wiggle to stay in place.

Honon reaches back with both hands, hooking them behind my knees and pulling me snug against his back.

"Wrap your arms around me and let your body lean into the turns with mine," he says over his shoulder.

"Don't you have a helmet?" I ask when I notice he's not wearing one.

His longish hair is tied back at the base of his neck with a leather string.

"You're wearing it."

"Isn't that dangerous?"

He turns to look at me again. This time I swear he's smiling, even though all I see is the crinkles around his eyes.

"Been a good twenty years since I last wiped out. I'll be fine."

"Famous last words," I can't resist mumbling against his back.

His only response is to grab my hands, which I have lightly resting on his hips, and pull them all the way around to rest on his stomach.

"That's better."

The next thing I know, we're whizzing through the

almost deserted streets of Durango, the cool wind stinging my cheeks.

I fucking love it.

It's a bit dicey when we leave the town and the street-lights behind and head up the mountain. I keep checking the side of the road, afraid some wildlife—an elk or a deer —will jump out in front of us. Wouldn't be the first time something like that happened. I'm relieved when we reach my turnoff without incident but sad the ride is almost over.

I can't remember ever mentioning where I live, but I'm not surprised Honon seems to know exactly where to go. If I've learned anything about the members of Arrow's Edge over the past few years, it's that not much escapes them, and if one knows something, they all do.

When he stops the bike in front of my house, I quickly dismount and try to undo the strap under my chin.

"Here, let me get it," he offers, reaching out to do it for me, but his eyes remain on my face. "I'm guessing you enjoyed that?"

"It was okay." I shrug, trying to make myself look casual as I hand him the helmet, but the big grin on my face is a dead giveaway. "Appreciate the ride, though."

He doesn't say anything when I turn and head for the house, but I don't hear him driving off until I close and lock the front door behind me.

# CHAPTER
# THREE

*Honon*

I knock on the door of the nondescript apartment in the new building, near the hospital, on the south side of town.

I take a step to the side, out of view of the peephole, and listen to footsteps approaching before the door opens.

"What do you want?"

Daylight doesn't do this guy any favors, and I try not to get distracted by his appearance. I'm here to deliver a message.

"Hear you're back to work tomorrow."

He plants his hands on his hips and tilts his head.

"Yeah? So? I don't see how that's any business of yours."

Still with the attitude.

"That's easy, I sign your paychecks."

He scoffs, clearly not buying it, but when I continue to quietly stare him down, I see doubt creeping in.

"Sophia signs my checks," he finally sputters.

I shake my head.

"And who do you think signs hers?"

He shrugs like he doesn't care, but I can tell I've piqued his interest.

"You don't have a clue, do you? Let me spell it out. Arrow's Edge MC owns the restaurant. I'm Arrow's Edge, therefore—technically—I'm the one signing your paychecks. See how that works?"

He nods, clearly not as stupid as he looks. It's not necessarily common knowledge the club owns the Backyard Edge. Not that it's some big secret, but it's also not something we advertise. There are still plenty of people with negative associations when they hear the club's name.

"Right, glad we've got that cleared up. Seemed important for you to know before you return to work tomorrow. If it had been up to me, your ass would've been fired after what happened Friday night, but Emme decided to give you a little leeway. I'm here to make sure you don't abuse her goodwill and make trouble for her."

"I would never—" he blusters, but I cut him off.

"Oh, I think you would have. Don't forget, I heard what you said to her in the alley," I remind him. "That said, I think we've come to an understanding. Yeah?"

"Of course," is his immediate answer.

Still don't trust the guy, but at least he knows who he's dealing with and that should give him pause.

I can feel his eyes on my back as I make my way down the stairs to where my bike is parked.

The past two nights I hung out at the Backyard, keeping Mack company at the bar and making sure there'd be no more disruptions like Friday night. It didn't hurt I could quietly observe Emme going about her business.

Other than saying hi when I walked in, she kept her distance, working on the other side when she was behind the bar, and generally avoiding me. When I showed up last night, she didn't even say hello, just shook her head as if my presence annoyed her and mumbling something about scaring the customers.

During lulls I'd chat with Leah—she's the wife of one of my brothers and works there—or Mack, which is how I found out Fred would be back on Tuesday. He'd called in, saying he felt better and would be in for his next shift.

It wasn't hard to find his address through employee records stored on our server, and since I had nothing better to do this morning, I decided to pay him a visit.

Mondays the restaurant is closed, and as I pull away from the apartment building, I wonder what Emme is up to today. For some godforsaken reason, my thoughts keep drifting to her. It's starting to piss me off.

Still, when I drive past a shopping plaza and spot the sign for a new barber, it's her comment about scaring customers that has me pull into the parking lot.

"Oh my. You need some work, honey."

The effeminate voice is a surprise from the rotund man, who looks up when I walk in. With a shaved head, ample tattoos, and heavy rings on almost every finger, he looks pretty rough. You'd expect a big booming voice to match the look, and not that high-pitched lilt.

There is no one else in the small shop, which has a retro look to it.

"I need a cut."

He makes a clicking sound with his tongue.

"I can *see* that. Come sit here and let Bruno take care of you."

He pats the backrest of one of two red leather barber chairs with one hand, while motioning me over with the other. I'm guessing he's Bruno.

This feels a little like being lured into a spiderweb, but I force my feet to move and take the offered seat.

His hands land on my shoulders, giving them a little squeeze.

"You look worried, but there's no need to be," he coos, leaning close. "We'll get you looking like a million bucks without taking away from that badass appeal. Just lean back, honey, I'm gonna make those baby-blues shine."

Any other man might've taken that as his cue and beelined it out of here, but I'd like to think I'm tougher than most, and force myself to lay my head back when he reclines the chair.

Half an hour later, he sits me back up.

"Well, look at what was hiding under all that fur. Two of the most adorable dimples I've ever seen."

*Adorable.* Yeah, just what I was going for.

A little worried, I glance at my reflection. It's not too horrible, at least I still have a full head of hair, even though it seems to have all gone gray. What beard I have left is little more than scruff, but at least I don't look near as threatening. I'm not sure whether that's a good thing or not.

That scale quickly heads toward regret once I get back to the clubhouse.

The first person I see is Lisa who nods and mumbles, "Much better," before disappearing into the kitchen. But when I turn toward the large table and join a couple of the guys for lunch, the smart-ass remarks start flying.

Brick's mumbled, "Pretty boy," is a good reminder why I grew the full beard to begin with.

"Goddamn, you look like a choirboy, not a biker," and, "Did you get your nails done too?" are not unexpected. A little ribbing from the guys.

It's Ouray's "What's her name?" and Shilah following

up with, "Was wondering why you were suddenly spending time at the Backyard," that starts getting under my skin.

Rather than giving them a reaction—which is what they're hoping for—I grab a couple of sandwiches and get up.

"Leaving so soon?" Yuma taunts. "Or are we getting too close to the truth?"

Determined not to give him an inch, I flash my dimples.

"Don't flatter yourselves. I've gotta get up to the gun range. Couple of cops are coming in to run the practice course."

I'm not lying. I have bookings for several groups in the coming days. Refresher exercises for Durango PD officers, set up by Police Chief Benedetti. I spoke to him last week. Crime is on the rise in Durango, and the chief wants to make sure his officers are ready to face any situation.

The gun range at the back of the property used to be Nosh's baby, but with his failing health, membership had dropped to only a handful and the place had fallen into disrepair. Two years ago, Ouray brought it up during a club meeting and wanted a vote on whether to close it down completely or find someone willing to take it on. I volunteered, took over the daily running and, with the help of some of the guys, started making some upgrades and decided to build a course for firearms drills.

We finalized it fall of last year and it's regularly booked by local law enforcement or private groups. For the first time in years, we'll be recording a nice revenue, which I'm pretty pumped about.

I spend a lot of my time up there but I don't mind. The range has become my thing, and it's a good place to hide when I want to be alone.

Like now.

Ignoring my brothers' heckling, I turn and head for the door.

---

*Emme*

Of course.

I let fly a litany of profanities when I chip away the last of the old linoleum in the bathroom.

It had taken forever to clean up. Whoever put the stuff down back then made sure it would stay glued down forever.

Being careful with my limited budget, I'd tried to save some money by preserving the subfloor. It had looked to be in decent condition and the many, many hours I've spent picking away at the stubborn flooring seemed worth it.

Until now.

*Shit.*

I was so determined to finish it today so by Wednesday, when my cement board is delivered, I'd be ready to get started on the walls. Looking at the rotting portion of subfloor I uncovered today, I know that's not going to happen.

It wouldn't be so bad if it was limited to the bathroom, I could probably patch it up, but it looks like it extends under the wall to the bedroom closet on the other side. Now I'm going to have to pull up the old carpet there to assess the damage.

Disgusted, I toss the palette knife and small mallet on

the floor and get to my feet. I wince as I straighten up. Sitting on your knees for hours at a time really makes you feel your age. Not that forty is that old, but I'm definitely not as limber as I once was.

When I walk into the bedroom, my eye catches on the old alarm clock still plugged into the wall of the otherwise empty room. I've temporarily moved to the other end of the hallway, into one of the smaller spare rooms, while doing the work on this side and have been using my phone for my alarm.

Almost four thirty already. Where has the day gone?

I had so many things planned but the hours got sucked up by that damn linoleum.

My Mondays are always busy doing shit I don't have time for, or am too tired to do the rest of the week. Today that list included a run to see Brick up at the clubhouse and pay him for the new tires he put on my Ranger.

I tried paying the young guy who dropped the truck off Saturday afternoon, but he waved me off, saying I should take it up with Brick today.

I don't like owing anyone money. Maybe I can still catch him at the shop and get that settled up. Then I can take a quick run into town, grab some fast food to bring home, and have a look at the closet floor after I eat.

No time to clean up though, but I hardly think Brick's going to notice, let alone care, about a little dirt. I can hit a drive-thru in town and no one will be the wiser.

Rushing downstairs, I stuff my phone in my backpack, grab my keys off the hook, and head outside.

The prospect, who waves me through the gate at the club's compound, directs me to the auto shop next to the clubhouse. I find Brick inside, his head under the hood of what looks to be an old Camaro with two teenage boys looking on.

"Emme. What are you doing here?" Brick asks when he spots me.

"Came to settle my bill. What do you prefer? Check or credit?"

"What bill?"

He wipes his hands on a rag he pulls from his back pocket, keeping his head low, but I catch a slight smirk on his face.

"For the tires, Brick," I snap, irritated. "Don't pretend you don't know what I'm talking about."

I'm not some charity case. I can afford a set of tires, even if it means postponing some other stuff. Plenty of others are not as lucky.

"Oh, I know what you're talking about, but there's no bill to settle."

"Of course there is," I huff. "You had to buy the tires. Those are brand new."

"That they are, but I promise you I didn't pay a penny for them. Heck, I didn't even put them on." He juts a thumb at the two teens. "These two numbnuts did. They needed the practice. All I did was supervise."

I narrow my eyes at him, recognizing the pile of bullshit he's trying to feed me.

"Don't play me for an idiot."

He throws up his hands defensively.

"Hey, I'm not. It's the God's honest truth. These boys need to learn somehow."

Exasperated, I concede that point.

"Fine, but there's still the cost of the tires."

"I swear on my grandson, I didn't pay for them."

His eyes slide over my shoulder and one side of his mouth jerks up.

A ripple of awareness skates over my skin as someone walks up behind me.

"But why don't you ask him," Brick suggests, jerking his chin at the person I can sense at my back. "He picked them up."

I swing around on who I'm pretty sure is Honon, but the sight of him has me momentarily distracted.

"Whoa, what happened to you?" flies from my mouth before I can check it.

I've seen him around from time to time in the few years since I started at the Backyard, but I had no idea this was hiding underneath all that hair.

Hello.

Ignoring my comment, Honon darts a glare over my head at Brick's deep chuckle and a few snickers from the boys.

Then he grumbles, "It's called a haircut," and without looking at me, turns around and heads outside.

"Hey, wait just a minute," I call after him, belatedly remembering why I'm here.

I catch him halfway to the clubhouse.

"What?"

I jerk my chin up at his sharp tone.

"What do I owe you for my tires?"

"You don't owe me a thing."

I take a step closer and have to crane my neck to look him dead in the eye.

"I will if you won't let me pay, and I've worked too hard my whole life so I'd never be in anyone's debt to start now."

Something in his hard expression changes before he

drops his head and rubs a hand through his much shorter, but still fabulous hair.

"Christ, woman. I've never met anyone so eager to part with their money," he mutters.

"That's not it at all, I just—"

He cuts me off with a raised hand.

"Fine, I get it. Four hundred bucks."

I don't believe it for a second. I checked and the cheapest tires for my truck run more than a hundred bucks a pop. These are Goodyears, not cheap on the best of days. I'd figured I'd probably be out close to a grand, adding in labor.

He reads my dubious expression correctly and adds, "Buddy of mine works at Big O Tires. These were on sale and he gets a decent employee discount on top."

I'm not sure I trust he's telling the truth, but I don't know that I want to straight-out call him a liar. Besides, four hundred bucks would mean I still have a small buffer left in my savings.

Walking over to one of the picnic tables in front of the clubhouse, I pull my checkbook out of my backpack and write a check for the amount.

"Who do I make it out to? I assume Honon is not your full name?"

I watch his expression, fascinated by a pair of deep dimples appearing on the side of his mouth when he presses his lips together.

*Wow.* Who knew?

"Hank Wicks," he grinds out, not sounding too happy.

What a great name.

I write it in the appropriate space, tear the check out of my checkbook, and hand it over with a smile.

"Appreciate it."

Then I slip by him and head for my truck, noticing Brick standing outside the garage, a grin on his face.

Looking back at Honon when I open my door, I catch him staring.

"By the way," I call out. "Great haircut."

I can hear Brick laughing when I get behind the wheel.

# CHAPTER
# FOUR

*Emme*

I hate getting up early.

Unfortunately, I have no choice.

Some years ago, we had some issues at the Backyard with deliveries, and since then we make sure there are always two people at the restaurant in the morning. Sophia is usually there with one of the kitchen staff to receive supplies, but she's a morning person.

I'm not.

The final drops of coffee gurgle into my travel mug, and I yank it from the machine to take a greedy sip. *Fuck*, that's hot, but I drink it anyway. I need the shot of caffeine to get going, especially after last night.

Monday evening I spent ripping up the old carpet inside the main bedroom closet, finding more rotten subfloor. That led to ripping out the entire carpet in the room and taking down the wall between the closet and the bathroom.

Yesterday I had to work, but Mack was closing, so I got

out of there at a little after nine. I rushed home, determined to get the bathroom ready for cement board and tile before Durango Building Supplies drops off my order today.

It was after two when I finally got to bed and my damn alarm went off at five thirty.

Once in the truck, I drop my mug in the cupholder and rub my eyes with the heels of my hands to clear the grit. I'm just pulling out of my driveway when a bull elk saunters out of the trees on the other side and stops in the middle of the road, staring straight at me.

He's beautiful, almost mysterious as a faint halo of steam rises up from his hide in the pale light of a chilly May morning.

I don't move, watching as the animal seems to be gauging whether I'm friend or foe, until something spooks him and he darts back into the trees. He's long gone when I finally turn onto the road, feeling a whole lot better about my early start.

The lot is still empty when I arrive at the restaurant and park my truck. No sign yet of Terry, one of the sous-chefs. When I unlock the back door and walk in, I almost trip over a garbage bag someone must have forgotten to throw into the dumpster. Grabbing it, I head back out and wrestle the heavy lid up to toss the bag inside before letting go.

The lid slams shut with a satisfying bang, but when I take a step toward the back door, I hear a loud squeal. Almost like a trapped animal.

I quickly swing back to the dumpster when I notice a box wedged between the back of the bin and the wall. The squeals now sound more like crying, and they're coming from that box. The hair on the back of my neck stands on end, I'm pretty sure that's no animal.

I notice it has some weight to it as I carefully try to pull the box free. My stomach is in knots when I set it down and lift back the flaps. A red, scrunched-up face, eyes squeezed shut, and little mouth opens wide as the baby wails.

*Jesus.*

What sick fuck would leave a baby behind a dumpster in a restaurant parking lot?

Tiny fists are punching the air, working their way out of the pink blanket the baby was wrapped in. A girl? Poor little thing must be freezing. I reach for the box to take her inside, where it's warm, when I notice an envelope pinned to the blanket. Something is scribbled on the front and my heart almost stops when I read what it says.

For Emme,
In case of an emergency.

What on earth?

I'm trying to think of anyone I know who had a baby, let alone leave her for me to find. I can't come up with a single person. Granted, I've lost touch with a few friends these past few years, but I seriously doubt they'd pick me to leave a baby with.

Another loud wail has me snatch up the box, baby and all, and rush into the restaurant. By the time I get to the small office, the baby's crying seems to have slowed down.

I flick on the light, set the box on the desk, and reach inside. The moment I pluck the little body from the blankets and rest her against my shoulder, the crying stops. Then I reach for the envelope.

I didn't know where else to turn, should things go terribly wrong.

If you are reading this, they clearly have.

I've stumbled on something big that has put a target on my back, and I'm afraid my kids are in danger too.

Don't trust the authorities! Don't trust anyone!

I beg of you to protect my babies.

Athena is 6 months old and I'm sure you remember Malco.

Please, please, keep them safe and tell them I will always love them.

Rhea.

*Holy shit.*

"Emme?" Terry's head pokes around the door. "Whoa, is that a…"

"A baby, yes. It's my sister's," I blurt out, even though I don't have a sister. "I'm babysitting for a few hours."

I'm rattled by the letter, trying to wrap my head around what it all means, but until I know what the hell is going on, I need to come up with an excuse why I suddenly have a baby in my arms. This happens to be the first one that comes to mind.

It seems to satisfy Terry.

"Oh, cool," he replies easily, dismissing the baby and my pathetic cover story. "Sorry I ran a little late. The truck was just pulling in. I can take care of it. You look like you have your hands full."

"That'd be great, Terry, thanks."

As soon as he leaves, I close the office door for some privacy and sag down on the love seat. The baby feels heavy against my shoulder as my thoughts swirl.

Rhea?

I haven't seen or talked to her in at least a year, if not more. Hell, I didn't even know she was pregnant. Our last conversation ended in an argument when she mentioned the mystery man she'd started seeing was married. I warned her but she'd fallen for his stories. Believed he'd leave his wife so he could be with her. She didn't want to listen to reason.

Is this baby his?

And where the hell is Malco?

He was about seven when I moved out of the trailer and into my new place, so that would make him nine years old now.

Rhea and I had not only worked together at The Pink Petal, but we both lived at the Oxbow Trailer Park. We'd forged a friendship and, from time to time, I even looked after her kid if she had a shift when I was off.

Of course, we didn't see or talk to each other as much after I got this job, and especially once I bought my house, but we kept in touch until last spring.

Did she leave the little one in a box out back? I find that hard to believe. It makes more sense the boy did that, but why? And where is he?

I shift the baby on my shoulder so I can look at her. She's fast asleep, but eventually she's going to wake up and need a diaper change or food. Putting her carefully down on the couch beside me, I get to my feet and grab the blanket from the box to cover her with, moving the visitor's chair to block her in so she can't roll off the couch.

Then I sit down at the desk and read her note again.

*Holy hell*, I'm in over my head.

————

*Honon*

"Yeah," I groan, my eyes still glued shut as I answer my phone.

Didn't sleep a whole hell of a lot. Not with Nosh barging into my room in the middle of the night, confused and agitated. Woke up the entire damn clubhouse. It had taken Shilah and myself a while to get him settled back in his room, but each time I tried to leave, he'd start getting out of bed again.

I spent a good chunk of the night sitting on the floor beside him until he finally fell asleep and I could crawl back in bed.

"Honon?"

At the sound of Emme's voice, my eyes snap open and I'm suddenly wide awake.

"You're talking to him."

I lift the phone away to take a quick glance at my screen and see it's not even seven.

"I...uhm...I need your help."

Alarmed, I swing my legs over the side of the bed and reach down to grab my jeans.

"What's wrong?"

I put my phone on speaker so I can get dressed.

"I wouldn't have bothered you, but I can't seem to get hold of Leah. She's probably—"

"Emme," I interrupt her, shoving my legs in my jeans. "What is it?"

"It's easier if you come here."

"Where is here?"

"The Backyard."

"On my way. Give me fifteen minutes."

"Actually, Honon?"

"Still here," I grumble, grabbing a clean T-shirt from my dresser.

"Could you stop by the drugstore and pick up a baby bottle, some formula, and diapers for a six-month old?"

That certainly gets my attention as I struggle to get the shirt over my head.

I'm pretty fucking sure Emme did not have a baby the last time I saw her on Monday.

"Better have a good reason for sending me into a store to ask about fucking baby stuff."

"I do. I'll explain when you get here."

I grunt in response, shrugging into my vest, and shoving my wallet in my pocket.

"Oh, and, Honon?"

"Emme?"

"Please keep it to yourself."

Well, fuck.

———

She jumps up from behind the desk when I walk into the office, her index finger pressed against her lips.

Then she points to the couch.

I peek over a chair shoved in front of it and spot a little bundle under a blanket, only the top of a tiny head with a few whisps of flax-blond hair showing.

Emme waves me over to the other side of the office and takes the plastic bag from me.

"Who's the kid?" I ask, keeping my voice low.

"She's a friend's."

"Who's the friend?"

She looks at me like she's deciding whether I can be trusted or not. Then she sighs deeply, reaching for a piece of paper on the desk and handing it to me.

"Malco is her son?" I ask after scanning the note.

Emme nods. "He's nine."

"So where is he?"

"I don't know."

"Did you call her? This Rhea?"

"I've been trying. No answer."

I curse under my breath. Judging from that note, the woman worried she got herself in hot water. For her to dump her kids on Emme would suggest she may have had a valid concern.

The fact the boy is missing as well does not bode well for either of them.

"We've got to take this to the cops," I suggest.

"No!"

She snatches the note from my hand just as the baby starts crying.

"Shit," she mutters as she hurries to pick up the little girl.

Bouncing the fussy baby on her shoulder, she shoots me an angry glare.

"I thought I could trust you," she hisses.

*Fuck me.* Of all the things she could throw in my face.

I rub a hand through my hair and squeeze the back of my neck.

"It's the right thing to do, Emme."

"How can you say that? She all but spells out in the note not to call the cops or her kids could be in danger. We don't have any idea where Malco is. What if someone has him already?"

"Hold on a second," I try to slow her down. "You're jumping to conclusions here. We don't even know something has actually happened to her."

"Her baby wouldn't be here otherwise," she counters.

I can't really argue with that.

"Toss me a diaper, will you?"

I dig up the diapers and a pack of wipes I picked up and carry them over to where Emme is on her knees next to the couch, trying to get the baby to lie still so she can get the navy-blue romper off. The little spitfire isn't having it and keeps rolling out of reach.

"Here, let me."

Picking up the tiny thing, I sit down and lay her on my knees. The abrupt change seems to have quieted her. Big blue eyes observe me intently as I make quick use of what might be a brief respite and tackle her romper. It's one of those footed things with snap closures along the inseam. The poor kid's diaper is soaked.

It takes no time at all to slap a clean one on her.

"You look like you've had practice."

"Some. When Sophia and Tse's twins were little, I babysat a couple of times. Try wrangling two of these squirmy things at the same time."

I'm surprised the little girl hasn't put up a fuss yet when I start doing up those tiny snaps.

"What's that?" Emme asks.

She points at a dark spot I thought was part of some kind of pattern I noticed in the dark fabric of the romper. I touch the spot and it feels damp, as do some of the others. Then I rub it with a wipe.

"Oh no," Emme whispers when the wipe comes away pink.

In no time flat, I strip the baby down to her diaper and quickly check her for marks. There don't seem to be any.

"I need a towel, or a sheet, or something to wrap her in."

Emme nods as she gets to her feet and hurries out the door. I hold the little one against my shoulder with one hand, and pull my phone out with the other.

"Lisa, it's me. I need a favor."

Emme returns with a couple of kitchen towels and a tablecloth, just as I'm giving Lisa instructions to swing by the restaurant with some of Finn's old baby clothes and a car seat. She looks mad as hell as she takes the little girl from me and covers her up.

"Before you blow up," I quickly explain. "I only told Lisa we need her help with a baby. She didn't ask questions and I didn't volunteer more information. But," I add. "I think the safest place for the kid is the compound."

"Her name is Athena," Emme snaps.

"Yeah, but I'd keep that to myself as well, for now. Until we can figure out what's going on."

"Whatever." She jerks that pointy chin high. "But she's staying with me. Rhea asked me to keep her safe."

"Have you considered by doing that, your friend may well have put a target on your back as well?"

I can tell she hadn't thought of that yet, so I push on.

"How is that going to work anyway? You're already doing double duty with Sophia gone, are you gonna hide this little one in here all day? Face it, unless you pack your bags and disappear with her, there's no way you can keep her a secret." Then I play my trump. "And then there's the boy. He's still out there somewhere."

By the time Lisa walks in, Emme and I have agreed on a cover story. We're sticking as close to the truth as we can.

The little girl's name is Addy, and she was dropped off by her mother, an old friend of Emme's, who is dealing with a personal crisis.

I'm pretty sure Lisa doesn't buy into the story, but I trust her to sell it as best she can at the clubhouse. She doesn't say anything as she dresses the baby and straps her in the car seat, but before she leaves, she looks at Emme.

"The clubhouse door is always open for you. You wanna check on her, don't matter if it's day or night, all you gotta do is show up. In the meantime, she'll be well looked after."

"Thanks," Emme mumbles, her voice cracking.

To my surprise, this tough ballbuster of a woman has tears in her eyes as she watches Lisa walk out with the baby.

# CHAPTER
# FIVE

*Honon*

I don't have a good feeling about this.

The sliding door at the back is left open a bit, yet no one seems to be home. I tried ringing the bell and knocking a few times, to no avail.

Rhea's trailer is closest to the railroad tracks separating the trailer park from the river on the other side. It's fairly private—I can't even see her closest neighbor through the trees and undergrowth—but the downside is she'd have the train rumbling by at least a couple of times a day.

Just to be safe, I scan to make sure no one is looking before I carefully slide the door open all the way and step inside.

I can smell it right away; the coppery scent of blood and something else.

The smell of death.

I'm glad Emme stayed back at the restaurant. Not that she had much of a choice, with a restaurant to run and staff starting to filter in. It had still taken my reminder the boy might show up there looking for her to convince her to stay behind.

I understand her reluctance to trust anyone, but I still wish I had my brothers at my back. I don't like keeping shit from them, but if my instincts are right, I won't be able to for much longer.

Batting my hand at a persistent fly buzzing around my head, I move farther into the trailer, bracing myself for what I'm afraid I'll find. The moment I step around the island separating the small kitchen from the living area, I see the blood.

*Jesus Christ.* It's fucking everywhere.

She's lying facedown, halfway down the narrow hallway that leads to what I assume are the bedrooms. A bloodied baseball bat by her feet.

There's no way this woman is still alive, but I need to make sure.

I'm already dialing the police chief's direct line—I trust Joe—as I carefully make my way toward her, doing my best to avoid stepping in her blood.

"Benedetti."

I crouch down beside the woman and touch the cold skin of her neck to look for a pulse I know won't be there.

"It's Honon. I just found a dead body."

"Where are you?" Joe snaps.

"Oxbow Trailer Park. Unit twenty-seven," I rattle off the address Emme gave me. "I think the victim's name is Rhea Scala."

I spell the name, which Emme pronounced as 'Ray.'

"Who is she?"

"A friend of a friend. I came to check on her well-being, discovered the back door open, and found her inside. Looks like she's been dead for a while."

It's quiet for a moment and I wonder what he's thinking.

"You still there? Inside?" he asks, his voice all business.

"Yeah."

"Get your ass out of there and, for fuck's sake, don't mess up the crime scene. I've got a unit in the area I'll send over to secure the scene, and I'm on my way."

"Okay," I agree, but he's already ended the call.

Maybe I should've just backed out of here and put in an anonymous call—not looking forward to the questions I've got coming or the suspicious looks I'm bound to get—but it's too late for that now. Might be a good idea to give my president a quick heads-up, though.

I carefully retrace my steps out of the trailer, but it's not until I step down off the small back deck, I realize I should've checked the bedrooms to see if the boy is in there too. God, I hope not. The thought of a little kid meeting the same fate his mother did twists in my gut.

Turning to head to the front of the trailer to give Ouray a call and wait for the cops, I notice part of a bloody foot-print on one of the pavers that lead around the corner. Except the direction of the print is to the back of the property, toward the railroad and the river.

It looks small.

Child-sized. It may well have been left by the boy.

I wonder if he witnessed the attack on his mom. Or maybe he came back to check on her after dropping the baby at the restaurant and found her the way I did before running.

The Backyard isn't that far from here. A twenty-minute walk or so, faster if he followed the railroad tracks, which he may have done to avoid being spotted on the road.

I'm trying to think where a nine-year-old might hide.

That is, if he managed to evade whoever butchered that woman in there.

————

I'm leaning with my ass against Benedetti's cruiser, impatiently waiting for him.

The entire trailer is cordoned off with yellow tape and a couple of neighbors showed up to gawk at the police activities.

I spoke briefly with Ouray, giving him the same information I gave Joe but with the assurance I'd give him more detail when I can. I'm going to have to talk to Emme first, which is what I wanted to do as soon as the cops showed up but, of course, it wasn't as easy as that.

Thankfully, I'm no longer locked in the back of a patrol car where the first officers on the scene stuck me until Joe got here.

He had me go over my story twice, probing me on the 'friend' who asked me to check on Rhea, but I was hesitant to mention Emme by name. I could see that pissed him off, but with a woman dead inside, her note no longer seems alarmist. I may trust Joe, but I don't necessarily trust every other cop in town.

The first thing I need to do is talk to Emme, I don't want her to have to hear through the grapevine her friend is dead. That should come from me and in person, which is why I've ignored her two calls.

When I see Joe step outside, I push away from his vehicle, meeting him halfway up the path to the front door.

"Looks like there's two kids missing," he remarks, narrowing his eyes on me. "One is just a baby."

I try to keep a straight face.

"Domestic?" I toss out.

"No sign of an adult male in the house. We'll know more once we canvass the neighbors. Or talk to that friend of yours," he adds.

I ignore the probe.

"You know I can bring you into the station for questioning, right?"

I nod. "You could."

"Goddammit, Honon." He points a finger in my face. "Two kids' lives might be at stake."

I lean in and keep my voice low.

"I'm well aware, Joe. That's the point."

He looks confused at first, but then a flicker of understanding crosses his face.

"You know more."

I clamp my lips together and keep my eyes locked on his.

"Sonofabitch," he mutters, before grinding out, "We're spread so goddam thin, I've had to start taking on cases myself, so you keeping shit from me is not helping."

"I know and I'm sorry, man," I apologize. "As soon as I safely can, I promise."

I realize I'm putting him on the spot, but I'm also trusting him with more than is comfortable, and he knows that.

"Am I free to go?"

He shakes his head, muttering a few profanities under his breath.

"Don't go far. I don't want to have to chase your ass down."

I don't argue, but simply turn on my heel and head for my bike before he can change his mind.

---

*Emme*

I'm almost glad lunch was busier than usual.

It kept me from stewing in the office.

I'm not good at taking a back seat and waiting around, but Honon made his point earlier. I just wish he'd give me an update. Surely, he must've checked Rhea's place by now.

"Hey," Mack calls out when I pass by the bar with a tub of dirty dishes. "Didn't you tell me yesterday you had a delivery and needed to pop out at two? It's twenty after now."

*Shit*, my cement board.

I drop the tub on the bar with a clang and hurry to the back.

"Hold down the fort," I call over my shoulder.

I hear Mack's disembodied, "You've got it!" behind me as I dart into the office to grab my backpack.

Getting behind the wheel of my truck, I quickly give the building supplier a call, but someone other than Rick answers the phone.

"Hi, it's Emme Lightfoot, I have a delivery scheduled between two and five today, but I'm running a little late. I should be there in ten minutes, fifteen, tops."

"Oh, no worries. We're running a bit behind ourselves. The driver called in sick so we had to make other arrangements. We're just finishing up loading the truck and we'll be on our way. You'll have it well within the original window since you're near the top of the list."

As soon as I get home, I head for the garage. I was supposed to tidy it up and make room for the supplies, but with time getting away from me on Monday, I haven't had a chance. May as well make myself useful while I wait for the truck, but first I give Honon's number another try.

Five rings and again Honon's gruff voice with instructions to leave a message. I did that once already.

Ignoring the sour lump in the pit of my stomach, I punch in the code on the small keypad beside the garage door and wait for it to roll up.

It doesn't take long for me to work up a sweat, moving some of the heavy metal sheets and assorted scrap to one side. I'll probably need a quick shower before I head back to the restaurant.

Just then I hear the rumble of an engine and poke my head outside, watching the delivery truck pull into the driveway. Perfect.

"Nice place!" Rick calls out as he lowers himself from the cab.

"Since when do you run deliveries?" I ask, walking up.

"One of the guys called in sick. I was the only one available with a commercial license." He looks over at the garage. "Wow. You've got a decent collection of scrap metal. Need to get rid of that? I'd be more than happy to haul it out of here. We can use the truck if we do it after hours."

I bite off a grin. If only he knew how much that scrap metal can be worth once I'm done with it. Of course, given the recent detours in my life, it may be a while before I can pick up my welding torch. I have bigger fish to fry.

"Appreciate the offer, but I'm afraid it doesn't belong to me. I just store it."

A technicality but not a lie, and it makes for a good excuse. The metal is inventory for Twisted Rod Designs, never mind it's my company. That's not common knowledge, since most of my business is done online, and I'd like to keep it that way. For now, anyway.

"I see." He nods and studies me for a moment before he takes a pair of work gloves from his back pocket and pulls them on. "Okay, where do you want this stuff to go? In there?"

"Yeah, left side of the garage would be great."

I follow him to the back of the truck where he starts pulling three sheets of cement board at once. When I reach into the truck to grab one, he stops me.

"Don't worry, I've got it. No need for you to get yourself dirty."

I look down at the shirt I put on this morning and notice it's plenty dirty already, but whatever. I shrug at him.

"Be my guest."

He seems pretty determined to show off a little since one of those boards weighs over fifty pounds. He'll have to make the trip a few more times though.

Instead, I grab the handle of one of the five-gallon buckets of drywall compound and lift it out of the truck. The bucket isn't exactly featherweight either, but I'm stronger than I look. While Rick lumbers to the garage, I carry the bucket to the front door. It's May, the possibility of frost still exists and I don't want to take the risk of this compound freezing, so it's going inside.

I head out to grab the other bucket and Rick is already on his way with the second load. I hear the rumble of a motorcycle when I get to the back of the truck, and watch as Honon comes rolling toward me.

My breath catches in my throat when his eyes lock on mine. The steely expression on his face isn't telling me much so when he gets off the bike and starts walking toward me, I can't stop myself.

"And?"

It worries me when he doesn't answer, walking right up to me so I have to tilt my head back to hold his eyes.

When he whispers my name, I'm already shaking my head.

"No…please, no."

I never thought I'd say this, but I'm grateful for his arms wrapping firmly around me as my knees buckle.

"I found her at home. She'd been gone for a while already. I'm so sorry," he mumbles in my hair.

As I process the information, I indulge in the comfort he's offering for a second. Then a thought pushes to the forefront.

"What about Malco?" I ask, pushing him away.

"Hey! Get your damn hands off her!"

Before I know what's happening, strong hands grab me by the shoulders and shove me to the side. Rick immediately steps around me and moves into Honon's space, who is glaring at him with an icy expression.

Oh shit, this is not going to end well.

I quickly slip between the two men, facing Rick as I put my hands on his chest.

"He's a friend, Rick."

The man's eyes drop to my face.

"Then how come you're crying?"

The hand I lift to my face comes away wet.

"She just got some bad news," Honon rumbles behind me, before adding with a hefty dose of sarcasm. "So if you'll excuse us?"

Then another strong hand wraps around my upper arm, pulls me away from Rick, and steers me toward the house.

"Okay, I've had about enough of being manhandled, thank you very much," I mutter, jerking my arm free.

Honon doesn't object but I can feel him close on my heels as I rush up the steps and inside. There I immediately swing around.

"Malco?"

"Wasn't there," he answers. "But it looks like he may have been there at some point."

The wave of relief has me doubling over, my hands on my knees. Sucking in a few deep breaths, I straighten up.

"We need to find him. He's out there somewhere, Honon."

He nods.

"I know, and the best chance of finding him is to get more people involved."

"No cops," I remind him.

"Arrow's Edge. This is what we do, Emme. We find kids, keep them safe. But there's only so much I can do by myself. With the club involved, our chances of finding him increase exponentially."

I know what he says makes sense, but the more people we tell, the bigger the chance the information reaches the wrong person.

"One more thing," he continues. "I had to report finding your friend's body."

Oh God, I hadn't even thought of that.

"You called the cops?"

"I called someone I trust, who happens to be the chief of police. The only thing I told him was, I was doing a friend a favor checking in on Rhea when I found her. I didn't lie, but I wouldn't give him your name, and didn't tell him about the baby. However, it's not for nothing he's chief of police, he knows there's more to the story and is expecting answers."

I turn my back and press a hand against my forehead.

"I don't know what to do."

"I do. We find the boy, and get him safely to the compound. We'll figure out the rest after."

I feel his hand drop onto my shoulder, giving it a squeeze.

"But we need to tell my brothers."

*Jesus*, how can my life spin out of control so suddenly?

"I don't think we have a choice," I admit grudgingly.

# CHAPTER
# SIX

*Emme*

"Hey, Emme!"

I lift my hand to Kaga, Leah's husband, who's sitting at the bar beside an older man.

I've only been in the clubhouse a couple of times before, but I know quite a few of the guys, by sight anyway. Some of them have popped into the restaurant to sample the brisket at one time or another.

A few more hellos go up as Honon puts a hand on the small of my back and nudges me ahead.

"Ouray is gonna be in the back," he says behind me.

It had been his idea for me to come along and decide for myself how much to tell his brothers. I took him up on the offer, but don't have a lot of time. Mack is expecting me back at the restaurant before the dinner rush gets crazy.

As we pass a couple of kids sitting at the large harvest table, bent over what looks to be homework, I can hear the sound of crying coming from the kitchen.

My feet automatically carry me in that direction.

"Emme…"

I glance back at Honon, holding up a finger.

"Give me one sec."

In the kitchen I find Lisa, bouncing the wailing baby on her shoulder, while stirring a large pot on the stove.

"She hasn't been able to settle since her last bottle," Lisa explains when she spots me.

I have next to no experience with babies, but still find myself reaching for the little one. The moment I lift her on my shoulder, stroking a hand up and down her little back, she seems to quiet down.

Lisa grins at me.

"She likes you."

"She doesn't really know me," I tell her.

The older woman shrugs as she turns back to the stove.

"Don't seem to matter to her."

"Bring her with you," Honon suggests behind me, "We're meeting in Ouray's office."

I catch Lisa's eye.

"May as well," she agrees, motioning to the baby. "She's comfortable now."

I follow Honon through the clubhouse to a hallway at the back. I've never been here, and it feels like being led into an inner sanctum of sorts.

The office he shows me into is large. Ouray is sitting with his feet up on a desk on the right, and across from him a few of the guys are hanging out on a pair of old couches. I know the big, black guy they call Trunk, as well as Paco, who comes into the Backyard regularly with his wife, Mel. I recognize the younger guy, but don't know his name.

I hate to admit I'm a little intimidated. I may be tough but there's a lot of free-flowing testosterone in this room full of brawny men, who all easily tower over my modest five foot five. Nevertheless, I square my shoulders while clutching the baby a little closer.

"I see you've got the touch," Ouray observes as he drops his boots down from the desk and gets up.

"Sheer luck," I return with forced ease. "She probably cried herself out."

He grins at me before moving his eyes to Honon, his expression turning serious.

"Want the room cleared?"

Honon glances at me, his eyebrows raised. He's leaving the decision up to me. I glance over at the guys to my left, some of whom are already getting to their feet.

"It's okay, there's no need," I answer, turning back to Ouray. "Honon convinced me we stand a better chance with the club involved, and I trust him."

"A better chance of what?" he wants to know.

"Of finding this little one's nine-year-old brother. He's missing and I'm afraid he's in danger."

The atmosphere in the room changes perceptibly from laid-back and casual, to serious and highly charged.

"Here, sit down," Trunk's deep voice rumbles as he gets up to make room for me on the couch. "I'll go grab the other guys, and call Yuma to get his ass over here."

The large office is starting to feel crowded when Kaga closes the door behind the last of the men. Some have pulled over chairs from the beat-up conference table on the other end, while others have opted to lean against a wall or a piece of furniture.

Through all of the commotion, little Athena sleeps peacefully on my shoulder, her body like a little oven against me.

"Want to walk us through?" Ouray invites me.

I glance to my side at Honon, who's taken a seat on my armrest. He nods at me with a hint of his dimples.

*Yowza.*

Taking in a fortifying breath, I start recounting how I found the baby next to the dumpster this morning and discovered the note pinned to her blanket. At some point Honon takes over, telling them about the blood we discovered on her romper, his subsequent trip to the Oxbow Trailer Park, and what he discovered there. When he provides details he hadn't shared with me yet, the involuntary shiver running through my body doesn't go unnoticed.

"You okay?" Honon asks quietly, leaning toward me.

Pushing the mental images his description initiated aside, I steel myself and nod.

"I'm fine."

Not really, but I can't afford to be anything else. Emotions will have to wait until that little boy is safe.

"How well do you know the kid?" Ouray asks me. "Any thoughts on where he might've gone to?"

I shrug. "Not that well. I mean, I haven't really seen him since I moved to my new place, but that was two years ago. I remember he liked dinosaurs and fire trucks, for what it's worth."

"Any family you know of?"

"No. Rhea wasn't from here. She told me she was a product of the foster system somewhere in the Midwest."

"Any other friends you know of? Neighbors the boy may have gone to for help? People at work?"

"Not really. I mean, she was friendly with a couple of the girls at the club back when I was there, but she kept mostly to herself. The only other person I know she was close to was Mrs. Sanchez—she was a neighbor at the trailer park—who would sometimes watch Malco, but she passed away not long after I moved. I'm sure she must've had a babysitter, but I don't know who that might've been."

"Where did she work?" Paco asks.

"She's been working at the club for years. The Pink Petal."

I can tell from the reactions, they're familiar with it, which doesn't surprise me. Most adult males know The Pink Petal, and I'm willing to bet most, if not all, of these guys have visited the gentlemen's club at one point or other.

"Used to belong to a guy I know," Ouray shares. "Sold it a couple of years ago."

"Ben Maverick. Yeah, he sold it maybe six months after I started working at the restaurant," I confirm.

"Didn't realize you bartended there," he observes.

"I didn't," I clarify, my head held high. "I was a stripper."

Most would choose to use the term 'dancer' as a euphemism, but I'm not ashamed of any of the jobs I've worked at to get where I am today and refuse to be made to feel that way.

I look around the room, daring each and every one of the guys to show judgment but don't see any reaction, except from Yuma. He throws his head back and starts laughing.

"What the fuck's so funny?" Honon barks at him.

"This is hilarious," Yuma sputters. "I always thought some of those tats looked familiar. Fucking Vixen. You remember her, don't you, brother? Picture Emme with black hair and a welder's mask. She's her."

Great. Now they'll all have mental images of me strutting around the stage in my tiny leather thong, black wig, and welder's mask. It was a great costume the guys went nuts over. I made a lot of bucks wearing it, and yet it allowed me anonymity outside of work.

"Can we get back to Malco?" I snap sharply. "I have to get back to work."

"Maybe it's better if you stay here," Ouray suggests.

"Not if there's a chance the boy might come back to look for me," I counter.

─────

*Honon*

"Dude, I remember you crushing hard on Vixen."

I turn a glare on Yuma, who doesn't hesitate to rib me the moment Emme leaves the office to hand the baby back to Lisa.

"Don't start," Ouray intervenes, calmly setting us back on track. "We've got a boy to find. Honon, I want you to go with Emme to the restaurant. She's right; if the kid dropped his sister at the restaurant, he may be back. Lots of places for him to hide and wait until dark."

I nod. Since Emme going back to the restaurant only echos the point I'd made to her earlier, I completely agree with him.

"Another possibility is the park along the river," I suggest. "The tracks are right behind his mom's trailer. All he'd have to do is cross them to get there. He might want to stick close."

Trunk clears his throat. "If the boy witnessed his mother's murder, or saw her body, he might not be easy to catch. The kid's gonna be spooked and will run when he feels cornered. I suggest you approach with caution, and monitor from a distance. There's only one person he trusts and that's Emme. Better to keep an eye on him until she can get there."

A few grunts of acknowledgement go up in response.

"What about the cops?" Brick directs at me. "Surely, they'll be out there looking."

"Probably. Benedetti knows there's more to my story, but let me go anyway. It's a matter of time until he loses patience and hauls me in."

"Why not tell him all of it?"

"Because," Ouray takes over addressing Brick. "If there is any truth to the warning the woman left in that note, it's possible someone connected to law enforcement might be involved."

"Isn't that a bit of a stretch?" Yuma comments. "I mean, we know almost all of those guys. Heck, most of them come here to make use of the gun range."

I get it. His wife is a former Durango Police Department detective, but he knows as well as I do, just because someone appears to be a good guy doesn't mean he is.

"Maybe," I concede, shooting a sharp look his way. "But are you willing to risk the life of a nine-year-old kid?"

"Unless he's already dead. A more troublesome prospect we haven't considered yet. It could already be too late if whoever killed his mother managed to get to him," Kaga offers somberly.

Something I refuse to consider yet. Mainly because of the impact it would have on Emme. She's been holding it together so far, but I fear any bad news around the boy would crush her.

The friendship between her and Rhea may not have ended well, but it's very clear to me she still cared a lot about the woman and feels a strong sense of responsibility for her kids. Hell, she seems to have bonded with the baby already. The little thing looked completely at ease in her arms.

"Has anyone checked the security cameras at the restaurant?" Paco suddenly brings up.

"Shit. Why didn't I think of that?"

I give my head a mental slap.

Security was tightened a few years ago when the restaurant found itself in the crosshairs of some drug dealers but we haven't had much going on since, and I'd all but forgotten about the cameras.

"Maybe we can get a glimpse of the boy. It'll help knowing what he looks like."

Ouray makes room for Paco, who takes a seat behind the desk and turns the large computer screen so the rest of us can see as well. Then he brings up the video feed from the rear of the restaurant.

"What time did she get there this morning?" he asks.

"Probably six or so," I'm guessing.

"I'll run it backward from there."

He speeds through the frames until the digital clock in the bottom corner of the screen shows four fifty-three, and a small figure steps out of the trees bordering the back of the property.

"That's gotta be him," I affirm, noticing the bundle the kid is cradling in his arms as he approaches the restaurant's back door.

For a few moments he disappears out of range of the camera, presumably as he places his sister behind the dumpster, which is only partially visible on the screen. Then he reappears, and hurries halfway across the parking lot before he stops and looks back. The images are grainy at best, but the poor kid's mental struggle is plain to see.

"Poor bugger," Brick mutters.

"Brown hair, slight build, I'm guessing four and a half to five feet," Paco observes. "White sneakers, dark pants, and a black hoodie with some kind of logo on the back."

On the screen, the boy disappears into the trees.

"Okay, guys, let's find this kid, get him to safety," Ouray jumps in. "As far as the cops go, if it comes to that, let me handle law enforcement."

He looks at me when he says it, looking for acknowledgement. I know there isn't much he keeps from Luna—his wife, who is law enforcement herself, albeit with the FBI—but I trust his judgment so I give him a nod.

"Right, now that we have that out of the way, Paco, can you pull up a satellite map of the park? And, Honon, you better get out of here before she takes off on her own."

I shoot him a mock salute and walk out to go in search of Emme.

———

There is only one table still occupied when I return to my spot at the bar. A couple so engrossed in each other; they don't seem to have noticed the place has emptied out.

"Beer?" Mack asks.

"Sure."

A moment later, he slides a cold bottle my way.

"Something going on I should know about? You've been in and out of here all night, and Emme is barely functioning, she's so stressed." He leans over the bar. "Emme is never stressed."

"For the last time, I'm not fucking stressed."

The subject of discussion slams a bin with empties on the bar, saving me a response.

Mack takes a step back, his hands up defensively.

"My bad," he mutters with a smirk. "Must be your time of the month then."

Emme climbs up on the footrail and almost launches herself over, but can't quite reach him.

"I'm this close…" She illustrates with her fingers. "…to showing you what happens when you really piss me off."

"You mean this isn't it?" Fred comments, walking up to the bar.

He clearly hasn't gotten any smarter in the past few days. For a moment, it looks like I might have to grab her before she does him bodily harm, but then she lets out a frustrated growl before dropping down and stomping off to the back.

Contemplating whether to let her cool off on her own or follow her, I decide on the latter. Grabbing my beer, I slide off the stool and make my way around the bar.

"You're a braver man than me," Mack comments.

I answer by flipping him the bird before I head after Emme.

I find her sitting at her desk, staring at the little blue romper the baby was wearing this morning.

"Emme?"

She startles at the sound of my voice.

"Did you find anything?"

I approach the desk and sit down in one of the visitor's chairs.

"Not yet."

"Anything from the others?"

"They'll call me as soon as they have something," I assure her and then point at the scrap of material. "You know we should probably put that somewhere safe, in a plastic bag or something. It may be important."

"I know," she agrees, her voice as dull as her eyes.

"Are you okay?"

She looks at me and visibly pulls herself together.

"I'm fine," she lies.

# CHAPTER
# SEVEN

*Emme*

The coffee I made doesn't even make a dent in the thick fog hanging around my head.

I barely got any sleep, dozing off every so often only to startle awake again.

After we closed the restaurant last night, I'd wanted to join the search for Malco, but Honon convinced me to go home. He suggested if I did anything outside of my normal routine, it might put me on the radar of whoever killed Rhea and could be looking for her kids.

It pissed me off to be sidelined like that—not doing anything makes me feel like I'm failing my friend—but Honon was right, I can't risk drawing any attention to myself when it could put the kids at risk. He followed me home, promised they wouldn't stop looking for Malco and would call me if they found him. Like earlier, he waited until I'd gone inside and locked the door before driving off.

Restless, I'd started peeling the old wallpaper in the main bedroom until my arms were so sore, I could barely lift them over my head anymore. It was after two before I rolled into bed, exhausted, but sleep wouldn't come.

I've been sitting here, sipping my coffee and staring outside as I watch the morning sky slowly brighten with the rising sun, while waiting for time to pass. It's Mack's turn to receive deliveries at the restaurant this morning so I'm not expected in until eleven or so, which is hours away yet.

It's just after six and there's been no word from Honon.

The thought of that poor kid, alone out there somewhere and probably scared out of his wits, is eating at me. If I don't find something to do, I'm going to go out of my mind.

I thought of giving Lisa a call to see how the baby is doing, but I should probably wait until a more decent hour.

I'm just getting to my feet when I see something move in the trees bordering my backyard. The same elk I saw earlier in the week on the road steps out into the clearing. I recognize his antlers. He stops, raising his head and slowly looking around as if surveying his domain. His breath is visible as it puffs in small clouds from his flared nostrils.

Then, something seems to startle him and as suddenly as he appeared, he's gone again.

Maybe it's a sign I should get my ass in gear and do something productive instead of moping around. I dump out the rest of my coffee in the sink and rinse out my cup, setting it upside down in the dish rack.

I'm on my way to get dressed when I hear the rumble of an engine.

Rushing to the front door, I pull it open just as the bike turns up my driveway.

"Did you find him?" I yell out the moment Honon removes his helmet.

His eyes snap to me, instantly narrowing as he sets the helmet on his seat and starts stalking toward me.

"Get inside," he snaps. "It's freezing."

My bristles go up right away. Who the hell does he think he is ordering me around?

But before I have a chance to retort, he's already crowding me back inside, kicking the door shut behind him.

"You're half naked for fuck's sake," he mutters, his eyes scanning down my body.

I'm not sure whether the shiver rippling down my spine is from the cold or his scrutiny, but I'm suddenly aware of the thin material of my well-worn sleep shirt, which barely covers my thighs.

Either way, it doesn't stop me from reacting.

"Well, maybe next time you show up on my doorstep at six in the fucking morning, I'll make sure I'm appropriately dressed. Now," I follow up right away. "If you wouldn't mind, I'd appreciate an update on Malco."

For a moment he simply looks at me, before lowering his gaze to the floor.

"Not yet. We went up and down the riverside, walked the railroad tracks, and checked every hiding spot between the trailer park and the restaurant, but the kid must've hunkered down somewhere for the night."

Unless, of course, someone already got to him. Honon isn't saying the words, but I hear them in his voice anyway. There's a sound of defeat, or maybe I'm reading too much into what might be simple fatigue. After all, the man's been out looking all night.

"There's still some coffee in the pot," I tell him, turning my back. "Help yourself while I get cleaned up."

I try not to think about the boy—or the man currently

rummaging around in my kitchen—as I quickly rinse off in the shower and get dressed. My morning routine is pretty basic and it doesn't take me long to get ready.

When I walk into the kitchen, I'm surprised to find Honon didn't stop at helping himself to coffee. Apparently, he's helped himself to the meager contents of my fridge as well. He looks quite at home, flipping French toast in my favorite frying pan on the stove as he stifles a yawn.

"You're out of bacon," he tells me without turning around.

"Missed my grocery run this week." I move past him to make a fresh pot of coffee. "Most of the time I eat at the restaurant anyway."

When the coffee machine starts gurgling, I turn and lean against the counter facing him.

"Why are you here?" I ask.

He turns his head to look at me, his expression inscrutable.

"Killing two birds with one stone. Been a long night. I needed to refuel and wanted to touch base with you." He turns off the burner and lifts the pan. "Plates?"

I swivel around, open the cupboard, and grab two plates I hand to him.

"Syrup?" is his next question.

I grab the bottle from the fridge door and join him at the kitchen island.

"It's tasty," I mumble, a mouth full of fluffy goodness.

He grunts in response, busy stuffing his own face.

Funny, twenty minutes ago, eating had been furthest from my mind and here I am, inhaling the unexpected breakfast.

"So what's next?" I ask, clearing the empty plates and dropping them in the sink.

"Same thing. We keep looking, widening the circle. The kid's gonna surface sometime. One of our guys is keeping an eye on the trailer, in case he comes back there looking for food. He'll be getting hungry."

Hungry, thirsty, cold, and scared out of his mind.

Or maybe he's not feeling any of those things anymore.

The thought hits me like a punch in the stomach and I grab the edges of the sink, doubling over.

"Hey…" Honon's strong hand curves around the back of my neck. "Don't go there. He's a smart kid, he got his baby sister to a safe place, right? I bet you he's laying low, biding his time until he feels it's safe."

"But he's only nine," I argue, straightening up.

Unfortunately, I lose the warmth of his touch as he drops his hand.

"You'd be surprised what a nine-year old kid can handle."

Something in the tone of his voice has me turn to look at him. All I catch is a glimpse of dark shadows in his eyes before they disappear as he flashes me a grin.

An effective distraction with those dimples on full display.

———

*Honon*

A Durango PD cruiser is parked by the back entrance of the restaurant when I follow Emme's truck onto the parking lot.

She'd insisted on coming, saying she'd go nuts at home, and I didn't have the heart to try and talk her out of it.

I get the need to stay busy, do something constructive when you feel out of control. Emme's life has definitely been tilted on its axis. In a lot of ways, we are alike; we take our responsibilities seriously and are loyal to those we care about. If I were in her shoes and a friend placed their most valued treasures in my trust, I wouldn't be able to sit still either. I'd feel the weight of that responsibility to my soul.

When I got to her place this morning, I'd been worn to the bone until she stormed out her front door wearing nothing but a shirt that hid little. That sure woke me up, at least it did certain parts of me. Those strong legs had been fodder for some energetic fantasies I harbored back when I had no idea who she was. At the club, she'd stood out from the other—mostly slender—dancers. More compact and powerful, she danced with a confidence that had been a total turn-on for me. The mystery of the welder's mask she used to wear only added to the overall appeal.

Emme pulls into her usual spot while I park my bike beside the dumpster. I wait for her, watching her walk toward me. I'd already been more drawn to Emme than I was comfortable with, but discovering she's hiding that enticingly curvy body underneath those plain T-shirts and shapeless cargo pants makes it even harder to look away.

"What do you think they want?" she asks, nudging her head toward the cruiser.

"Not sure. Only one way to find out."

I open the back door for her and follow her inside.

I'm relieved to see the cop we find sitting at the bar, talking with Mack, was here the night Emme had her run in with that group of punks. He was the one I pointed out the damage on the vehicles to.

The man only gives me a cursory glance before focusing his attention on Emme.

"Ah, Ms. Lightfoot," he begins, getting up from the stool and offering her his hand. "Officer Conley. If I might have a moment of your time?"

"Sure. Why don't we use the office?"

Thank God I tucked that little blue romper under the seat of my bike last night.

Emme darts me a pointed look before heading down the hallway. The cop follows and I bring up the rear. Outside the office, he stops and turns to me.

"I think I should speak with Ms. Lightfoot in private."

Fat chance I'm going to let that happen, but before I get a chance to convey that message, Emme speaks up.

"Actually, since Honon was here that night, I'd prefer he stay."

There's no reason why that comment should make me feel good, but it does.

"Very well," he concedes, but he doesn't look happy about it.

I'm pretty sure it has little to do with Emme and everything with me. Some of the cops who have been around a while still view Arrow's Edge members as a bunch of criminals.

Emme invites him to take a seat as she rounds the desk to sit down behind it, assuming a position of control. Smart girl.

I opt to stay in her line of sight, leaning against the wall.

"I just have a few follow-up questions related to the altercation that occurred here last Friday," Conley starts. "Did you know David Hines prior to your encounter with him that night?"

She shakes her head.

"Is that the guy? This is the first time I've heard his name."

"We picked him up for questioning yesterday. He says this wasn't his first time at the Backyard Edge."

"I guess that's always possible. I just don't remember him. It's a busy restaurant, a lot of people come through here, I can't remember them all."

"Fair enough. He seems to recall you from his prior visits, though. Claims you had it in for him ever since he turned down your advances."

"Bullshit," I bark, ready to jump to her defense.

But Emme doesn't seem to need it as she bursts out laughing.

"In his dreams, maybe," she mocks. "Have you seen the guy? He can't be a day over twenty-five. I could almost be his mother, for fuck's sake. Besides, I don't flirt with customers. Ever," she emphasizes. "Feel free to check with the rest of the staff."

"I already did, I just wanted to hear it from you," the officer admits, just as my phone buzzes in my pocket.

It's Kaga.

"Hold on a sec," I mutter, glancing at Emme and nudging my head toward the exit. "I've gotta take this, I'll be right outside."

She gives me a nod and I take off down the hall and duck out the back door.

"Talk to me."

"I have an idea where the kid might be."

"Where?"

"You know how Emme said she remembered the boy liked dinosaurs and fire trucks? My boys were much the same at that age. Their favorite thing was to ride their bikes to the firehouse and hang around on the sidewalk in hopes they'd catch a glimpse of the firefighters, or better yet, the trucks driving off, running their sirens."

My interest is piqued.

"Station 3 is closest. Still a heck of a walk for a little kid," I point out.

"Not if he's scared and believes he'll be safe there," Kaga argues. "I already called the station. They haven't seen the boy, but one of the guys came in this morning and mentioned he thought he heard an animal rummaging through the dumpster on the side of the building."

It's always possible it could be an animal, but my gut tells me something else.

"Meet me there, but keep your distance. I'm bringing Emme."

I end the call and turn to go back inside, just as the door opens and the cop walks out.

"That sniveling little fuck is feeding you a line," I inform him. "He's just pissed a woman half his size got the better of him. You're barking up the wrong tree."

He holds up his hand.

"I'm well aware, and I'm not barking up any tree. The man's arm is broken, I'm simply doing my job and verifying statements."

With that clear, he continues to his vehicle while I head inside to get Emme.

I find her talking to Mack at the bar.

"Everything okay?" she asks when she spots me.

"We've gotta go."

Her eyes go big.

"Now?"

"Right now. It's an emergency," I enforce.

She turns back to Mack.

"I'm sorry. The schedule will have to wait, I've gotta run."

The guy looks annoyed.

"What's going on with you? You're not yourself."

"I'm sorry, there's some stuff going on, I wish I—"

"It's personal," I abruptly cut her off, feeling the urgency to get to the fire station. "I'll have her back as soon as I can."

Before anyone has a chance to say anything else, I take hold of her arm and spin her toward the back door.

"Did you find him?" she asks the moment we step outside, an anxious expression on her face.

"Maybe. Give me your keys, we'll take your truck."

"I can drive my own truck."

Of course she would protest.

"Except you're vibrating with adrenaline and are likely to cause an accident. Besides, I know where I'm going."

We stop in front of her vehicle and I hold out my hand.

She tries staring me down but quickly gives in, fishing the keys from her pocket and handing them over.

As I peel out of the parking lot, I can feel her eyes on me.

"What?"

"Is he okay?"

I reach my hand out and give her knee a light squeeze.

"Hopefully, we'll have the answer to that soon."

# CHAPTER
# EIGHT

*Honon*

In the five minutes it takes us to drive from the restaurant to the fire station, I'm able to fill Emme in on what's happening.

The moment I pull up alongside the curb around the corner, she's ready to jump out of the truck.

"Hold on. We've gotta wait for the guys, plan how we're gonna do this."

"Why can't I just walk up to the dumpster and call his name?"

"Because if you end up spooking him and he runs, we may not get a second chance. First of all, I want to see if we can get someone on the roof. From that vantage point we should be able to see inside the bin to confirm if he's in there. If it turns out he is, we can keep an eye on him in case he bolts when you approach him."

She doesn't say anything, but lets go of the door handle and straightens, her eyes scanning our surroundings and her hands clasped tightly in her lap. She's like a live spring, and almost jumps out of her skin when a knock sounds on my window.

It's Kaga.

"We're parked at the apartment building on the other side."

Good. That's the side where the dumpster is.

"Who's we?" I want to know.

"Yuma, Lusio, and Shilah."

Glad to hear Shilah is here. He's the youngest and probably most fit of the guys. I shoot him a text to meet us here, then I get out of the truck.

I'm not surprised when I hear the passenger door slam on the other side seconds before Emme joins us on the sidewalk.

"So what's the plan?" she asks, bouncing on the balls of her feet.

To save myself having to go over twice, I wait until Shilah comes jogging around the corner before I answer her question.

"Shilah and I are gonna walk into the firehouse, talk to whoever is in charge, and see if there's a way to get on the roof. The boy won't be able to see us if we approach from this side. Then we'll wait to see if Shilah can get eyes on him."

"Figures I'm the one going on the roof. I don't like heights," he grumbles. "Should've worn my fucking sneakers."

"I'll go," Emme volunteers.

I shut that down right away.

"Over my dead body."

"Suck it up, Buttercup," Kaga taunts our younger brother, jabbing an elbow in his ribs.

Ignoring Emme's mutinous scowl, I forge on.

"I want you to drive the truck around to the apartment building. Park it as close as you can to the wooden fence shielding the dumpster, but make sure you can see enough of the front of the fire station to catch my signal. Kaga and the others will cover any escape on the side and at the rear, and I'll make sure he can't get away in the front."

She glances over to the firehouse.

"Are you sure he's here?"

"Can't be a hundred percent sure, but my gut says he is."

Her eyes find mine, searching for I don't know what, but it appears she's found it when she gives me a sharp nod.

"When I signal you, get out of the truck, walk around the back of the bin, and call for him. We want to stay out of view of the road and draw as little attention as possible. As soon as you have him, get him into the passenger side of the truck, and tell him to get down on the floor and out of sight."

"Okay."

I can tell she's nervous, so I lean in a little.

"It's gonna be fine, Emme. Trust me."

I wait for her to confirm with a tight little nod before I turn to my brothers, both of whom are wearing stupid grins on their faces.

"Quit standing around like idiots. Let's go."

Shilah falls into step beside me as I round the corner.

"Guess I know why—"

"You wanna stick around to take your next breath, I highly recommend you shut your piehole,"

From the corner of my eye I see him pretend to zip his lips, but the shit-eating grin remains.

*Asshole*.

The first person we bump into is Evan Biel, Trunk's brother-in-law. Luckily, it's his crew on shift, I know most of those guys. Evan takes us upstairs, where I explain to his captain what we're after. I don't even have to go into detail. All I tell him is we think a kid we've been looking for is hiding in his dumpster, and he simply assumes it's another street kid or runaway.

"Text me when you get in position," I tell Shilah before he climbs out of one of the skylights and onto the roof.

I leave Evan to keep an eye on him and make my way down to the large bay doors.

I've only been waiting a few minutes when his message comes in.

He's here. Sleeping from what I can tell. Covered himself with cardboard.

I immediately check in with Kaga, who messages right back to let me know they're in place.

When I stick my head around the corner, I can see part of the pickup, the rest is blocked by some bushes. Emme's silhouette is visible behind the wheel. I stretch out my arm and give her a thumbs-up. A second later, I see the driver's side door open and Emme slipping out.

She's smart enough not to slam the door shut and disappears around the back of the truck, and out of sight.

Keeping my ears peeled, I wait to hear her call out before slipping around the corner of the building and inching toward the bin.

"Malco, are you in there? It's Emme, remember me?"

She's keeping her voice low, but it sounds like he heard her, judging from the faint rustle inside the dumpster.

"I want you to know your sister is safe. You were so smart to drop her off for me to find. She's still so little, and lucky to have a brother like you to take care of her."

She quiets for a moment and I listen for any sound of movement from inside, but it stays silent.

"Malco? I found the note from your mom. She asked me to look after both of you. I know you're probably scared, but I promise I just want to keep you safe."

This time when she pauses, I hear a sniffle.

"Do you remember I used to babysit you when you were younger? You had a dinosaur hand puppet you liked so much you tried eating pizza with it on. It looked like the dinosaur was eating the pizza instead and it made us laugh. Do you remember that?"

I can hear him moving around inside and then the sound of something banging against the metal side of the bin.

"Where is Athena?"

I blow out the breath I've been holding when I hear the timid voice.

"Hey, buddy," Emme coos. "A good friend of mine is keeping her safe so I could come and get you. Her name is Lisa and she lives just up the road from my house. Do you want to see your sister?"

"I can't. It's not safe."

"It is," I hear her persist. "I have friends there and it's the safest place in this whole town. It even has a big fence around it and a guard at the gate so no one else can get in. My pickup is right here. All you have to do is climb out of here and you can hide on the floor of the truck and I'll drive straight there. No one will even know you're hiding inside."

Another few clangs and then I hear Emme's voice again. "Hold on to my hand."

———

*Emme*

That poor boy.

He's red-eyed, with tear-tracks streaking through the dirt on his cheeks, and he's covered in filth.

His hand grabs on to mine like a lifeline.

I take a quick glance around, rush him to my truck, and help him duck down under the dashboard. Reaching over the seat, I grab an old flannel shirt and cover him with it.

"Stay down," I tell him right before I close the door and rush to the other side.

Honon startles me, already waiting by the driver's door.

"You get in first, sit in the middle and keep him calm, I'll drive," he whispers.

This is not the time for an argument, so I resort to narrowing my eyes at him before I climb inside. Afraid Malco might try to get out, I reach over to lock his door. The moment Honon gets in beside me, the boy's head shoots up, his eyes wide when he catches sight of him.

I lean over, my face inches from his to try and draw his attention.

"That's Honon. He's one of those friends I told you about."

As Honon starts the truck and backs out, I shoot off a

silent thanks at least the large man had a haircut and a beard trim, and no longer looks like a yeti.

"He and some other friends have been helping since yesterday to try and find you."

Honon looks over and flashes his dimples at the boy.

"We looked everywhere," he explains with a grin as he turns his eyes back to the road. "Pretty smart of you, hiding at the fire station, but I bet you're hungry. Don't worry, you won't be for long, Lisa will try and stuff you so full you won't be able to take another bite. She's a good cook. The best. Wait until you get a taste of one of her cinnamon rolls, they're so nice and gooey, you'll have icing dripping down your fingers. Word of warning though, she's probably gonna have you wash up first, 'cause, kid, you smell like swamp water. We don't really have alligators in this part of the country, but one whiff of you and they might just decide to come here on vacation."

I'm surprised by Honon's easy ramble, which seems to ease some of the panic on Malco's face. When I reach out my hand to him, he grabs on to it again.

"Alligators?" he asks in a wobbly voice.

"He's just kidding," I quickly assure him, before turning my head to look at Honon. "Right?"

"Yeah, kid. I'm messing with ya, but I'm dead serious about Lisa making you wash up first, so best be prepared."

On the drive to the compound, I become increasingly aware of Honon's impressive thigh pressing against mine. The cab of my pickup isn't that big and with Malco ducked under the dashboard beside me, I can't exactly move over. At least not easily, I've tried.

Honon's hand slips down the steering wheel and lands on my leg.

"Stop fidgeting."

"I'm not fidgeting, I'm trying to give you some more room."

"Got plenty of room." He glances at me from the corner of his eye before dropping a heavy arm over my shoulder, tucking me close. "There, is that better?"

Better?

I open my mouth to tell him what I think but snap it shut again when I catch Malco looking on with interest. The last thing the boy needs to hear is me bitching at Honon about personal space.

The poor kid just lived through a nightmare.

It's not long before we turn up the driveway to the compound.

"It's safe to sit up now," Honon tells him. "We're here."

Malco lets go of my hand and pulls himself up, poking his head out from under the dashboard to look out of the window.

"Is that a prison?" he asks, staring wide-eyed at the eight-foot-high, chain-link fence and gate coming into view.

"No. The gate is to keep people out, not lock them in," I hurry to explain.

"This is a safe place," Honon adds, as one of the teenagers I saw with Brick the other day swings the gate open. "We're like a big family. Even got a couple of kids around your age living here."

"Is this where I'm going to live?"

His question hangs heavy inside the cab of the truck.

"For now, anyway," the man beside me answers when I can't find the words. "We'll help you figure the rest out later."

I swallow down the lump in my throat. When the truck stops in front of the clubhouse, I glance over at Honon, who is looking back at me.

"Come on. Let's get this boy to his sister."

Honon gets out of the truck and I reach in front of Malco to unlock the passenger door, before I scoot over and get out the driver's side. I round the vehicle to help the boy down when the door of the clubhouse opens and Lisa steps outside, baby Athena in her arms.

Suddenly, Malco comes flying out of the passenger side, but even though his eyes are fixed on his sister, he stops short of rushing up the steps.

"This is Lisa, the friend I told you about," I tell him gently.

"And you must be the big brother," Lisa takes over. "I have a feeling this little girl was missing you something fierce."

On cue, the baby seems to catch sight of Malco and squeals loudly, stretching her arms toward him. That triggers the boy, who races up the couple of steps to the porch and takes Athena from Lisa's arms. The baby immediately grins big, slapping her hands on Malco's cheeks.

"Oh my," Lisa mumbles, apparently as moved by the scene as I am.

"Sheesh, kid," Honon comments dryly. "Now your sister's gonna need to get hosed down as well."

# CHAPTER
# NINE

*Honon*

I watch Emme take Malco's hand as the two follow Lisa out of the clubhouse.

"Joe will want to talk to the boy," Ouray warns behind me.

"Not today. He's been through hell already. Give him a break."

It's the reason why Emme is helping Lisa take the kids to her cottage. Things are about to get real at the clubhouse, and the children are better off not being around for that.

Luna had already been inside when we got here earlier. Ouray called her as soon as he got word we found the boy. While I stayed with the kid as he took a quick shower in my bathroom, Luna had taken Emme aside in her husband's office across the hallway.

Time to pay the piper.

With the kids safe in our care, there's really no excuse to delay filling law enforcement in on what we know.

I talked to Luna after she spoke with Emme. I shared

what I knew and handed over the baby's romper and the note, both of which I'd kept safe in the seat of my bike.

The next step had been calling Joe Benedetti, which Luna took care of, insisting he come alone.

It's going to be a long afternoon either way.

"The restaurant is going to be shorthanded," I realize out loud, turning to Ouray.

"I sent Mika over, he's good behind the bar, and Leah was supposed to be off today but she's heading in to help out with the dinner rush. It's covered," he informs me.

Good. That'll be one less thing for Emme to worry about.

———

"And you say you have no idea what she's supposed to have been looking into?"

I bristle at the tone of Joe's question, but a sharp glance from Ouray has me hold my tongue.

I shouldn't have worried, because Emme seems well-equipped to deal with the probing questions.

"As I've indicated before, I hadn't spoken to Rhea in over a year. That shouldn't be too hard to verify," she adds testily.

"Right, a falling out over her relationship with a married man, you mentioned. You have no idea who this married man is?"

"She never said his name."

"Do you think it's likely he's the father of the six-month-old?"

She shrugs. "Your guess is as good as mine, but the timeline fits, and Rhea wasn't one to sleep around. In fact, she hardly dated at all."

"To your knowledge," Benedetti fills in. "But you hadn't seen or spoken to her in over a year, so you can't be sure."

I can see Emme's nostrils flare as she takes a deep breath, probably trying to keep her cool.

"Which is why I told you your guess is as good as mine. Look, I can't tell you what I don't know, and I have no idea what she's been up to this past year. Maybe you should talk to some of the girls at the club," she suggests. "I know she was friendly with a couple of them, but I don't know if they're still there. I remember Mandy Lewis was one, and the other girl's name was Cher. I can't recall her last name though."

"Cher Valente," Joe fills in. "I spoke with her at the club last night, she didn't have much to say, nor did anyone else for that matter. Although, it might've been different if I'd known what I know now. I could've asked more specific questions."

Unlikely, but I don't bother pointing out people associated with an establishment like that—whether employees or patrons—wouldn't exactly stand in line to cooperate with law enforcement. Benedetti knows that.

I'm sure the chief already had enough on his plate being short-staffed, but now he has to worry about the possibility someone in, or with influence on, his department could be involved. His frustration is palpable.

"I can give it a try," Luna offers. "They may be more inclined to talk to a woman."

Benedetti turns weary eyes on her.

"Are you asking or telling me?"

"Still your case, but you know as well as I do if there's any hint of police entanglement, the FBI gets involved. But what may be of benefit is the fact you're understaffed," she adds. "It's actually a great cover to get me in on this case without raising any flags. As far as the outside world goes, I'm on temporary loan to the police department."

"We'll do what we can to help as well," Ouray offers.

Joe raises an eyebrow. "You've got those kids safe?"

"As safe as they can be."

"I'm going to have to talk to the son. We need to find out what he knows or may have seen."

For the first time since stepping into Ouray's office, I speak up.

"It'll have to wait; the kid is traumatized enough."

"He could have information that may help us find his mother's killer," Benedetti counters.

"He probably does, but his momma won't be any deader tomorrow or next week. He's not ready, and if you force him to relive that trauma now, the damage you'd do could be lifelong."

I watch a muscle tick in Joe's jaw as he appears to battle an internal struggle.

"Fine," he grudgingly agrees, getting to his feet. "I'll hold off, but let me know if he volunteers any information."

"You bet."

Luna follows him to the door before turning around, pinning Emme with a look.

"You should be careful too."

Emme nods. "I know."

"Good. Best thing to do is stick to your regular routines, but I'd suggest you keep your distance from the kids. For your safety, but theirs as well."

It's like someone punched her in the stomach, Emme's expression registers shock as the blood seems to drain from her face. She's so damn capable and strong most of the time, you'd almost forget she's had a traumatic twenty-four hours as well.

Luna's face softens before darting a glance at me.

"Unless, of course, you can come up with a plausible excuse why you're becoming a regular at the clubhouse." Then she turns to her husband, a smirk on her face. "Worked for us."

Ouray chuckles as she pulls the door closed behind her, leaving only the three of us in his office.

"She makes a good point," he comments, getting up from behind the desk.

"I'm not sure what that means."

Emme looks confused, but I know damn well what those two were referring to.

Years ago, the FBI was investigating a chain of robberies and murders along the Highway 550 corridor and suspected the involvement of an MC. To infiltrate that world, Luna went undercover, riding the back of our president's bike as his old lady. We all know how that ended.

"Honon will explain," Ouray says, walking out the door as well.

*Bastard.* He knows damn well what he's setting me up for.

"What they're suggesting is a fake relationship with someone in the club to justify the time you spend here with the kids."

My words are met with silence and I brace myself for her outrage at the mere suggestion, but once again Emme surprises me.

"Pretending to be in a relationship?"

"Yes."

"With *someone*?" she probes, but her eyes are sparkling.

"Me, all right? A relationship with me," I snap.

"You mean a *fake* relationship."

"Fucking hell. Yes, of course a fake one."

"That might actually work, although you seem less than excited at the prospect," she observes, getting to her feet. "But don't worry, I can just ask one of the others to be my fake boyfriend."

*Over my dead body.*

―――――

*Emme*

I don't make it to the door.

"Like hell, you will."

His hands grab me by the shoulders, whipping me around. The scowl on his face is quickly replaced by a look of confusion as he takes in the grin on my face.

"You played me," he growls.

"You made it easy," I counter, patting his chest with my hand, but he's not letting go of my shoulders.

His eyes drop down to my mouth, and my breath catches in my throat. Suddenly it doesn't seem funny.

"I'll do it."

"Look, I can't ask that of you. I'm sure—"

"Shut up, Emme," he mutters as his mouth closes over mine.

*Wow.*

Could well be because it's been a hell of a long time, but I'm pretty sure I've never been kissed this thoroughly before. Definitely not on the first try.

There is nothing tentative or unfamiliar about the way Honon melds his mouth to mine. The confident stroke of his tongue and the accompanying possessive growl spread molten heat through my body. There's a barely restrained hunger I can almost taste on his fantastic lips.

The experience seems as oddly familiar as it is new, and despite myself, I can't help but cling onto him for the ride.

Sanity returns as soon as he ends the kiss.

The fact *he* was the one who ended it—because I'm ashamed to admit I would've happily stayed attached to his lips indefinitely—annoys me.

I'm mostly pissed at myself for losing control, but it's easier to take it out on him.

"What the hell was that?"

"Practice," he explains casually, flashing an easy grin as he grabs for the door. "We've gotta make it believable."

As if what happened just now didn't affect him in the least, he waves me out the door. But when I stalk past him, I notice the rapid rise and fall of his chest.

The man is not nearly as unruffled as he'd like me to believe.

When I walk through the clubhouse, I notice it's busier now than it was earlier. A couple of older kids are playing on a gaming system in the living area, and a few of the younger ones are sitting at the dining table. Homework again, I guess.

"Emme," Ouray calls from the bar, where he is sitting beside the old man. "Come have a drink."

A couple of the other guys are standing around, but I don't see Luna or the police chief. They must've left.

I walk over to the bar, the sound of Honon's heavy boots following me.

"Thanks," I tell Ouray. "But I'd like to go check on the kids and then I should probably get going. Thursday nights are busy at the Backyard, and with Sophia gone—"

"You don't have to worry about the restaurant, we've

got it covered," he interrupts. "Plus, Lisa said she'd bring the kids over when the little one wakes up. We ordered a huge stack of pizzas, enough to feed an army, so there's no reason to run off."

*Shit.* If I insist on leaving now, I'm going to look like an asshole.

Resigned, I hoist my butt on a stool and accept the beer Honon slides across the bar.

---

"You're leaving?"

Jesus, the kid is killing me.

Malco hasn't been far from my side since he saw me sitting at the bar when he walked in with Lisa. He hasn't said much though. During dinner, when we joined the table full of kids, he seemed content to listen to them talk while eating his pizza. There's definitely nothing wrong with the boy's appetite.

But his face dropped when I told him I had to go home and would stop by to see him and Athena tomorrow.

"I don't live here, buddy. My house is right down the road though. I won't be far."

"Why can't you stay here?"

"Because I have to wake up early tomorrow morning to go to work and all my things are at my house."

"Can we come with you then?"

I throw a desperate look over my shoulder at Honon. How am I supposed to explain to a nine-year-old it's in part for his sake I'm trying to stick as close to my normal routine as I can?

Honon walks over to Malco's side and crouches down to his level.

"Hey, I told you this is the safest place in town for you, didn't I?"

The boy nods.

"Right, and it is. But until we can catch the person you were hiding from, it's safer for you, your sister, but also for Emme, if she stays at her own house and goes to work tomorrow like it's any other day."

There is a lot Honon leaves out of his explanation, but Malco has already proven he's clever. I can tell by the concerned look he throws me; he understands the gist of what was left unsaid.

"I'll be fine," I tell him, taking his hand in mine. "And when this is over, I'd love for you to come see my house. It's a bit of a mess now because I'm trying to fix up the bedrooms, but it's gonna be great once it's all done."

Talk about an incentive to get my butt in gear on this reno.

He returns my hug awkwardly, but when I glance back as I reach the door, I see he's already turned toward the group of kids playing a board game at the big table.

Honon follows me outside, a backpack slung over his shoulder.

It doesn't really surprise me, I figured he'd probably see me home safely. I'm starting to discover the man has a protective streak a mile wide. Three days ago, that would've annoyed the shit out of me, but since then my sense of security and my view of the world have tilted a bit.

"I'll drive," he announces. "I still have your keys."

Right, I forgot his bike is still parked behind the restaurant.

"We should pick up your bike," I suggest when I get in the truck.

"I'll drive in to work with you tomorrow morning and grab it."

That explains the backpack, he plans on staying the night at my place. I'm not sure how I feel about that, but I'm not sure I want to waste energy arguing. I'd love to get a few good hours of work in before I collapse in bed.

Alone.

"Make yourself comfortable," I tell him when we walk into the house. "You've already seen the sorry contents of my fridge, but I think there may be a stray beer in one of the vegetable drawers. I'll be right back."

I dart down the hallway to the spare bedroom to change into work clothes. This room is a disaster, my clothes draped over the stationary bike I haven't used since I moved here. When I emptied the big bedroom to start renovations, I made the mistake of tossing out the old rickety dresser since I was planning to buy new furniture anyway. Of course, that left me with no place to store my clothes, hence the mess.

It takes me a few minutes to dig out my bib overalls and my favorite holey shirt before I quickly get changed and duck inside the main bedroom and flick on the light.

*Yikes.* I forgot I'd been too tired to get rid of the wallpaper mess from last night.

I grab a few garbage bags from the bottom of the hallway linen closet and get busy, eager to tire my body out so my mind will let me sleep tonight.

"Whatcha doing?"

I jump at the sound of Honon's voice.

"Geeze, you startled me." I blow out a deep breath and finish tying up the last garbage bag. "I wanted to clean up the mess I left last night and start putting up my new cement board in the en suite."

He ducks his head in the bathroom door.

"You did all this? By yourself?"

"Yeah, why wouldn't I? It'll probably take me a while—the kitchen and living room took me almost two years—but I'm not in a hurry." I quickly rethink that statement when I realize my lazy timeline may well have changed. "That is, I *wasn't* in a hurry, but now…"

"I'll help," Honon offers, shoving the sleeves of his Henley up to expose his forearms.

His very fine forearms.

"Do you know what you're doing?" I ask him, crossing my arms over my chest.

His eyes crinkle as he smirks at me.

"I think I can handle myself."

# CHAPTER
## TEN

*Honon*

I hear her moving around the room and crack one eyelid.

The only light source is the one on the hood above the stove, but it's enough to see her standing by the counter making a pot of coffee.

She's wearing the same nightshirt as the other day, her sleep-tangled hair is hanging to the middle of her back. I can't really see her legs from my vantage point, but I have a clear enough recollection to be able to imagine the view. It's enough to stir certain parts of my anatomy I've been keeping a tight rein on all night.

Everything I learn about this woman only intrigues me more. I got a kick out of watching her in action last night hauling, measuring, and screwing down those heavy boards. I'm used to working with Tse on some of his jobs, I like the physical work, but working side by side with Emme was an unexpected blast.

We didn't talk a whole lot, but I got her to divulge her

plans for of the house, and time seemed to fly. It was already after midnight when we called it quits, by which time we'd managed to get half of the bathroom done.

I'd been tempted to make a move on Emme, but she'd been swaying on her feet, and after I took my turn in the shower, she'd already gone to bed. I settled in on the couch, but despite my own exhaustion, sleep hadn't come readily.

Swinging my legs off the couch, I approach her on bare feet. I can tell she's aware of me when her hands still, just as I slip my arms around her body, trapping her against the counter. Lowering my head, I press a kiss to her soft skin where the shirt has slipped down her shoulder, exposing more of her intricate tattoos.

She smells amazing.

"Morning."

"Morning," she echoes, her voice a little hoarse.

"It's funny," I murmur, lifting my hand to trace a vine curling up to her neck. "I used to imagine exploring this beautiful ink on Vixen."

I hear her little gasp.

"You saw me dance?"

I chuckle, easing her around to face me.

"Oh, more than once," I admit.

She raises an eyebrow.

"You're a regular?"

"Nah. Yuma dragged me there the first time but I occasionally came back after that." I duck my head so my eyes are level with hers. "Stopped going when Vixen stopped dancing."

She's trying hard—and failing—to hide a satisfied little smirk as she turns her face away.

"Yeah," I rumble, pulling her tighter to me. "Can't

believe I didn't recognize you. The tattoos should've given you away."

"In all fairness, I've added quite a few since. Plus, I suspect you weren't necessarily focusing on my ink back then."

I shoot her a wide grin.

"You would be correct."

Curling a finger under her chin I lift her head, bringing her eyes back to me and giving her a chance to stop me before I kiss her.

Since the coffee is gurgling and I know she needs to get going soon, I keep the kiss light and my hands on top of her shirt. It's a struggle.

"I feel I should point out once again, there's no one here to see," she repeats when I finally let her go.

"Just getting you used to my touch for when we do have witnesses."

It's obvious from the roll of her eyes, she's not buying what I'm selling.

Guess I've already confessed too much for that.

––––––––

My bike is still parked where I left it when we get to the restaurant half an hour later.

"Do you have to get going right away?" Emme asks. "I can whip you up a quick omelet or something."

I have a group coming in this morning but not until nine. I'll have plenty of time to get to the range.

"Sure."

Getting out of the truck, I'm just handing Emme her keys when my phone rings. I check the name on the screen and hold my phone against my chest.

"I've gotta take this. I'll be in shortly."

She nods and I wait until she's halfway to the back door before I answer.

"It's been a while, brother."

The familiar chuckle on the other end puts a smile on my face.

"No decent cell reception in Denali National Park."

"You're in Alaska?"

"Was. Spent the winter there."

"Jesus, you're a sucker for punishment."

"Not really. Beautiful up there, man. So vast, you don't ever have to see another person if you don't want to. Feels like you're at the end of the world."

"That's 'cause it is, you stupid fucker. Did you rent a place or something?"

He barks out a laugh.

"More like a shack, brother. An old hunting cabin in one of the Denali National Preserves. No running water, no electricity, but views forever. Lived off what I could trap or shoot. It was amazing."

Doesn't sound like a particularly good time to me. I like the outdoors just fine and am always up for a trek into the mountains or a week-long hunting trip, but not for months. I happen to enjoy my creature comforts; my beer, my bed, and my regular meals.

"So how come you left?"

"The snow was melting, which means the return of the tourists. Besides, I felt a hankering for home. One of Lisa's meals, shooting the shit with the boys, a beer with the old man."

At the mention of Nosh, I feel a pang of sadness.

"About the old man," I start.

"Ah, shit. Don't tell me…"

"He's still alive," I quickly assure him. "But for how long is anyone's guess. He's not well, doesn't know whether he's coming or going, and can barely take a piss by himself anymore."

"Fuck, man. That's sad."

"That it is," I agree. "So whereabouts are you now?"

"Canadian Rockies. Jasper. Cool place. I was thinking of hanging around here a few days, make my way down to Montana, maybe check out the Kootenai, and then follow the mountains home. I figured I'd take a couple of weeks, a month, but maybe I should rethink my plans."

"Nah, don't do that. The old man could kick around for another ten years and you'd have wasted the chance. If anything happens, I'll get in touch. Just make sure you check your fucking messages once in a while."

"Will do. Everyone else okay there? Anything new?"

For a second I'm tempted to tell him about Emme, but decide against it. Nothing really to tell. Instead, I give him a quick rundown on the welfare of the club, before we say our goodbyes and end the call.

He'd been flying under the radar for six months after he first took off, before I heard from him. We'd started getting worried when his phone number was no longer listed and we lost track of where he was. He apologized for going dark, said he needed to stand on his own two feet for a while—which is something I understand—and promised to check in with me every couple of months. He's done so faithfully over the past few years and I've left him alone. Until I realized a couple of months ago, I hadn't heard from him in a while and left him a message.

I should probably let Lisa know; she's been asking about him.

"I'm busy," she clips as she answers the phone. "What do you want?"

I hear the baby crying in the background.

"Thought you might wanna know Wapi is okay. He's in Canada but making his way home."

I hear her exhale loudly.

"Well, thank the Lord for that."

"Everything all right over there?" I ask when I hear pots clanging in the background.

"You try cooking breakfast for an army while wrangling a bunch of rowdy kids and a crying baby," she snaps. "I'm about to go on strike."

I grin at the thought. Lisa is all bark but no bite.

"You worry about the kids. I should be there in half an hour to cook for the troops."

———

*Emme*

"Glad to see you're in a better mood."

It's after lunch and I was on my way to check on the kitchen but stop to glare at Mack.

"And yet here you are trying to piss me off again."

He shrugs, unimpressed.

"Hey, if I'd known you were actually seeing the guy, it would've explained your bad mood."

I see word of the wet kiss Honon laid on me in the kitchen before he rushed out the door has made its way through the restaurant grapevine. Terry has a big mouth.

"Oh yeah? And how is that?"

"Easy, relationships are messy. Guys always fuck up. Believe me, I know."

"Since when are you an expert on relationships?"

Mack calls himself a serial monogamist, which is basically code for bed-hopping. He's hardly ever without a girlfriend, but every few months he trades them in for the next model.

"Since Becca broke up with me last weekend and told me almost the same thing every other woman who dumped me has said: I'm a fuckup. I wish someone would write a handbook because I'm clearly not understanding the rules."

*Wow.* Okay, I guess I totally missed the mark on that. Mack's a fun guy, personable, tall, pretty good-looking, although a bit too preppy for me. However, I would never have guessed he was the *dumpee* and not the *dumper*.

"I hear you, brother. I have exactly the same problem."

We both turn to Fred, who slides a tray of empties on the bar before looking at us. I'm guessing he was in a hurry this morning since his eyebrows are a little lopsided. One of them arches substantially higher than the other, making him look like an angry Vulcan.

It's not easy imagining Fred with dating problems. Or dating at all.

I press my lips together, nod, and escape to the office before I burst out laughing in the poor man's face.

Making use of the after-lunch lull, I start working on a big order for tomorrow and try to catch up on some paperwork I've been avoiding. At some point Lauren, our other sous-chef, sticks her head in the door.

"Sorry to bug you, but I'm getting low on a few things and I've got stuff in the oven. Any chance someone could run out to the Natural Grocers?"

"Got a list?"

She walks in and hands it to me. Looks like pretty basic stuff.

"I'll run out, Mack and Fred are doing liquor inventory."

Maybe I can zip up to the club for a quick visit before I hit up the store, and still get back before the rest of the staff gets here at four thirty. It's Friday night, and it'll be too late to drop by after we close.

Since it's the middle of the afternoon, the clubhouse is quiet. Soft snoring comes from the living area, where an episode of *Dateline* is playing on the large screen TV and a pair of boots are just visible resting on a footstool. The only other noise I hear is coming from the kitchen, where I find Lisa emptying out the dishwasher.

But my attention is instantly drawn to a folding baby crib in the far corner.

"She just started to fuss," Lisa explains, looking up. "She's probably getting hungry. If you want to grab her, I'll get a bottle ready. Check her diaper though, there's a bag on the floor beside the cot. Safest place to change her is right in there, at least she can't get far. She's a mover, that one."

I'm greeted with a pair of bright blue eyes and a watery smile. Being a mother was never really on my radar. I was too busy meeting the life goals I set myself to consider the possibility. But I'm feeling pretty maternal smiling back at this little girl.

I quickly unzip her sleep sack and change her wet diaper, which Lisa probably could've done in two minutes but takes me much longer. The other woman doesn't interfere though, and by the time I lift Athena out of the crib, she's already chopping vegetables at the counter.

"Left the bottle on the table for you."

I take a seat at the kitchen table, tilt the baby in the crook of my arm, and aim the bottle at her pursed pink mouth. As soon as the nipple disappears between her lips, those little hands grab the bottle and shift it to a position she apparently likes better.

No doubt who's in charge here.

"Where is Malco?"

"Honon took him for a ride on the ATV up to the over-look, they shouldn't be long. The boy was a little lost. Trunk tried talkin' to him a bit this morning, but he just curled up in a tighter ball. Hasn't said a peep to me either. I've only heard him talk to you and Honon."

As if she conjured them, I hear the door of the clubhouse slam shut and footsteps running this way.

"You came."

Malco stops in the doorway, his face flushed from the outdoor air.

"Told you she would if she could," Honon explains, walking up behind him.

He throws me a wink and turns to Lisa.

"What are the chances for a couple of adventurers getting a hot chocolate?"

"I'd say pretty good," Lisa plays along. "As long as y'all wash your hands before you sit your butts at my kitchen table."

It's already three forty-five when I rush out of the club-house and I'm probably not going to make it back to the restaurant in time. I don't care though, I feel a lot better having seen the kids.

That feeling lasts about as long as it takes me to get down to the store, toss what I need in my cart, and rush it to the checkout.

"Hey, Emme."

I turn to find Luna at the checkout next to mine, pulling a few things out of her basket.

"Oh, hi."

"I was actually on my way to see you and just stopped in to grab a few things for dinner. Let me cash out and I'll catch you outside."

She's waiting for me when I walk out the doors, balancing three big bags in my arms, and wondering what it is she needed to talk to me about.

"Here, let me help you."

Taking one of the paper bags, she walks beside me to my truck without speaking. After we've loaded the groceries on the passenger seat, I turn to her.

"You said you were coming to see me?" I prompt her, bracing myself.

"Yes," she confirms, a sympathetic look on her face. "We received the preliminary report from Rhea's autopsy this morning."

"Oh," is all I manage.

Then, to my absolute horror, I burst into tears. Big gasping sobs.

It's not that I haven't thought about Rhea these past few days, but I never allowed my thoughts to go very far. I tried to shove those thoughts and feelings down for the sake of those kids. Hearing an autopsy was done on her body is like getting slapped in the face with the horrible reality of her death.

"I'm so sorry," Luna mutters.

"Not…your…fault," I sob.

She opens the truck and urges me to sit down on the running board. I'm grateful for the open door shielding me from curious eyes.

I force myself to take deep breaths through my nose to regain some control.

"It's been a crazy few days," I share when I've calmed down a bit. "I feel like I got knocked into a raging river and I'm still barreling downstream. I've been so busy keeping my head above water, I haven't had time to let it all sink in."

"Well, I'm still sorry I brought that on."

I force a smile when I look up at her.

"Had to come out one way or another, I suppose. Was there anything specific about the…the report?"

Luna sits down beside me, her elbows on her knees and her hands clasped between.

"The cause of death was blunt force trauma to the head, but she had bruises and abrasions on other parts of her body as well. She also had bruising around her neck," she tells me in a gentle voice.

The overwhelming sadness of moments before is replaced with an intense anger burning my gut.

I surge to my feet and take a few steps before I swerve around, launching my fist into the side panel of my truck. An impulse I immediately regret, cradling my fist in my other hand.

"That's gonna hurt," Luna observes dryly.

"It already fucking does," I admit through clenched teeth.

# CHAPTER
# ELEVEN

*Honon*

"Has he eaten at all?"

I glance at Lissie, Yuma's wife, sitting beside me at the bar with her eyes fixed on her father-in-law.

Nosh is sitting with Lusio and Yuma at one of the smaller tables, playing with the food on his plate. He's been staring off into the distance, away in some alternate universe. He doesn't even seem to register when either of the other men try to engage him in conversation.

Lisa had voiced concern earlier and raised the alarm. Nosh had not touched either his breakfast or lunch today and had been asleep in front of the TV all afternoon. She'd become worried when he hadn't woken up when the kids filed in after school, which would've meant the end to any peace and quiet in the clubhouse. It had taken Lisa and my combined efforts to rouse him.

After putting a call in to Yuma, he ended up bringing his family over for dinner. Despite Nosh's recent cognitive issues, he still dotes on his grandkids, but tonight he's barely even acknowledged them.

"Not a single bite," I tell her.

"I know Yuma doesn't want to force his dad into care, but I wonder if we've reached a point where he doesn't have a choice."

Lissie voices what I'm sure has been on all our minds.

"It's possible," I concede. "But he could also just have an off day. Maybe a bug or something. Let's see what he's like tomorrow."

"I guess."

I'm trying to stay positive, but I think we both realize it's only a matter of time.

The front door opens and Ouray walks in, his eyes scanning the clubhouse. He lifts an eyebrow when he catches sight of me and comes straight for the bar, pulling me aside.

"Thought you'd be at the Backyard Edge by now."

That had been the plan, but worry for the old man is keeping me here.

In his heyday, Nosh may have been a hard man, a firm taskmaster, but he also took on the role of parent. Something I desperately needed in my life back then. He's always been there for me, looking out for me, and since his health started failing a few years ago, it seemed like a natural development for those roles to switch.

Yuma is his son by blood, but the old man is a father to most of us.

Which is why I'm torn.

"I'll check in there later," I tell Ouray, who shakes his head.

"Luna just got home. Told me she saw Emme earlier."

"Oh?"

I haven't spoken to her since she left the clubhouse.

"She says she shared the outcome of the postmortem on her friend with Emme. What killed her was the bastard caving her head in after he'd worked her over. She had some older injuries as well, so it probably wasn't the first time."

Having found her body, that conclusion doesn't surprise me.

"I hope Luna was a little less fucking descriptive talking to Emme," I grumble.

"What do you think, asshole?" He throws me a scowl before he continues, "She needed to know if Emme knew anything about possible prior abuse and discuss a few other things with her. They found fingerprints on the baseball bat."

That gets my attention.

"And?"

"Same prints were all over the house, but mostly in the boy's room. It's a small hand, it looks like they belong to him."

Something about the way he says it has my hackles go up. I don't like where this is going.

"So? The bat was probably his. Makes sense his prints would be on there as well."

"Except, his are the *only* prints on there."

"The killer could've worn gloves," I suggest.

"Believe me, I just had this same discussion with my wife. Problem is, those fingerprints were ridged in blood. His mother's blood."

I immediately look over my shoulder to find Malco sitting next to his sister, who is in a high chair at the dining table, those wide eyes fixed on me.

*No way.*

"There's no way," I hiss at Ouray. "Not a chance in hell. They're barking up the wrong *fucking* tree."

"Calm down, brother. No one is saying he had anything to do with it, but they're gonna need to talk to him. Find out how those prints ended up on the murder weapon."

"Not without me there, they're not," I insist.

The kid needs someone to protect him.

"Funny, Luna mentioned that's the first thing Emme said." Ouray claps me on the shoulder. "Speaking of Emme, Luna mentioned she was upset. You should probably check in on her."

I glance over at Nosh, who looks like he's already nodding off. He'll need to be helped to bed soon.

"Nosh has a clubhouse full of people who can look after him," Ouray points out, not missing a thing. "Emme does not."

———

I find Emme with Mack behind a busy bar.

Only standing room left. Some wannabe tough-guy yahoo with ink down to his fingertips, skull rings, and a goddamn Fu Manchu stache with braided goatee is occupying my stool at the end. He's also eye-fucking the woman behind the bar.

"That's my spot."

He turns his head slowly, looking me up and down before returning his attention to Emme.

I drop a heavy hand on his shoulder, dig my thumb into the pressure point at the base of his neck, and bend down.

"She's mine too," I growl by his ear.

I catch Emme shaking her head as she watches me straighten up and give the guy a firm slap between the shoulder blades. Smarter than he looks, he vacates my seat without argument and moves to the other side of the bar, where he appears to settle up with Mack before leaving.

"Chasing off my customers better not become a habit." She bangs a bottle of beer on the bar in front of me. "And as an FYI, chest-pounding and knuckle-dragging are not in the least appealing."

It's not until she starts walking away, I catch sight of her bruised and swollen hand.

"What the fuck happened to you?"

She rolls her eyes as she turns back to me.

"My bad. I should've added snarling and barking to that list."

I suck in air through my gritted teeth and try again.

"Emme, what happened to your hand?"

She holds her mangled hand up and studies it like it's an alien object.

"Argument with my pickup. The truck won."

Then she turns her back and heads for a waiting customer.

*Jesus.* Even with her claws out I want to jump her.

I must be further gone than I thought.

―――

*Emme*

I'm dead on my feet when I lock the back door a little after eleven.

It was crazy busy tonight, but it suited me just fine. It

was a good distraction and left me no time to worry about some of the things Luna told me today.

Despite barely talking to him, I'm not surprised to find Honon already sitting on his bike, waiting for me. He'd spent the night nursing a beer at the end of the bar. I'd occasionally glance over to find him watching me with narrowed eyes.

He was probably pissed I was ignoring him, but I didn't want a repeat of what happened in the parking lot of the grocery store this afternoon. One kind word or gentle gesture might've opened those floodgates again, and that's not something I can afford. Not at work, the one part of my life where I at least have the illusion of maintaining some modicum of control.

Still, pissed or not, somehow, I have no doubt he'll be following to see me safely home.

I set the radio to an oldies station before I pull out of the parking lot, and sing along loudly all the way home to avoid letting dark thoughts swarm me. Those will have to wait until I'm in the safety and privacy of my own four walls.

Although privacy may be relative, since five minutes later I don't even attempt to stop Honon from following me into the house.

I barely have a chance to dump my backpack on the floor and shrug out of my hoodie when I'm pushed face first up against the wall, Honon's heavy breathing in my ear.

"What happened to your hand, Emme?"

He repeats his question from hours ago in a low, threatening voice.

Anger at being manhandled abruptly changes into a

different kind of fire when I feel the evidence of his state of mind press against my ass.

Would it be so bad to keep this fucked-up world at bay a little longer by indulging in a physical release?

Because I know that's all it can be. He may be attracted to me, ready to live out a fantasy he's harbored since my dancing days, but I'm pretty sure he's not in the market for anything more.

Then again, neither am I.

Instead of answering him, I twist around, loop my arms around his neck, and lift up on my toes so I can sink my teeth into his plump bottom lip.

His deep guttural groan sends a tingle through my body, and I jump up, clamping my legs around his hips as I mold my mouth to his. With large hands cupping my ass, he marches me to the couch and drops down with me straddling him.

I immediately tug up my shirt, briefly letting go of his lips to pull it over my head. His hand shoves down the back of my cargos and straight into my panties, his long fingers easily finding the wet gathering between my legs. I'm still struggling with the clasp of my bra when he shoves two fingers inside me, and my back arcs at the sudden intrusion.

"Yesss…" I hiss into his mouth.

This feeling of fullness, the slight burn of tissues stretching to fit; it's perfect.

Just like the first time he kissed me, I love his possessive confidence. Not a hint of hesitation in the way he claims me.

I drop my bra, reach for his fly and rush to open it, ready to do some claiming of my own. My fingers wrap around silk steel.

He pulls his hand from my pants and drops his head back, hissing sharply between his teeth.

"Goddammit, Emme... Should'a known you'd be feral."

Then he grabs my hip and urges me to my feet.

"Drop the pants."

I don't hesitate, shoving them down along with my panties, and kicking them aside. Honon's gaze never leaves me as he pulls a condom from his jeans before shoving them partly down his hips.

"Wanna do the honors?" he asks, a half-smile on his face as he flicks the foil packet.

I'm standing here buck-naked. I know what I look like; colorful ink pieces cover both of my arms and go halfway down my back, but the rest of my body is untouched. With the exception of my very first one; a broken chain tattoo around my ankle I got at sixteen in an act of rebellion.

I have no problem letting him look his fill, but this isn't a one-way street.

"I will if you lose the shirt."

For a moment he looks torn, but then he tosses me the condom and strips off his shirt.

"Hop on."

He doesn't give me much time to take stock but I like what I see. A lot.

He has some kind of snake curling up his left upper arm, the tattoo of a dragon on his right shoulder, and an intriguing abstract piece, which runs from his right hip bone up his side.

He holds out his hand and I grab on, straddling his thighs before I rip the foil pack and roll on the condom. Then I stroke my fingers up his hip bone to the abstract tattoo, feeling dips and ridges of scarred tissue underneath.

"What hap—"

Before I can finish my question, he grabs my hips, lifts me up, and lowers me on his erection.

"Talk…is…for…later," he grunts, bucking up as he pushes inside me again and again.

Not like I'd be able to utter a single coherent word at this point. My body is taken for a wild ride, and all I can do is grab on to his shoulders and hang on.

I catch a glimpse of his turbulent eyes, which seem to swirl with a mix of lust and unfamiliar shadows. The next moment I lose them, when he closes his lips around my nipple, and I'm overwhelmed with sensations.

Letting go of his shoulders, I lift my arms in the air, and trust him to make me soar.

———

"Are you gonna tell me about your hand?"

I'm sprawled on top of his body as his fingers draw lazy circles on my ass.

I'd almost forgotten.

Lifting my hand off his chest, I flex my fingers a few times. It hurts a little, but nothing is broken. I was lucky.

"I was angry. I punched the side of my truck."

He takes my hand and examines it, pressing a kiss on my bruised knuckles.

"That's a fucking boneheaded thing to do, Wildcat."

I raise my head and throw him an incredulous look.

"Wildcat? Seriously?"

His eyes sparkle mischievously as he flashes a grin.

"That's what you remind me of. You've got a fierce temper on you, you use your claws when someone gets too close, and you go wild when I touch you just right."

I can't decide whether to be insulted or flattered, so I opt for ambiguity.

"Whatever."

He gives my body a little shake before he asks, "What got you riled up?"

"I bumped into Luna at the grocery store after I left the clubhouse. Turns out someone had likely been using Rhea as a punching bag for a while. Some of her injuries were old."

My blood stirs even talking about it.

He nods. "Ouray mentioned Luna had talked to you."

"Did he tell you they want to interview Malco?" The muscle ticking in his jaw tells me he's heard. "Did he tell you why?" I follow it up with.

"Yeah, he did."

Agitated, I roll off Honon and grab the throw off the back of the couch to wrap around me. Then I pad to the kitchen and start wiping the counter.

"It's bullshit. He's a little kid, for fuck's sake," I rant, looking over at the couch where Honon is just pulling up his jeans. "It doesn't make any sense."

"I know it doesn't," he agrees in a conciliatory voice as he walks over. "But Malco is the only person who can explain what actually happened."

"So you're saying you're good with it? Interrogating an already traumatized kid?" I snap, annoyed he's being so rational.

"No, I'm not good with anything that kid went through, and I don't want to put him through more, but I don't think there's any choice."

I hate that he's right. I hate it so much.

"He's gonna be so scared," I whisper as he folds me in his arms.

"We'll be there the whole time," he assures me.

I drop my head to his chest and let him hold me for a bit.

Then I lean back to look up at him.

"Hey, I'm curious… What were we practicing for this time?"

Honon throws his head back as he bursts out laughing.

The next moment I'm picked up off my feet and flung over his shoulder as he marches me to the bedroom.

# CHAPTER
# TWELVE

*Honon*

"Told you he wasn't ready."

Trunk pats Luna's shoulder before taking a seat at the bar beside her.

Because Saturdays are busy at the Backyard Edge, and Emme wouldn't be able to take time out of her day, Luna had agreed to wait until this morning to interview Malco. That had given Trunk and me a little time with him yesterday, to see if he'd be comfortable enough to answer even simple innocuous questions from Trunk, but all he did was nod or shake his head.

"I know. I had to try though," she explains. "He's the best lead I've got. So far, I don't have a whole lot else to go on. No computer or cell phone was found on the scene, and I don't have unlimited time or resources—with everyone stretched so thin—to have someone go through the pile of her paperwork and correspondence back at the office. I'm feeling the pressure."

On the other side of the clubhouse, I see Emme coming out of the hallway, her arm around Malco. Needless to say, the interview hadn't gone well. Not really talking to begin with—only a few words directed at Emme or myself—the moment his mother was mentioned, the kid seemed to completely shut down.

We'd left Emme alone with him to see if she could pull him back from wherever he'd retreated to. Apparently with some success, since he appears to be responding to something she says with a nod.

"What about those other two dancers?" I ask, turning back to Luna. "The ones Joe said he'd already interviewed? Nothing useful from them?"

"Just a whole lot of 'I don't know anything.' Neither were particularly convincing, though. I got the sense they were holding back."

"Maybe we can try," I suggest. "If it's just a matter of not wanting to talk to cops, they may feel safer talking to one of us."

"Who is they?" Emme asks, as she joins us at the bar.

Looking behind her I see Malco has joined some of the other boys playing some kind of video game.

"Mandy and Cher," Luna answers her. "They're still not saying much."

"I'll do it. They know me."

I'm getting ready to object when Emme puts a hand on my arm.

"I'm one of the girls. At least I was. It's more likely they'll confide in me than any of you guys."

"She's got a point," Luna agrees.

"And before you say something about me taking any kind of risk," Emme jumps in, reading me well, since that's exactly what I was about to point out. "There is nothing unusual about me touching base with the girls I used to dance with after a mutual friend has died."

"She's got you there, brother," Trunk contributes.

I opt not to react and instead listen to Luna instruct Emme on what kind of information she's looking for, while I finish the dregs of my coffee.

A little while later I walk Emme outside. She has to be at the restaurant at eleven. Luna already left a few minutes ago.

"When do you plan on talking to them?" I ask when we get to her truck.

"I'm off tomorrow, I'll try them in the morning. Luna forwarded all their contact info, so I thought I'd try them at home instead of the club. They may be more inclined to talk there."

"I'll come with you," I announce. "I don't have anything scheduled at the range until the afternoon, and one of the other guys can handle any walk-ins in the morning."

Emme rolls her eyes.

"That would defeat the purpose, now, wouldn't it?" she mutters with a touch of sarcasm.

"Then I'll wait in the truck," I persist, tugging her into my arms.

"If I say no, you're gonna follow me anyway, aren't you?"

I grin down at her upturned face.

"Probably."

Wolf whistles go up from the direction of the garage when I kiss her. As she gets in behind the wheel—slightly flushed underneath the freckles I've only recently noticed— I aim a glare at Brick and Mika who are standing in the bay door, giving me a thumbs-up.

"Why don't you put those thumbs back up your asses where they belong," I call out.

Of course, that only adds to their hilarity.

Too late I decide to ignore them and duck my head inside the cab of the truck.

"I'll come by later," I tell Emme, leaning in for another peck before I slam the door shut.

I'm watching her drive off when I hear the door to the clubhouse open behind me, followed by Lisa's voice.

"We need you in here. The old man's collapsed."

I find Trunk already crouched next to Nosh, who is sprawled on the floor next to the small table he was sitting at earlier. I'm relieved to see his eyes open, but he's got a nasty cut on his forehead.

"What happened?"

"Don't know. Didn't see it but I heard the bang. Looks like he hit the table going down."

Nosh groans and when he tries to sit up, I press down on his shoulder. Trunk leans over him so he can read his lips.

"Stay down, old man. You're bleeding."

"Calling Yuma," Lisa announces, her phone already by her ear.

"That's gonna need stitches," I observe.

The gash looks quite deep and is bleeding like a mother-fucker. Of course most head wounds do.

"Could be the least of his worries," Trunk mumbles. "He's gonna need to get checked out. Make sure he stays down."

Then he gets to his feet, pulls out his phone, and walks away a few steps keeping his back turned. I can hear him talking to a dispatcher.

When I turn back to Nosh, I see his eyes are closed, but his chest continues to rise steadily. Thank fuck for that.

Twenty-five minutes later, the old man is loaded into an ambulance with Yuma by his side. Ouray showed up as well and plans to follow them to Mercy.

"Agah!"

Athena slaps her tiny hand on the surface of the table.

Lisa ordered me to keep an eye on the baby while she took Malco, and a few of the younger kids, out the back door to watch TV at her place. Of course, the little one started screaming from her crib in the kitchen the moment Lisa walked out the door.

A diaper change and a bottle later, she's pretty comfy sitting on my lap.

"Too bad it's too early for a beer," Brick groans as he gets to his feet. "But I've got a few customers waiting for their vehicles, so I'd better get to it. Hope the old man will be all right."

Fuck, I hope he'll be all right as well.

"Ouray said he'd keep us updated," I tell him. "Hopefully, we'll hear something soon."

Trunk and Brick may not have grown up in the club as a lot of us have, but they know the role Nosh played and respect the Arrow's Edge MC family he built. We're all worried. Losing him would be a huge loss for everyone.

"Bah!"

I look down at Athena's upturned little face and melt a bit when she flashes me a gummy smile.

The end of an era, and who knows, this little girl may be the beginning of another.

———

*Emme*

I saw Honon come in right around the time the kitchen usually starts slowing down, but the bar gets busy.

Other than a quick hello when he sat down, he hasn't said much and has been staring in his beer or checking his phone.

Something is up, but I don't get a chance to ask him until after I usher the last customers out the door.

He startles when I walk up and put a hand on his back.

"Everything okay?"

He turns his head to look at me. His eyes are clouded despite his smile.

"Yeah. You ready to go?"

Whatever is bothering him, he's not ready to talk, so I don't push it.

"Give me ten minutes."

"Sure."

I rush to check in with Lauren, who is the last one in the kitchen. The others left along with most of the waitstaff a while ago. She's already turning off some of the lights when I walk in.

"You'll be in on Tuesday?"

"Yes, I'll be in for morning deliveries, Terry has a dentist's appointment and he'll take the dinner shift. Chris left a note on your desk with a few schedule changes for the week."

"Great, thanks, Lauren. Have a good night."

I do a last walk-through and flick the switch for the overhead lights before I duck into the office and have a peek at the note our chef left behind. At the bottom he scribbled 'Sophia back on Friday!' with a smiley face beside it. I'm not sure if it means he's glad because I'm doing a piss-poor job of filling in for Sophia, or if he's happy for some relief for me. Either way, I can't wait for things to return to normal.

At least here at work.

After turning off the computer, grabbing my backpack, and locking the office door, I head back to the bar.

"You head out," Mack suggests when he catches sight of me. "I'll be right behind you. I'm just gonna finish the garbage and then I'll lock up."

After we say our goodbyes, Honon follows me down the hall and out to the parking lot.

"I'll make sure you get home safe," he promises when the door slams shut behind us.

I spin around.

"You're not staying?"

He shakes his head.

"I gotta check on something."

He glances at his phone again, which is still in his hand.

"Hey," I call his attention. "Are you sure you're okay?"

He stares off to the side, avoiding my eyes, and takes a moment to answer.

"It's Nosh, the old man."

"Did something happen?"

"He went down just after you left, knocked his head on the table, and cut himself pretty good." He runs a hand through his hair. "Anyway, he's been at Mercy for damn near ten hours, and all I know is they stitched up his head and were doing some tests, but I've heard nothing new since."

I open my door and unlock the passenger side.

"Come on, get in. Let's go."

He scrutinizes me for a moment before he appears to clue in.

"My bike is here."

"It was fine here before. We can pick it up later."

Coming to a decision, he nods and jogs around to the other side to get in.

When I pull out of the parking lot and turn south toward Mercy Hospital, he starts talking in a low voice, and I have to strain to hear him.

"Nosh found me on the side of Highway 550 when I was eight. I'd somehow managed to crawl out of the ravine my father threw me down."

"Your father? *Jesus*," slips from my lips before I clamp them firmly shut.

I know guys, I know to moderate any kind of reaction when they're talking about heavy stuff, or they'll clam right up.

"Yeah. He was a sick bastard. Was still pissed at my mother for leaving him and determined to make her hurt. So he picked me up after school for what was supposed to be a camping trip and headed for the mountains. I remember him telling me to get out of the car to see the waterfall from the outlook point, and the next thing I know I'm picked up and tossed over the edge."

"Holy shit."

I glance over and see he has his head back and his eyes closed.

"Like I said, don't know how I got to the side of the road, I was in pretty bad shape, but Nosh took me in. He eventually tracked down my father and told me that chapter of my life was over. I didn't ask what that meant and he didn't tell, but he gave me a home, a family, and my next chapter."

*Whoa.* That's a lot to take in.

"What about your mom?"

"She committed suicide right after my father told her I'd been killed in a tragic accident."

I find it hard to breathe and struggle to regain my composure.

"So, that's my messed-up past. What about you? You still got parents?" he asks as if he didn't just make my damn heart bleed for him.

"Jesus, give me a minute to recover from that," I mutter.

"It was a long time ago."

"For you, maybe. It's new to me and pretty horrific." I give my head a shake and blow out a breath. "Anyway, yes, I still have my parents, but I haven't seen them in years. They disowned me when I tasted freedom for the first time in college and went a little wild."

He rolls his head to the side and grins.

"See? Wildcat."

"Whatever." I wave him off. "Anyway, my father was a plastic surgeon and never home, so my mother had all the time in the world to try and mold me into her image. Still," I concede, "my childhood sounds like a fucking Hallmark movie compared to yours."

*Wow.* You can cover a lot of ground in a fifteen-minute ride to the hospital.

It's like everything I thought I knew about Honon shifts slightly and settles in a modified perspective, now I have a more detailed context.

"That spot's opening up."

He points at an SUV backing out of a parking space not far from the hospital's main entrance, and I pull in. When I get out of the truck, Honon is already waiting for me and we start walking toward the doors.

Halfway there he grabs my hand, slips his fingers between mine, and holds on tight. When I glance over, he's looking straight ahead, a faint smile on his lips. He doesn't let go until we walk into the small waiting room on the second floor, a helpful nurse directs us to.

I stand back while Honon greets Ouray and Yuma with one of those manly half-hugs that looks more like chest bumps accompanied by a couple of bone-jarring backslaps. When he leans down to kiss a seated Lissie on the cheek, Ouray throws an arm around my shoulder for a side hug.

"Appreciate you bringing him, darlin'."

"Yeah, thanks, Emme," Yuma adds, giving me a similar treatment.

Unsure what to say to any of that, I opt to stay quiet and simply flash a smile. I've worked for these guys for years and they're usually friendly enough, but other than Tse, I've certainly never been hugged by them. With the exception of Honon in recent days, of course.

"We've been waiting for an update," Yuma volunteers. "Last we heard he definitely has a concussion so he'll be here at least overnight, but they also said he was very dehydrated, which is why they're running a few more tests. The doctor says it's possible his kidneys aren't working too well. They took him up to radiology."

"Is he awake?" Honon asks him.

"Off and on, but very disoriented. More so than usual, he doesn't even seem to know where he is."

I feel a little uneasy—like an interloper—listening to them discuss a man I don't really know.

"Should I maybe get us some coffee?" I offer.

Before anyone has a chance to respond, the door behind me opens and I quickly step to the side.

The doctor walking in is an older gentleman wearing a somber expression. He glances briefly at Honon and myself.

"Everyone here for Robert Wells?" he asks.

"Yes," Ouray answers. "We're all family."

# CHAPTER
# THIRTEEN

*Honon*

"You're coming to the clubhouse right after?"

Emme sets her cup down on the counter and turns to face me.

"As soon as I'm done."

"Be careful," I mumble, drawing her in my arms.

"Honon…"

"Humor me."

She sighs.

"I'll be fine."

I give her a stern look before bending down to brush her lips.

"Go." She gives me a little shove. "You're going to be late."

Plans have changed since last night, so instead of tagging along with Emme, I'm on my way to the clubhouse.

Ouray called a club meeting for nine this morning. We have some difficult decisions to hash out, and I'm not looking forward to it.

*Jesus*, end stage renal failure. It had been a hard pill to swallow, but even harder will be trying to figure out what to do now.

I was able to see Nosh briefly last night, but he was out of it. Yuma insisted on staying the night, and we ended up leaving at the same time as Ouray, who was taking Lissie home.

After picking up my bike at the restaurant, we didn't get in until well after two. Emme had gone straight to bed, but I wanted to try and get a hold of Wapi again and ended up having to leave him a message, which I'd hoped to avoid.

Emme was asleep by the time I crawled into bed, and didn't even stir when I wrapped her in my arms. That was a new experience for me; sharing a bed with a woman for the sole purpose of sleeping. It was nice—really nice—which, I'm sure, had everything to do with the woman I was with.

It's one thing to get to live out a fantasy, but it hits a whole other level when reality turns out to be so much better. I wonder if that's why I'd always kept my distance from Emme, maybe on some level I knew she'd be the one who'd burrow deep under my skin.

I pull up to the clubhouse and a very full parking lot. Even Yuma's truck is already here.

Inside, I'm surprised to find everyone gathered around the large table. Normally, we get together in Ouray's office for club meetings. Also unexpected is the presence of the old ladies. Even Mel, Paco's wife who has a busy law practice in town, is here. The only ones missing are Wapi, Tse, and Sophia.

"Where are the kids?" I ask Lisa, who is sitting beside her husband.

Most of the kids would be in school except for Lettie—

Yuma and Lissie's youngest—and, of course, Malco and his sister.

"The baby's asleep in the crib in the kitchen and the boy is watching movies with Lettie in Ouray's office."

"All right. Everyone," Ouray calls the group to attention and points at a Bluetooth speaker in the middle of the table. "We've got Tse and Sophia on speaker, this way we only have to do this once." He looks up at me. "Any luck with Wapi?"

I shake my head.

"Left him another message to give me a call, but I haven't heard."

"All right. We'll have to proceed without him. Yuma?"

"Right. No easy way to do this. Turns out, Nosh's kidneys are failing. The doctor called it end stage renal failure."

I hear some gasps and muffled curses, see some wet eyes, which is much how we reacted last night when the doc gave us the news.

It had been Yuma who preferred to hold off telling everyone until this morning. I think he needed time to process it all himself first. His relationship with his father had never been the best. It was only in recent years, after Momma's death, those two were able to mend some fences, and now this.

"Y'all know how he feels about doctors and hospitals," Yuma continues. "Hard to know how long he's been sick. Not that it matters anymore. The doctor says he's got weeks, at most."

"Is there nothing they can do?" Paco wants to know. "Dialysis or something?"

"It would only prolong the inevitable," Lissie speaks up.

"In his condition, at his age, and in this advanced stage, they're not even sure it would do any good at all."

"We should've forced him into the damn nursing home," Kaga grumbles. "Maybe then they would've—"

"He would've hated it and you know it."

Tse's voice sounds tinny over the speaker.

"He would've," Ouray agrees. "Besides, woulda, coulda, shouldas are not gonna do him, or us a lick of good. This is where we are now, and forward is the only way to go. So, we've gotta put our heads together and figure out what we're going to do."

"Isn't that Yuma's decision?" Mel points out, in typical lawyer fashion.

"Technically, I guess so," Yuma responds to her. "At least for the outside world. But since it will impact all of us, we all weigh in."

"Right. We have a few options," Ouray takes over. "Keep him in the hospital where they'd treat him, try to squeeze out some more time for him, if possible. Also, Yuma was given a list of possible hospice care places in town this morning. The focus would be to keep him comfortable, although, according to the doctor, renal failure often means a fairly painless and peaceful death. And finally, our last option is to bring him home."

Yuma had brought up the final option last night, but didn't feel he could make that call without everyone's consent.

"Home," Lisa declares firmly. "He belongs here."

"Home," Luna echoes.

"Home," Paco agrees with a nod.

One by one everyone weighs in, the answer the same.

Then Ouray looks at me, waiting for my vote.

"Bring him home."

He nods. "Very well. It'll mean everyone chipping in, working in shifts to make sure he has around-the-clock care."

Voices of agreement go up around the clubhouse.

I don't think there's ever been a time I've felt the bond that ties us together quite as strong as I do now.

"Nosh built this place," I find myself saying. "He forged this brotherhood. He brought us in, gave us a home, and raised us into this family. It's only right we all guide him on this final road trip."

"Amen, brother," Tse speaks up. "Amen."

————

*Emme*

"We're on our way home."

I had an awkward chat with Mandy on the doorstep of the surprisingly upscale townhouse she apparently shares with her fiancé. She claimed she hadn't really spent much time with Rhea outside of work in the last year or so. I walked away without anything useful.

I'd hoped to have more luck with Cher Valente but spent ten minutes fruitlessly ringing the bell and banging on the door to her apartment on W. 32nd Street and just got back to the truck when my phone rang.

"I'm sorry," I tell Sophia, easily guessing their reason for cutting their vacation short.

"You already heard?"

*Shit.*

Now I have to explain how I got to be at the hospital

with Honon last night. I didn't want to tell her what was going on at home because I knew she would've insisted on coming back as soon as she heard. She's a good friend and will be pissed I kept the events of the past week from her.

"Yeah. I happened to be at the hospital with Honon last night when the doctor passed on the news."

It's quiet for a moment.

"You were with Honon?"

"He, uh, was at the Backyard last night, and—"

"Honon? Wow, he usually makes it a point to avoid the restaurant."

Makes it a point? Well, whatever his hang-up was before, in recent days he seems to have become a regular.

"Well, we had a bit of a situation last week Honon has been helping me with."

I proceed to giver her an abridged version of the events, aware the kids might be listening in, interrupted by her occasional outbursts of disbelief or anger.

"You should've called me."

"And you would've done what? Throw the kids in the car and make Tse drive you home? I know you; you'd have been back here the next day. At least now you've had a decent chunk of time to visit with your parents."

"She's got a point, Fee," I hear Tse telling her. "And Emme? Glad Honon's got your back. He's a good man, so don't bust his balls too hard, will ya?"

Ha. If only they knew.

From the corner of my eye, I catch a glimpse of a familiar figure moving gingerly into sight from the far side of the apartment building. She appears to scan the street before she veers right and hurries down the sidewalk.

"Guys, I have to run. We'll talk later."

Without giving them a chance to respond, I end the call

and slip my phone in my pocket. Then I get out of the truck and dart diagonally across the street.

"Cher! Hold up!"

She speeds up even as her head whips around. The panicked look on her face is quickly replaced with relief when she catches sight of me.

"Oh my God, Emme," she blurts out, pressing a hand to her chest. "What are you doing here?"

"I was actually hoping you'd have a minute to talk to me. It's about Rhea."

As soon as I mention Rhea, she blinks a few times before turning her eyes away.

"Were you just at my front door?"

"Yeah, that was me. You were home?"

"I thought you were someone else."

"Someone you're trying to avoid?"

I have to step aside to get out of the way of two teens walking down the sidewalk, when Cher grabs my arm.

"Let's get off the street."

It's obvious Cher is worried about something or someone. Why else would she first refuse to open the door and minutes later slip from the building and scurry down the street?

I'm no detective, but my gut tells me to let her pull me along to a walkway between the apartment building and the houses on the side street. Halfway down she stops and turns to face me.

"What do you know about Rhea?"

Bingo.

Now I have to figure out a way to get her to talk to me without revealing too much to her.

"I heard Rhea was murdered. As you know we were friends, but unfortunately last year we had a bit of a falling out. I haven't spoken to her since." I shake my head and let my eyes drift off over her shoulder. "I guess I just wanted talk to someone else who knew her." Then I turn back to Cher. "I feel kinda guilty, you know? The argument was so stupid, over some guy she was seeing."

Cher's attention seems to be piqued.

"A guy?"

"Yeah, I never met him, but she seemed over the moon for him. One of those married guys promising to leave their wife but they never do."

She rolls her eyes. "I know the type. I knew she was seeing someone but she never talked about him. I don't think it lasted long, but I figured he must've been the father of her baby."

"Baby?"

Normally I can't lie for shit and I'm sure it's written all over my face, but Cher isn't paying me much attention as she seems to be watching a few cars drive by on the street.

"Yeah, she had a little girl about six months ago. Athena, sweet little thing. It's funny, I always thought Rhea had no family, but this cop came around asking questions at the club and told us both kids were with family."

"She never mentioned anything to me either. So, the cops were at the club?"

"Twice. Except the second one was a woman, an FBI agent."

"Do they think someone at work had something to do with it?"

She gives me a sideways glance and shrugs.

"Who knows? Things haven't been the same since the new owner took over. Brought in a bunch of new girls, some of them barely legal, for cripes' sake. Stuck Rhea in the office for minimum wage when he found out she was pregnant, even though she had two kids to support. And then, to top it all off, Mandy hooked up with the owner's son and became a royal bitch, walks around like she owns the place and the rest of us are dirt under her shoes." She snorts. "Only reason I still have a job is because I know when to keep my mouth shut."

"Why would you have to? Is there fishy stuff going on? It used to be a clean club."

She scoffs. "Used to be, yeah. These days, though, you don't wanna know. I go in for my gigs, don't make waves, and don't ask questions. I was hoping I could dance for another year, sock enough away so I could maybe move somewhere else, start over, but now…I can't wait to get far away from fucking Don Hines."

"Don Hines?"

The name sounds familiar, but I can't place it.

"New owner," Cher clarifies.

Ah, that makes sense. If Luna hasn't already looked into him, she probably should. It sure sounds like something is going on at The Pink Petal.

"And, Emme? Do yourself a favor: don't be going around asking questions about Rhea. It may reach the wrong ears."

"What ears?"

She shakes her head and glances toward the street again.

"Trust me, the less you know, the better it is. I've gotta go."

She turns her back on me and starts jogging to the other side of the alley.

"Cher!" I call after her. "Who are you afraid of?"

But she's already disappearing around the corner and out of sight.

# CHAPTER
# FOURTEEN

*Emme*

"Did you say Hines?"

I finish slipping another spoon of mashed sweet potatoes in the baby's wide-open mouth before I aim my eyes at Honon. He's leaning against the kitchen doorway.

I've just been updating Luna on my strange but informative encounter with Cher Valente. She joined me in the kitchen so I could feed Athena while Lisa ran into town to pick up some supplies.

"Don Hines, yeah. He owns The Pink Petal."

"Why?" Luna pins him with a look. "Do you know him?"

"No, but I've heard the name." He glances at me. "The moron causing trouble at the restaurant, wasn't his name Hines?"

That's why it sounded familiar.

"David Hines," I confirm.

"That the guy who gave you the shiner?" Luna asks me.

My free hand inadvertently lifts to touch my face where the mark the guy left has already mostly faded.

"I prefer to think of him as the guy whose arm I broke, but yes."

"I'll check into it. See if he's any relation. I was planning to have a talk with Don Hines anyway. I haven't had a chance yet—the guy's been out of the country—but his manager mentioned he'd be back this week," Luna explains.

"I wonder if it's possible Don Hines is the married man Rhea'd been seeing," I muse out loud. "Maybe the *authorities* she warns about in her note refer to her boss? You know, since Mandy is apparently involved with the guy's son, I could try—"

"Emme?" Luna cuts me off. "I think, until we figure out what is going on at The Pink Petal and how it could be related to your friend's death, you should heed Cher Valente's caution and keep your head down. There's a reason the woman is spooked. We have no way of knowing if her fear is valid and if she's being watched. Don't start drawing attention to yourself."

"Ah-bah!"

Athena slaps her little hand in the plate of sweet potato, splashing the orange goop all over me.

"That's my cue to get back to work," Luna announces, barely missing the spatters flying. "And, Emme, I'm serious. Don't take any risks. You've got these kids to worry about now."

Nothing else she could've said would have me snap my mouth shut any faster.

Honon is already mopping up Athena with a kitchen towel he'd wet at the sink. The baby got as much gunk on herself as she did on me, the entire front of my shirt is splattered.

"Third door on your right, down the hallway," he directs me without taking his eyes off his task. "Clean shirts in the top drawer of the dresser. I've got her."

Yes, he does. His confidence when handling the little one is a surprising turn-on. Who'd have thought?

I move through the clubhouse, stopping only to check in with Malco, who is sitting in the corner of the couch, a book on his lap.

"What are you reading?"

Instead of answering, he shows me the cover. It's the first book in the Chronicles of Narnia, *The Magician's Nephew*. C.S. Lewis's fantasy world is a perfect place for him to escape from reality. I spent quite a bit of time there when I was growing up.

"I think I've read that book and all of the others in the series at least three times," I tell him. "Are you enjoying it?"

"It's okay," he mumbles softly.

Then his eyes drop to the blotches of orange on my shirt.

"Your sister, I'm afraid," I explain. "Apparently she enjoys playing with sweet potatoes more than eating it."

"Applesauce," he suggests. "She likes that."

"Applesauce, huh? We'll have to try that next time. Maybe, when you have a minute, you could write down the things you and Athena like to eat? I think that would help Lisa and me a lot."

He nods, and I dig a small notepad and a pen from the dungeons of my backpack and leave them beside him on the couch. He's already grabbing for them when I duck into the hallway.

The second door is partially open and I catch sight of

Ouray sitting on the edge of a neatly made bed. His elbows are resting on his knees and his head hangs down. Grief speaks from the slope of his shoulders. Last night he'd seemed so controlled and practical, but I guess even the strongest among us have moments of weakness.

I quickly dart by and duck into the next room, closing the door behind me.

The layout seems to be a mirror image of the room next door but the setup is little different. The bed is also neatly made, covered with a drab, army-green comforter, but it's against the back wall, under the window. A few coats and a sweatshirt or two are hanging from a row of pegs along the wall on my left and on the opposite wall, next to an open door revealing the bathroom, sits the dresser.

A few well-read paperbacks are stacked on top, along with a small wooden tray with a collection of change and other flotsam. On the wall above the dresser hangs a collection of framed photographs. One of a group of boys sitting on the porch of the clubhouse, shucking corn. I have no problem picking out Honon. He can't be much older than ten or twelve, and already he had a killer smile with those dimples.

There are a few other snapshots with him as a younger boy, but my attention is drawn to a picture of Honon in uniform, his arms slung around the shoulders of two other soldiers as they smile and squint into the sun. All three look to be in their early twenties.

I didn't know he was a veteran, although it doesn't really surprise me. It somehow fits him.

The sudden sound of water running startles me into action and I open his top drawer, grabbing the first shirt I see. I take it into the bathroom and flick on the light. It's as tidy as the bedroom is, but despite my inherent curiosity, I hold myself back from peeking into the medicine cabinet.

I whip my dirty shirt off and quickly check my reflection to clean up anything left behind before I pull Honon's T-shirt over my head. It's a navy shirt with the logo of The Edge Boxing Club, which is hanging halfway down my legs. Fishing an extra hair elastic from my pocket, I quickly gather up the excess material and fashion it into a knot at my hip bone. It looks only moderately better but that can't be helped.

"Find everything okay?"

Honon is waiting for me when I walk out of the bathroom, Athena sitting on his arm.

"Yeah. A little big, but it'll do until I get home. I need to do laundry anyway, so I'll wash it quickly and get it back to you.

"Keep it, I've got ten others like it," he remarks with a smirk. "Maybe it can be a replacement for when that old, ratty nightshirt of yours finally falls apart."

I shoot him a look, but secretly I like the idea of having something of his to hold on to after this is over.

My phone starts ringing as I'm stuffing the dirty shirt in my small backpack, but I don't recognize the number.

"Hello?"

"Is this Ms. Emmeline Grace Lightfoot?"

The man's voice is friendly enough, but still, I feel a little uneasy. I look over at Honon, who's closely watching me.

"This is she."

"Ms. Lightfoot, my name is Nick Flynn, and I'm a lawyer in Cortez. Rhea Scala is…*was*…my client."

———

*Honon*

"I could've gone by myself."

Stubborn woman.

"Going off to Cortez by yourself to meet some guy you've never met before? Given the circumstances, I'd think that qualifies as taking a risk, Emme."

"He's a lawyer, for heaven's sake," she sputters. "Mel said she knew the name."

Calling Mel was the first thing I'd done when the guy asked Emme to meet him at his office. Emme ended up leaving a message for Luna, who wasn't picking up, but she wasn't waiting around for a call back.

"Nick Flynn may be a lawyer in Cortez, but how the hell do you know for sure it was him you had on the phone? And even if it was, how do you know he's not somehow involved?"

Her knuckles turn white against the steering wheel, but she doesn't seem to have an argument for that.

I get her need to be independent, I understand pride, especially after she shared some of her background with me. Heck, I didn't say anything when she got behind the wheel and left me scrambling to get into the passenger seat before she drove off, but I wasn't about to let her take off on her own. Safety trumps everything else.

"Hey." I twist in my seat and put a hand on her knee. "It has nothing to do with you not being able to handle things on your own, and everything with me wanting to see you safe. Nothing wrong with that."

"Why?" she asks, darting a quick glance at me before focusing on the road ahead.

"Not sure what you're asking."

"Why do you feel my safety is your job?"

"Job? I said I want to see you safe, that's a wish, probably a need, but definitely not a job."

When she throws me a quick look, I catch a hint of uncertainty in her eyes.

"Okay. Then I guess I'm confused. Sophia called me this morning," she explains. "They're on their way home, by the way, but you probably already knew that. Anyway, I told her you were at the restaurant and she seemed surprised at that. She mentioned you always made it a point to avoid going there."

"I did," I admit.

There's no point lying about it.

"This is probably gonna sound stupid, but did that have anything to do with me?"

"Not anything…everything."

Her head whips around and she stares at me openmouthed.

"Emme, car," I warn her as the vehicle in front of us hits the brakes, trying to catch the turnoff to Mesa Verde at the last minute.

We narrowly miss it by swerving into the passing lane, which is blessedly empty. That could've been ugly.

"Oh shit," she mutters, looking back at the road, her face turning pink.

"There's a rest area up ahead. Turn in there."

A few minutes later, she pulls the truck into a spot at the rear of the rest area, away from the restroom facilities, but her hands stay on the wheel and her eyes face forward, staring at the mesa through the windshield.

"Are you okay?"

"You didn't even know me, why would you want to avoid me? Did I piss you off in a previous life or something?"

I bark out a laugh.

"Not likely. Look, I guess you've always held my attention."

She finally lets go of the steering wheel and turns to me, a look of disbelief on her face.

"Yeah, because that's a good reason to avoid someone," she snipes.

"That depends."

"On what?"

"On whether you're looking to get involved."

Now it's her turn to respond with a scoff.

"Gee, thanks."

"I'm not talking a one-night stand, Emme. I'm talking about getting hooked on someone. The kind of hooked that burrows deep under your skin and leaves a permanent scar when it's ripped away. That's what I was avoiding. I've seen the damage that can do."

I see the wheels turning, and then her eyes widen.

"Oh."

"Yeah. The fact we're sitting here talking about this shit, just a week and a half since I got a call you got yourself into a brawl, should tell you something. Now, do you think you can manage to keep your eyes on the road, or do I have to take over?"

"It wasn't a brawl," she snaps in a mutinous tone.

I'm starting to suspect being contrary is her default setting when she feels unsettled.

"And I'm driving," she adds.

I lean back in the passenger seat as she backs out of the

parking spot. Maybe I should feel unsettled too, but I'm feeling pretty good.

For a man who, for the past twenty years, has done everything to avoid a heavy conversation with a woman, I think I did well.

The remaining drive to Cortez is silent, which is fine by me.

"You don't have to come in," Emme tells me when we get out of the truck.

I don't bother answering that and follow her into the small storefront law office. An older lady sits behind a desk against the wall.

"Can I help you?"

"I'm here to see Nick Flynn. He called and asked me to come in."

"And your name is?"

"Never mind, Janet. I've got this."

A tall, bald man, around my age, walks into the small reception area. He gives me a brief glance before turning to Emme, offering his hand.

"Ms. Lightfoot, correct?"

"Emme, please. And this is…my friend, Honon."

He gives me a friendly nod.

"Please come in. Janet? Hold my calls."

"First of all, my condolences on the loss of your friend," he starts, when we take a seat in his office. "I'm afraid I didn't know her well; she was only in my office twice." He flips through a desk calendar. "The first time was March 17th. She basically walked in off the street without an appointment. She asked me to draw up a fairly straightforward last will and testament and insisted on waiting so she could sign it right away."

He opens a folder on his desk and pulls out a document he appears to scan.

"Like I said, her will is straightforward. In it she appoints you as guardian of her minor children, Malco and Athena, and leaves all proceeds of her estate in trust to you for the benefit of her children until they reach the age of majority, which is eighteen years of age in the state of Colorado."

Emme starts to fiddle beside me, a nervous scratching of her nails on the fabric of her pants as she stares at the document, so I cover her hand with mine.

"The second and last time she was in my office was three weeks ago," Flynn continues. "She showed up, seemed somewhat distressed, and asked me to hold on to an envelope for her. She left me with instructions to contact you—and only you—should anything happen to her, and to hand this over to you in person."

He pulls a thick manila envelope from his desk and slides it across the top to Emme.

"Should I open it here?"

"That's up to you."

She starts peeling back the flap, but I stop her.

"Before you do that, hire him."

She looks at me confused.

"Your friend has a point," Flynn concedes. "As your lawyer, I'd be bound by attorney-client privilege and nothing would leave this office."

"Okay, but don't you need a retainer or something?"

I fish my bill clip from my pocket, pull out a couple of C-notes, and toss them on the desk.

"That enough?"

By way of response, he hits a button on the phone on his desk.

"Janet? Start a new client file for Emmeline Grace Lightfoot, please? And if you would pull together an introduction package for her to pick up on her way out?"

Then he turns to Emme.

"That's taken care of."

Emme glances at me and at my nod, rips open the envelope.

# CHAPTER
# FIFTEEN

*Emme*

"Thirty-four thousand, seven hundred and eighty-six dollars."

Luna places the stack of bills back on the table.

"According to her financial records, that's exactly the amount she withdrew from her savings account before she shut it down three weeks ago. Our office uncovered another roughly eighty thousand in government bonds and mutual funds, and she had a little over six hundred dollars in her checking account."

I nod, still reeling from seeing that whack of cash in the envelope. Also included had been copies of the kids' birth certificates, a letter for each of them, and an envelope addressed to me I haven't had the heart to open yet.

Honon drove us back to Durango and I didn't object. I'd been stunned, feeling like I'd been hit with a few thousand volts.

Heck, I'm still stunned, sitting here in Ouray's office.

Being responsible for those children became even more

real after finding out I'm their legal guardian. There's so much to think about. Finishing my house so the kids have a place to sleep, furniture, getting their belongings from the trailer, school for Malco, medical care, my job. I'm the most ill-prepared person in the world for this.

What the hell was Rhea thinking?

"My head is spinning," I tell Luna. "There's so much I don't know. What am I supposed to do with all that cash? I mean, I'd open a bank account for the kids, but that might not be a smart thing to do right now."

"Yeah, don't do that," she agrees. "Listen, I recognize the panic in your eyes. Take it from someone else who also never expected to find herself a mother figure overnight— tackle one thing at a time. Right now, that's dealing with probably the most important job of keeping those kids safe. Everything else comes after."

She picks up the money, shoves it back in the brown envelope, and does the same with the copy of Rhea's will, the letters for the kids, and their birth certificates.

"These we put away in the safe for later. There's nothing of immediate concern."

I watch as she walks over to her husband's desk and opens a safe hidden in the credenza against the wall, stuffing the envelope inside.

"But this…" She points at the only thing left on the table in front of me, the envelope addressed to me. "…could contain information we need."

It had been heartbreaking enough to read the two hand-written sheets of paper she'd left for her kids. I haven't been able to bring myself to open the note she left me.

The door to the office opens and Honon walks in, his eyes immediately zooming in on me. When we pulled up to the clubhouse earlier, Luna—who'd received my message and called while we were heading back—was already there. When she took me into the office, Honon was called over by Paco and Ouray who were bent over some blueprints on the large table.

"Everything okay?"

"Fine," I lie, grateful for a moment's reprieve. "Everything okay with you?"

"Yeah. Ouray wanted to see if it's possible to add some doors in the next day or so. One connecting my room to Nosh's, and he also talked about putting in a door from the hallway directly into the suite and maybe close this door off."

He cocks his thumb at a door I thought was maybe leading to a bathroom.

"What the hell for?" Luna wants to know.

"Guess he figures it'll be busier in the clubhouse when Nosh comes home and doesn't want everyone going through his office when they're looking for a bed to crash in. The connecting door between the other two rooms is so it can be left open during the night. My room's gonna be used by whoever's turn it is to look after the old man."

"And where are you going to stay?" she asks.

Luna's eyes sparkle with a mischievous glint.

"Don't you worry about me," Honon returns without elaborating, but he glances in my direction.

I guess that's clear. Not that I have a problem with it, he's been staying at my house the past few nights anyway. I don't mind having him around.

"Emme was just about to open her envelope," Luna prompts.

*Great.* Reprieve is over.

I'm glad when Honon sinks down in the empty chair

beside me. He's not touching me but his presence feels supportive.

Grabbing the envelope from the table I rip it open and pull out a single folded sheet.

I hope with all my heart there will never be a reason for you to read this.

I have so many regrets, one of which is not listening to you when you gave me advice I should've taken.

Another is cutting you off afterward. I can come up with excuses, but I won't because in the end those won't change anything anyway.

I regret I let stupid curiosity get the best of me, putting myself and maybe even my kids in danger.

But what I regret most of all is putting my faith in a man who'd already let me down.

I made my bed; I have to lie in it.

But I can never regret my two beautiful children.

Malco is a sweet boy, smart too, and I have to believe he'll be able to get himself and his sister safely to you if it comes to that. He remembers you and I know you'll watch over him.

My little girl, Athena, I want her to know what a blessing she was.

She wasn't planned and my choice to keep her had been a purely selfish one, but no matter what the outcome of my bad decisions turns out to be, she was very much wanted.

Which brings me to this next part, where—despite already having pushed you to, or perhaps even over the edge of trust—I'm asking you to trust me once again.

Athena's father is not a good man, despite appearances. I
can only give you my word on that.
Believe me when I say everyone is better off not knowing
who he is, but in case his identity comes out somehow, I
need you to know you cannot trust him.
And lastly, this money I'm leaving to help with the care of
my children I honestly earned.
You're the closest thing I've ever had to family, and I don't
doubt you will take the best possible care of them.
I know I'm asking too much, but there is nothing I won't do
for my children, even if it means placing you in an
impossible position.

I'm sorry,
Rhea.

I'm not sure what to think or feel. So many emotions hit
me at the same time: confusion, anger, sadness, helpless-
ness, frustration.

Mostly the latter.

"This letter was written a little over two weeks ago, why
the hell didn't she come to me then?" I complain, tossing
the letter and envelope on the table.

"Fear," Honon suggests.

"Yet she writes a letter with vague references and that's
supposed to help me? It's useless. It's not telling us anything."

"She may not have left you a name, but that doesn't
mean the letter is useless," Luna suggests. "Let me take it
back to the office, I'll have a closer look at it."

A loud banging comes from the hallway and shakes the
walls.

"Are they taking down the walls now?" Luna asks Honon.

He shrugs. "No, just a new door opening, I hope."

A bit of demolition sounds like a great way to work out my frustration, so I shove my chair back, get to my feet, and head for the door.

"Where are you going?" Honon calls after me.

"To find another sledgehammer. I've got some energy to burn."

———

*Honon*

"Take a break."

Rather than going back and forth through the clubhouse, we propped open the back door and set up the table saw on a stack of pavers on the patio.

I watch Emme cut lengths of two-by-fours with an easy skill that is sexy as hell. There isn't a whole lot this woman can't do. Hell, she even looked good swinging the sledgehammer.

We've already framed out a standard-sized door opening connecting my room with Nosh's. Ouray called for a break while Paco went to pick up some doors at Home Depot. I thought Emme was right behind us but when she didn't show up after a few minutes, I went in search and found her out here.

"I just wanna get these lengths done so when Paco gets back, two of us can quickly frame the second one out, while the others start on the first door."

She turns back to the table saw and grabs another length of wood. I patiently wait until she turns off the saw and marks up the board, but when she starts loading the cut two-by-fours on her shoulder, I intervene.

"Hey, what are you doing?" she protests when I take them from her and lean them back against the outside wall. "I was just gonna put them inside."

"Right, and next thing I know you'll be hammering in the frame. We're taking a break, Wildcat."

I grab her hand and lead her down the hall to the clubhouse.

"God, it smells good in here," she comments, as the aromas of dinner waft out of the kitchen.

"Lisa's chili and cornbread."

"I should relieve her of the baby for a bit."

"You go take the load off—Ouray has a beer ready for you at the bar—I'll grab Athena."

I give her a little shove in the right direction, which earns me a flash of eyes over her shoulder, before I make a detour into the kitchen.

The baby is sitting in the high chair, banging a plastic cup on the tray when I walk in. The moment she sees me a big, gummy smile spreads on her face.

"Lord," Lisa mutters. "He charms another one."

I give her shoulder a little bump.

"You're just jealous."

"Damn right I am. Done all but stand on my head to get that girl to smile," she grumbles. "All you do is blink those baby blues of yours."

"She's a girl, she recognizes an easy mark."

Lisa snorts.

"Got a point there."

"Where's Malco? I thought he was in here with you?"

"Kid was bored. Trunk took him out on the ATV for a bit until the kids come home from school."

"Good, I'll take the baby for a bit so you'll really have your hands free."

I lift Athena on my arm and head for the door.

"Never thought I'd see the day, but I gotta say, a kid looks good on ya."

I shake my head and look back.

"Bite me, Lisa."

I walk into the clubhouse just in time to see Emme leap off the barstool and throw herself into the arms of a rough-looking guy in leathers. I watch as Ouray rounds the bar and pulls the guy away from Emme and hugs him as well, slapping him hard on the back.

*What the fuck?*

It's not until he steps back and grins when he catches sight of me walking up that I recognize him under all that facial hair.

Wapi?

"You've been holding out on me, brother!"

Emme reaches for the baby and the moment she's out of my hands, I'm wrapped in a bone-crushing hug.

"You're breaking my ribs, you hairy fucker. You've been eating your Wheaties."

"Wheaties, my ass," he snorts when he lets me up for air. "Deer, elk, caribou, grouse, hare, fish. You name it, I've hunted, cleaned, and eaten it."

He certainly looks like he's put on a few pounds, in all the right places. I move over to Emme who is back on her barstool, the baby on her lap.

"What the hell are you doing back here?" Ouray asks Wapi. "Honon said you weren't answering your damn phone again."

He shrugs out of his jacket and hangs it over the back of a chair. Definitely bulked up since he left.

"I was already on my way back when I got his message. Ended up staying just one night in Jasper but my hankering for home won. Been driving for three days straight. I'm beat."

"Well, sit down and I'll grab you a beer."

Wapi pulls out the stool on Emme's other side and sits down, grabbing the beer Ouray hands him, tilting the bottle back, and draining half of it. Then he lets his gaze roam over Emme and Athena before fixing his eyes on me.

"Seriously, I should kick your ass for taking the last good woman left in town off the market. And a baby? Already?"

I'm spared from responding when Lisa comes out of the kitchen and sees Wapi.

"Well, I'll be a dirty bird. The prodigal son returns."

Wapi is up in a flash to give Lisa the same treatment he gave us.

"Missed your cooking something fierce," he tells her.

She shoves him back a step and makes a face.

"Then you'd better get that road dirt scrubbed off 'cause you'll not be eating at my table reeking like that."

She turns on her heel and heads back to the kitchen. The door to the clubhouse flies open; kids come streaming in, followed by some of the brothers, and chaos ensues.

"I see not much has changed," Wapi observes.

The next second he's lifted off his feet by a widely-grinning Trunk, while Shilah and Brick pound on his back.

My eyes immediately scan for Malco, and I find him standing in the middle of the pandemonium, looking a little forlorn. I quickly head toward him.

"Hey, have a good time with Trunk?"

He nods, but doesn't take his eyes off the cluster of brothers.

"Are they fighting?"

"No, bud. They're celebrating." I crouch down a bit and point at Wapi. "See that big hairy dude in the middle?"

I get another nod.

"That's my good friend, Wapi. He just came home from living up in Alaska in the wilderness."

That gets his attention and he lifts his head to look at me.

"Alaska? It's cold there."

"Sure is. He stayed the whole winter. Had to hunt and fish for his meals."

His eyes widen, then he returns his focus to the group of men.

"Cool."

# CHAPTER
# SIXTEEN

*Emme*

"Get up here."

I look up and meet his eyes, defiantly sliding my mouth back down the length of his cock.

"Fuck, Wildcat, I'm gonna blow."

That's the plan, but apparently Honon is not on board. He abruptly sits up, grabs me under my arms, and unceremoniously hauls me up his body before rolling me under him.

"Brace, baby."

The last man who tried to call me baby and order me around in bed lived to regret it when I bucked him off. He ended up with a gash that required stitches after hitting his head on the corner of his nightstand. He'll bear the scar as a harsh reminder. Somehow, Honon doing the same has the opposite effect on me.

The difference is trust; something I don't give easily, but Honon clearly has laid claim to in record time.

Compliantly, I raise my arms and grab on to the slats in

my headboard as he kisses and licks his way down my body. When he nudges my legs, I let them fall open willingly. I'm like putty as I give myself up to his thorough explorations.

At the first firm stroke of his tongue along my slit, a full-body shiver runs the length of my frame. There's no fumbling to find his way around my nether regions as he zooms in on my clit with pinpoint precision. Then he pulls it firmly between his lips, humming against me. The soft vibrations raise goosebumps all over my skin, and I moan when his fingers fill me, overwhelming me with sensations.

Of course, the moment he has every muscle in my body trembling with the need for release, he backs away. My eyes snap open to find him upright on his knees, watching me, a satisfied smirk on his lips as he reaches for a condom he left on the nightstand.

"I hate you," I hiss in frustration, as he rolls it on.

Then he hooks his hands behind my knees and pulls me toward him until my ass rests on his thighs.

"No, you don't. Or won't, once I'm done with you."

Then he slips his hands under my butt cheeks, lifts me up, and drives himself home.

———

He brushes my lips again when we get to the door.

"Before I forget, do you have an extra key? I was gonna pack up a few of my things to bring over before I have to be at the shooting range. I've got a couple of guys coming in to run the course at around noon."

"You'll be staying here?"

Not like I hadn't already figured it out but it's something you'd normally ask, isn't it?

"Planned to." He tilts his head slightly to the side and narrows his eyes. "Didn't think you'd have a problem with it. Do you?"

*Ugh*. I'm not trying to be an asshole, but I also don't want to be taken for granted.

"Well, no, but it's nice of you to ask."

He rubs his hand down his face.

"Guess I shoulda done that in the first place. My bad."

Instead of belaboring the point, I turn and head back to the kitchen, grabbing my spare key from a basket on top of the fridge.

"Here." I hand it over. "And thanks."

He hooks me around the waist and pulls me in for another kiss.

"Work in progress, Emme."

I grin up at him.

"So am I." Then I give him a little shove out the door. "I've gotta get ready for work. See you later?"

"I may have dinner at the club—they're bringing Nosh home this afternoon—but I'll be there to pick you up."

With a wave over his shoulder, I watch him walk to his bike before closing the door.

Twenty minutes later, I'm about to pull out of my driveway when my phone rings. I don't recognize the number.

"Hello?"

"Is this Emme Lightfoot?" a woman's voice asks.

"It is."

"Hi, this is Meredith Carter, we've met a few times at the Backyard Edge. I come in with my husband, Jay VanDyken, from time to time."

I have an immediate recollection of the woman, a stocky frame, mop of unruly silver curls, red-rimmed glasses, and always wearing those red Doc Martens I'm a little jealous of.

"Hi, yes, I remember. What can I do for you?"

"Chief Benedetti told me to contact you. I happen to be the medical examiner for La Plata County and I'm calling about Rhea Scala. I understand you're her next of kin?"

"We're not related, but she was a friend and she didn't have any family, other than her children."

"Yes, the chief mentioned you're the legal guardian of her two minor children."

I guess Luna must have passed that information on to Benedetti, which makes sense, but it still makes me a little uneasy.

"I am."

"Well, let me start by saying how sorry I am for your loss."

"Thank you."

"I was wondering if you'd have a chance to stop by my office this morning. I promise it won't be long, but I have a few items belonging to Ms. Scala I'd like to give you."

A glance at the clock on my dashboard shows ten to eleven. I'll have to be a little late.

"I'm just on my way to work, but I could stop by now?"

"Now is fine. I'll leave word at the reception desk to expect you. See you shortly."

She's already ended the call when I realize I have no clue where her office is. A quick Google search gives me the address and before I pull onto the road, I shoot off a quick text to Mack to let him know I have an errand to run and might be a few minutes late.

I'm lucky to find parking across the street and rush into the building.

"Hi," I greet the woman behind the desk. "I was called

by Meredith Carter to come in? My name is Emme Lightfoot."

She smiles as she gets up.

"Yes, Dr. Carter said to be on the lookout for you. I'll show you to her office."

"Please come in," the older woman invites when her receptionist shows me into a modest office. "I appreciate you coming on such short notice. Have a seat."

The thought somewhere in this building Rhea's lifeless body is kept makes me nauseous. The pervasive smell of chemicals I noticed the moment I walked into the building doesn't help.

Behind me I hear the door close with a soft click as I sit down on the edge of the chair. Meredith slides a Ziploc bag with some jewelry across the desk toward me.

"The earrings and necklace belong to Ms. Scala. They've already been examined by the police lab and were returned here to be kept with her body until next of kin was found for funeral arrangements."

God, her funeral, of course. It hadn't really occurred to me that responsibility would be mine, but I guess it is.

"I haven't made any. I mean, I just found out about the guardianship yesterday. Quite frankly, I haven't been able to wrap my head around a lot of this."

"I understand," she sympathizes, leaning forward with a kind smile. "And trust me, I normally wouldn't have brought it up, but the reality is our morgue isn't really set up for long-term storage. Right now we're at full capacity."

"Of course, yes. I'll…um…contact a funeral home."

Google will have to come to the rescue again, because I haven't had any dealings with one.

"Unless you have a preference, I can highly recommend Hook Funeral Home. I work with them all the time and they're caring and respectful. It's just down the road from here. Ask for Gemma Hook, she'll be able to guide you through the process."

A few minutes later, I walk out of the building, Rhea's jewelry in my pocket, along with a business card for the funeral director. Maybe I'll see if I can sneak out for half an hour after the lunch rush later.

To my surprise, Sophia's SUV is parked behind the restaurant when I pull in. I find her in the office.

"What are you doing here?"

They got back Monday night when we were just finishing up the installation of the new doors at the club-house. Sophia said she'd probably be in on Friday to help with the weekend rush.

She shrugs. "I was restless. Tse is home with the kids and doesn't have any work scheduled until Monday, so I figured I'd come in, see if I can get us some more coverage here."

"What do you mean?"

I take one of the chairs and sit across the desk from her.

"Simple, I'm no longer the only one who has to contend with young kids. Listen, I've been lucky for the few years I had you to back me up, but going forward we're going to need more staff to fill those holes."

I'd avoided thinking too much about that, sticking to what Luna suggested about dealing with whatever is right in front of me first. I've been working since I was nineteen, sometimes two jobs at a time, I've never had to worry about my schedule impacting anyone else. Guess that's changed now.

"How do you plan on doing that? We had a hard enough time getting a server and we ended up with Fred," I point out.

Sophia snickers.

"Mack told me what happened. How has he been since?"

"Thank God, no meltdowns since that night, but he's still an odd duck."

"He should fit in just fine, then," she teases before turning serious. "And to answer your question, I just found out from Mack that rib place on Florida Road is closing. He happened to talk to the daughter of the owner yesterday. A girl he dated a few years back, remember? Ashley or Amber or something?"

"Aster," I fill in, remembering the pretty doe-eyed girl. Not the brightest bulb in the pack as I recall.

"Right, that's her. Anyway, the place had been going downhill while her father was ill, to the point it was costing them money to keep it open. Last month her dad passed away and now the family is shutting the restaurant and selling the building. All staff is getting their pink slips tomorrow."

"You want to be ready to scoop them up."

"Yup. The good ones anyway. Some of them have apparently been working there for years. Anyway, the girl was broken up about having to let people go, so Mack is going to suggest she send some of her more experienced staff our way when she lays them off."

"Shit. That would be perfect."

"I know," she agrees, a big grin on her face. "Would be great to have a more flexible schedule. Now, what was this about you stopping in at the morgue?"

I tell her about my meeting.

"I've never planned a funeral before. I don't even know what she would've wanted," I vent my concerns.

I was thinking about that on my way here.

"My guess, as a mom? She'd have wanted something small and simple for the boy. The baby won't remember a thing, but he's already been traumatized enough."

"God, I don't even know if it's wise to have a funeral, given the circumstances."

"Emme, go talk to the funeral home. Get an idea of what is possible."

"I'll do it this afternoon when it quiets down."

She gets up and rounds the desk, perching her butt on the edge, right in front of me, with her arms crossed over her chest.

"You'll do it now," she insists firmly. "Otherwise, you'll be agonizing over it all day. Get the information you need, and then I want you to go home and take a few days to think about it."

My instinct is to blow her off, but I've learned a thing or two this week. Mainly that I couldn't have managed this past week without help.

"Are you sure?"

"Positive, now go."

I stand up and give her a quick hug before heading back to my truck, admittedly feeling a little less weighed down.

Gemma Hook is a treasure, that's all I can say. The woman put me at ease, had me sign some papers, arranged to have Rhea's body collected from the morgue first thing tomorrow morning, and took the time to walk me through all the different options. When I told her I needed some time to think it over, she was very accommodating and explained she'd be able to keep Rhea for up to four weeks, if needed.

Still, when I walked out of there, I was bone-tired.

It feels a bit like skipping school—which I did enough of back in the day—when I get behind the wheel. Suddenly

I've got nowhere to be. Maybe I'll run over to City Market and load up. I don't usually buy a lot at once, but if I'm gonna be home for a couple of days, I'm going to need to eat and so does Honon. I'd almost forgotten he was bringing over some things.

By the time I walk out of the grocery store, my cart is loaded to the brim. I got a shitload of food plus a couple of six-packs with a variety of beer. I realized in the middle of the produce section I don't really know his likes or dislikes, so I probably bought too much, but whatever.

I quickly load the bags into the passenger seat and on the floor, returning the cart to the corral a few parking spots over. When I walk back to the truck, I notice whoever parked beside me didn't leave me a whole lot of room to get in.

Silently cursing the idiot, I carefully open my door so I don't scratch his, when I hear a noise behind me. Swerving around, I find myself staring into the barrel of a gun. The guy holding it is standing behind the opened rear passenger door, effectively blocking me in. The bottom of his face is covered with some kind of scarf, and he has a black hoodie pulled down over his eyes.

The first thing that comes to mind is that he's been waiting for me. I don't for a second believe this is random, which is confirmed when he opens his mouth.

"Get in the fucking car."

The voice is gravelly, but it sounds intentional. Like he's masking it.

"What do you want?"

There's no fucking way I'm getting in. Instead, I pretend to stumble back and hit my door, which smacks into the car's fender. Hope it leaves a mark.

"You bitch. Get in the car or I'll shoot you in the fucking leg and throw you in myself."

"Hey, Bill. How are ya?" I yell, waving at an older man pushing his cart to the corral. "Haven't seen you in forever!"

The man looks confused, but slowly starts walking this way.

"Is everything all right over there?"

*"Fuck,"* the guy in the hoodie hisses as he tucks the gun away and ducks back into the car.

The next moment it backs out of the spot, almost taking out my Good Samaritan, and peels out of the parking lot. I look to see if I can read his license plate but there isn't one.

Then I sink my ass down on the running board and pull my phone from my pocket.

"Are you okay, Miss?"

"Do you know what make that car was?" I ask the man.

"Looked like an older model Corolla to me."

"Thank you," I manage, then I dial Luna, who answers right away.

"Someone just tried to grab me in the City Market parking lot. There's two of them, one in the back seat and one driving an older model, navy Toyota Corolla, they turned right onto East 32nd Street. Didn't see the driver, but the gunman was Caucasian, about six, maybe six one, black hoodie, no markings, and I'd guess twenty-five to thirty-five."

"Holy fuck, Emme. Sit tight, I'll be right there. Are you okay?"

"Yeah," I mumble, aiming a weak smile at my savior. "It's been a day."

# CHAPTER
# SEVENTEEN

*Honon*

It's as if even more of him has disappeared these last few days.

He doesn't even look anything like the mental image I still seem to hold on to of the larger-than-life man he once was.

"Holy fuck, man," Wapi whispers, appearing beside me in the door opening. "I shoulda come back sooner."

"Bullshit. If he could, Nosh would kick your ass for saying shit like that. Besides, it wouldn't have changed a thing."

I get it though, I get the guilt, but I also know how useless and unproductive it is.

"Maybe not, but I'm here now and I plan to carry my weight. I'll be looking after him."

"Brother, we've already agreed we'll all chip in."

Wapi shakes his head. "You all have shit going on in your own lives and I have some time to make up for. I wanna do this."

He brushes past me and takes a seat on Nosh's old recliner we dragged into the room, making his point clear.

I take one more look at the sleeping man in the bed and head toward the bar.

Yuma, Ouray, and Kaga are quietly nursing drinks when I perch a hip on a barstool. Without a word, Kaga reaches down behind the bar and grabs me a cold one from the cooler. I take a deep swig and set the bottle down on the counter.

"Wapi's in there. Seems to feel he's got something to make up for and says he's gonna look after Nosh."

Yuma grunts.

"Wait 'til he finds out what's involved. He'll sing a different tune."

"Oh, I don't know," Ouray disagrees. "From what I can tell, he's done a bit of growing up while he was away. I say, let him. Plenty of bodies ready to jump in if need be."

"We'll see," Yuma grumbles in his Coke.

If it's tough for me to see Nosh like this, I can't imagine what it must be like for him. As a recovering alcoholic, times like this it's got to be tempting for him to fall off the wagon. We're going to need to keep a close eye on him.

"By the way," Ouray addresses me. "Was this the last of the groups Benedetti sent you?"

"One more on Friday, and then he wants me to run any guys who didn't perform well through a bunch of drills before letting them tackle the course again."

"Joe isn't messing around getting the department in shape," Kaga observes.

"He's got no choice," I point out. "Crime's gone up in recent years and he's short on manpower. He has to work with what he has."

"Yeah, city council recently voted down a proposed increase in the budget to cover those shortfalls," Ouray contributes. "Bunch of hypocrites talking publicly about being concerned at the rise in crime, calling on the chief of police to do something about it, but behind closed doors they fucking tie Benedetti's hands behind his back. Politicians give me a goddamned headache. Next elections—"

His rant is interrupted by the ringing of his phone.

"Hey, Squirt." His eyes zoom in on me. "Yeah, he's here —You're shitting me…"

The hair on the back of my neck stands on end. Something's wrong.

I'm already on my feet when I hear him say, "Okay, we'll be right there."

"What? Emme?" I blurt out the moment he shoves his phone in his pocket.

Ouray stands as well, his hands up to calm me.

"She's fine. Someone tried to force her into a vehicle at gunpoint in the parking lot of the City Market but didn't succeed, thanks to some quick thinking on her part."

I'm already moving toward the door.

"I'm driving," Ouray announces right behind me. "Luna says she's a little shaky and she doesn't want her to get behind the wheel of her truck."

I don't argue. I'm going to be fucking glued to her side until this mess is over anyway, so I won't need my bike.

I count three patrol units in the parking lot when we pull in. A couple of DPD SUVs and Luna's ride are clustered around Emme's parked truck at the back of the lot. A uniformed officer tries to redirect our vehicle, but Ouray ignores him and veers around. The moment he stops I jump out, leaving him to deal with the pissed-off cop.

Benedetti is there and so is VanDyken, one of his detectives. Luna is standing by the driver's side door, a phone to her ear, and I finally spot Emme sitting on the truck's running board beside her.

"Fucking hell, Emme. Are you okay?"

She sways a little when she gets to her feet and I grab her arm to steady her.

"I'm fine."

"Don't bullshit me, you're shaking on your feet."

She flashes me an angry look.

"That's because I'm so pissed, I'm spitting nails."

Yeah, me too.

"Who was it? Who was the sonofabitch?"

"Hey, Honon," Luna snaps. "Cool your damn jets. We're on it. Your job is to take her home so we can do ours."

Luna Roosberg may be a pixie of a woman, but she's a force to be reckoned with, especially in official capacity.

"Here." Ouray offers me his keys. "Get her back to the clubhouse, I'll store her truck somewhere safe and get one of the guys to pick me up."

"Wait a minute, clubhouse? I thought I was going home? And why can't we take my truck?" Emme demands to know.

"Because they clearly know your truck and we don't want to make it too easy for them to find you," Luna answers her. "And the clubhouse is the safest place for you."

Emme stubbornly shakes her head.

"No way. The clubhouse is the safest place for the kids. If I have a target on my back, the last thing I want to do is risk leading whoever it is straight to the kids, endangering them or anyone else there. I have to stay away from the clubhouse."

"And what? Go home where they might come looking for you?" I point out sharply.

She turns to me and jerks her chin up.

"Yes," she argues defiantly. "It's not like these guys are particularly savvy if they tried to take me in a busy grocery store parking lot in the middle of the day. I got away, didn't I? And I'll be better prepared next time."

"Next time they might fucking shoot first!"

Fear, frustration, anger, all explode as I yell at her, but she doesn't cower. Not Emme. She gets up on her toes and pokes a finger in my chest.

"Don't you yell at me like I'm some kind of idiot. The guy threatened to shoot me in the leg so I'd get in that car. They don't want me dead; they want something else from me."

"That's enough," Luna hisses sharply. "You two are starting to draw attention." Then she turns to me. "Emme has valid concerns about the clubhouse so I suggest, for now, you take her home, but be vigilant. I'll drop by as soon as I can."

Before I have a chance to object, Emme is already marching toward Ouray's Yukon. I grab her groceries before following.

The drive to her place is silent and I'm constantly checking my mirrors for anyone following. My blood pressure starts coming down when I turn onto her street and no one is behind me. Emme's place is the last house before Junction Lane stops in a dead end, which makes it a little easier to keep an eye on things.

Most of my anger has dissipated when I park the SUV in front of her garage, but Emme's still obviously pissed when she gets out and slams the door shut. She's already storming in the door by the time I catch up with her and disappears straight down the hallway to the bedroom. I hear that door slam shut as well, as I almost trip over the bags I dropped just inside the door.

I briefly contemplate going after her, but it's probably better if I give her a chance to cool off, so instead I head back out to grab her groceries from the back seat.

As I'm carrying the last bag into the house, I almost slam into Emme who was on her way out the door.

"Where are you going?"

She doesn't even slow down as she calls out over her shoulder, "I need to hit something."

I wait to see her head into the garage, before going inside to quickly unload this last bag in the kitchen. Then I take a beer from one of the six-packs she bought and bring it outside, grabbing a seat on her front steps where I can just see the garage. I've just had my first sip when a sound like metal banging on metal starts up.

Fifteen minutes later, one of the club's vehicles—an older black Jeep Brick keeps as a loaner—pulls into the driveway. I stand and walk toward the vehicle as Ouray and Shilah get out, and we exchange keys.

"Everything quiet?" Ouray asks, just as the clanging in the garage starts up again.

This has been ongoing as long as I've been out here, with brief breaks before the noise would start up again.

"That's Emme," I tell him. "She's been banging shit in there since we got home. Guess she's still pissed."

Ouray chuckles.

"Good luck with that one, brother. Looks like she's cut from the same cloth as my wife, and Lord knows I have my hands full with her."

I grunt in agreement and then watch them climb into the Yukon and back out of the driveway.

I still think she would've been safer at the clubhouse than here, but I doubt it helped my case that I yelled at her. Wouldn't be a bad idea to get Paco over here and see if we can't get some security rigged up, but before I make that call, I should probably talk to her.

The banging stops when I'm halfway to the garage, but this time I hear it replaced by hissing and popping noises. The overhead door is lifted a crack but the entry door on the side is open wide, random flashes of light visible. I walk over and poke my head around the corner.

Emme's back is toward me, little more than a silhouette backlit by the harsh glow of a welding torch. Sparks pop, creating the flashes of light I saw from outside. She's working on a metal shape trapped between two large vises. It looks like the branch of a tree. By her feet on the floor, I see a collection of tools. Mallets and hammers of varying sizes, chisels, and what looks like an extra-large pair of pliers.

I take a step inside, and suddenly the torch snaps off. Then she whips around as she lifts her welding mask to the top of her head. The same damn one I've seen her wear on stage too many times.

"Wow."

It's all I manage to say.

She looks a mess, with strands of her hair plastered to her cheeks and neck, and dirt and sweat staining her shirt. But her eyes are clear—almost too bright—standing out like jewels in her darkly flushed face, and she's easily the most stunning woman I've ever seen.

"The mask wasn't just a prop," I observe when I find my voice.

"No. Although, technically, it was for the purposes of dancing. I wanted something to cover my face so I wouldn't have to bother with stage makeup, and this was handy. It seemed to be a hit, tips were good," she adds as she whips off the welding mask and wipes the hair from her face.

"Oh, it was a hit all right," I tell her. "Even more of one now, knowing it revealed yet another layer to you."

My comments seem to throw her a little as she tosses the mask on her workbench and grabs a bottle of water, taking a deep drink.

I glance back at the shape suspended between the two large vises and walk toward it, reaching out my hand to touch it.

"Careful," she warns. "It could still be pretty hot."

Tapping the metal first to test, I run my fingers along the surface. It feels familiar. The texture is rough, much like the bark of a tree.

"This is really good. Amazing how you're able to make metal look like something organic."

I turn to face her.

"Thank you," she mumbles.

"Twisted Rod Designs. That's you, isn't it?"

As soon as I ran my hands over the branch I'd known for sure.

She seems shocked.

"How…"

"Last job Tse and I did before he left for Arizona was installing these custom-made rail panels for some rich guy up near Hermosa."

"Stoltenberg," she supplies.

"That's the one," I confirm. "Tse doesn't know?"

She shakes her head.

"Why?"

"I don't know. I was introduced to it when I did an art

course my first year in college. My parents were mortified when they discovered I wasn't painting sedate watercolors. I guess they felt that would've been more appropriate for their daughter than sculpting scrap metal." She chuckles dryly. "Clearly, they didn't know me very well. But it became a habit not to talk about it. I guess it stuck."

Her parents sound like pieces of work.

"Maybe I'm just a coward." She looks almost sheepish as she walks over to the sculpture and strokes a hand along its length. "It's surprisingly personal when you create something with nothing more to guide you than your own imagination. You put your heart and soul into it and it's scary to expose that to public scrutiny."

Then she turns to me and smiles.

"I figured if other artists could work under an alias—musicians, authors, actors, etcetera—then why couldn't I? So I became Twisted Rod Designs. It's why I bought the house with this great studio space. It brings me a little closer to my dream of doing this full time one day."

"You know Tse does a lot of custom work, right? He's making a name for himself in the more affluent neighborhoods in and around Durango. I'm not telling you what to do, but I bet if he knew Twisted Rod Designs is not only local, but you're the talent behind it, he'd be singing your praises to his clients."

She presses her lips together to hide the smile wanting to escape. Then she turns to grab a large sheet to toss over the sculpture and her workspace.

So that's why I didn't notice it when I was in here the other day to grab the cement board.

I wait for her to turn off the lights and follow her outside where the sun is starting to go down.

"Hey, Emme?" I wait for her to glance over her shoulder. "I shouldn't have yelled at you earlier."

She nods stiffly and I already regret bringing it up, but then she reaches back for my hand.

"I lost my shit too. Bunch of rookies we are."

# CHAPTER
# EIGHTEEN

*Emme*

It feels weird; normally when I wake up, I can't wait to get started on my day.

This morning, it's like I can't get myself to move. Not that I don't have anything to do—there's plenty, I have a house to finish—but somehow the motivation isn't there today.

Of course, that may have something to do with the man I'm currently snuggled up to.

"I can hear you thinking," he rumbles, his voice hoarse with sleep.

I lift my head from his chest and am met with a lazy smile.

"Only that I should probably get up and get productive instead of loafing in bed."

"Nothing wrong with a little loafing. Sometimes it's nice to just linger in a good moment."

His hand comes up to brush some hair out of my face before he adds, "I'd say this counts as one."

I drop my face to his chest to hide the smile he put there. The glimpse at this unexpected sentimental side only adds to the man's appeal, and I find myself falling deeper.

I'm not sure how long we stay like this, his large hand stroking my hair while I inhale his scent and listen to the steady safety of his heartbeat, but when he suddenly hisses and grabs for his side, I roll off him.

"What's wrong?"

He swings his legs out of bed and sits up, rubbing the tattoo on his side. The one covering a network of bumps and ripples I still don't know the origin of.

"Every so often I get a jab of nerve pain, which is weird, because the scar itself is numb to the touch."

"How did you get it?"

For a moment it looks like he's going to brush me off, but then he starts talking.

"Shrapnel." He throws me a glance over his shoulder. "I was part of an army reconnaissance unit in Afghanistan, post September eleventh. We were looking for possible access points to a network of caves and tunnels where a group of insurgents was reported to be hiding, when we ran into a mine. Potter and Santiago were killed, I survived."

"I'm so sorry," I mumble.

Then an image comes to mind of three uniformed men, arms around each other and smiling at the camera.

"The photo on your wall."

"Yeah, good friends. Brian Potter and Luis Santiago." He shakes his head. "Santiago had a young family: wife, two little ones under three. Brian got married two weeks before deployment. They left huge holes behind. There was no one special waiting for me, my loss would've barely made a ripple in anyone's life, and yet, I'm the one who made it out. Makes no fucking sense."

I simply place my hand on his shoulder and stay silent. He's not the kind of person who'd appreciate platitudes.

Still, there's a lot to unwrap here.

I don't have a psychology degree, but even to me it's clear he's still struggling with survivor's guilt. It may explain why he's avoided relationships for so long. Which locks in with what he said the other day, about getting hooked so deep it leaves a scar when it's ripped away.

At the time, I thought he might be talking from his own experience, but now I wonder if he was referring to the wives his friends left behind. Perhaps he feels he doesn't deserve what they lost.

He twists and takes my hand, pressing a kiss to my palm before getting to his feet.

"I'm gonna put some coffee on," he announces, shrugging into a pair of sweats he pulls out of one of his bags on the floor. "I'm thinking we can finish up drywalling the bathroom and get going on the tiling."

"I haven't ordered those yet," I explain, getting out of bed myself. "I first have to check if Stoltenberg finally came through with the money he owes me."

As I'm pulling on a pair of yoga pants and throw on an old shirt, I feel the temperature in the room dropping.

"You're kidding, right? That rich fuck hasn't paid you?"

An angry muscle ticks in his jaw as he glares at me from the doorway.

"Oh, I'm sure he will. He's probably just forgotten about it."

Last thing I want is for Honon to go off on one of my clients. It wouldn't be good for business.

"I doubt it, since every fucking time he goes up or down those stairs he's got his hand on that railing."

"Honon…" I start but he's already gone.

When I duck into the bathroom to get cleaned up, I can hear the rumble of his voice down the hall. Whoever he's talking to, at least he's not yelling.

When I walk into the kitchen a few minutes later, I'm greeted with the smell of coffee and bacon frying.

"Eggs, you want them poached, fried, or scrambled?"

"You poach your eggs?" I ask, surprised.

"English muffin, bacon, poached egg, cheese, avocado, and salsa. It's delicious."

"Sounds good to me."

I go about pouring us coffees while he busies himself at the stove.

Look at us, being all domestic. You'd think after living alone since college it would take some getting used to, sharing my space, but it doesn't feel awkward or invasive at all. Despite his size and his larger-than-life personality, I quite like him in my house.

"By the way, the money should be in your account."

My heart sinks.

"You called him. Please, tell me you didn't threaten him or something."

"Nope, I simply explained Tse and I weren't comfortable starting on his next project—a pool house with a guest suite—if invoices related to the previous job were still outstanding, as had come to our attention. Twisted Rod Designs wasn't even mentioned."

"What makes you so sure that did the trick?"

"Easy. He promised his wife she'd have it by summer." Then he throws me a grin. "And I've met his wife."

As promised, breakfast is delicious. I'm finishing stacking dirty dishes in the dishwasher, when Honon suddenly gets up from the island and marches to the front door.

"What is it?"

"Stay where you are," he snaps.

His tone sends a tingle of fear down my spine and my eyes stay fixed on the door until it opens again and Honon walks in with Luna.

"Sorry I didn't stop by yesterday," she starts as I slide a quickly poured cup of coffee in front of her. "I spent most of the night at a crime scene."

"Crime scene?"

"Hiker discovered the half-naked body of a woman a few hundred feet off one of the trails near the east Animas Mountain trailhead. She looked like she'd been there at least a few days. Benedetti was called to the scene and recognized the victim, so he contacted me."

Which means it probably has something to do with this case.

"I'm afraid it was Cher Valente."

A sick feeling curls in my stomach as I experience a flashback of me calling after Cher. Asking her what she was so afraid of.

"It looks like someone saw her, grabbed her off the trail, then sexually assaulted her before strangling her with the strap of her purse."

Oh, no. Poor Cher.

"At first sight it looked like a crime of opportunity," Luna shares.

"But you don't think so," I observe, hearing the hesitation in her voice.

"No, I don't. For one thing, no one in their right mind

would hike those trails in ballet flats, which is what she was wearing."

"I remember her wearing brown flats when I saw her on Monday." I close my eyes and pull up a mental image of her. "Also leggings, multi-colored with flowers or something. And she was wearing a knit brown sweater vest, or duster—it was one of those long ones—with just a plain white shirt underneath."

"It matches the clothes we found her with," Luna confirms. "We figure someone forced or carried her up that trail, her body showed evidence she'd been bound at some point. But we'll have to wait for the autopsy to confirm details."

"You think this could be connected to the guy with the gun at the City Market?"

"There's no way to know for sure, but it's a possibility we can't discount," she responds with an almost apologetic smile.

Remembering Cher's fear, I can't help wonder if someone was actually watching us, and grabbed her right after that. The thought sends chills down my spine.

"That's it," Honon grinds out. "I'm calling Paco."

———

*Honon*

I haul another couple of boards from the garage when I see Paco's truck pull into the driveway.

"Bathroom reno?" he asks when he joins me at the front door.

"Yup. Hang on a sec, let me get rid of these."

I carry the boards into the bedroom and stick my head inside the en suite. Emme started taping the far side while I'm finishing up the final boards.

"Paco's here."

She whips her head around.

"Let me finish this strip, I'll be right there."

I wasn't sure if she'd be up to it after Luna left a while ago, but she claimed she wanted to stay busy. Welcome news to me since I've never been good at twiddling my thumbs either.

Paco is standing by the sliding back doors, looking out at the view.

"Great location," he comments, turning around when he hears me come in.

"Yeah, it's a nice spot. Any thoughts on what would be needed?" I ask, getting right to the point.

"Doors and windows in here look fairly new."

"They are," Emme announces from behind me. "I installed them last year."

Paco turns around, one eyebrow raised.

"You did?"

Before she has a chance to climb up one side of him and down the other, I hurry to intervene.

"She did all the work in here. The windows in the bed and bathrooms are new as well, right, Emme?"

"Figured I'd do them all at once," she admits, still eyeing Paco, who quickly recovers.

"Good. All sliders?"

"Yup, all double latched and a pin lock into the base of the frame."

"Great. Now, what are you looking for in terms of added security?"

I leave it to Emme to list of basic things she and I discussed last night; door and window motion sensors, a few cameras, and motion lights by front and back doors.

Paco goes through the house and around the outside to take some measurements and make notes.

"So, can you give me an idea how much it'll be?"

His eyes immediately shoot to me.

"Don't look at him, I'm paying for it myself," she assures him, as adamant as she was last night.

I didn't fight her then either.

However, when she returns to her mudding and I walk Paco out to his truck, I make sure he understands who'll be footing the bill. At least the bulk of it.

"I figured as much. Let me see what I can scrounge up back at the clubhouse to get started today, but I'll probably need to order some stuff. I can have it overnight couriered, though."

"That's fine. I appreciate it, brother."

I clap him on the shoulder and head back inside. Emme looks at me funny when I walk into the bathroom.

"What?"

"Don't think I don't know what you're up to," she warns, wagging her finger at me before she turns back to taping.

I figure the best way to handle this is keep my trap shut, but I do walk up behind her and press a kiss behind her ear.

"And I'm immune to bribery," she mumbles.

Chuckling, I turn to the nearly finished wall.

———

That afternoon we made a good dent in the work.

All the drywall is up and the taping is done everywhere except for the wall where the shower tile is going up, that only received a skim coat of mud. Now we have to wait twenty-four hours or so for it to dry. It won't be until after the weekend when we can start tiling.

"You should order that tile," I remind Emme. "Do you know what you want?"

"Yes. Hang on."

She pulls a laptop from a drawer in the TV stand and brings it back to the island, just as Paco walks in from the bedrooms.

"I've done as much as I can today. The rest of the equipment is supposed to be delivered to the clubhouse before noon. It'll take me a couple of hours to install so it should be done end of tomorrow."

"Appreciate it, brother. Beer?" I hold up my bottle.

He lifts a hand.

"Nah, I've gotta run. Mel's daughter is coming over for dinner. One pissed-off Morgan woman is bad enough, pissing off two of them is suicide."

No sooner has he left and my phone rings. It's Luna.

"What's up?"

"Is Emme there?"

"Yup."

"Put me on speakerphone."

"It's Luna," I tell Emme, putting my phone on the counter.

"I want to give you a heads-up. On a hunch, I went over the report of the altercation at the Backyard Edge a few weeks ago, since that's the first time the name 'Hines' popped up on our radar. Turns out one of David Hines's buddies who was there that night is a Christopher Sampson who owns a 2006 navy-blue Corolla. I started off asking him how they ended up at the Backyard the night of the altercation. He said that hadn't been planned. They'd been looking for a place to grab a bite and it was the first restaurant they bumped into. However, when I confronted him with the attempted abduction at the City Market, Mr. Sampson turned out to be a fair-weather friend and was quick to point the finger at Hines. He admitted to being the driver, but claims he was told it was only a prank and was shocked when Hines pulled out the gun."

"So you picked up Hines?" Emme asks.

"I've been looking for him, but no luck. He hasn't been at The Pink Petal since Monday. His father claims he doesn't know where his son is. When I went to talk to Mandy, she said he left for a fishing trip, but I noticed two packed suitcases by the door."

"Getting ready to run," I observe.

"Looks like it," Luna confirms. "I took Mandy in for questioning, but she's clammed up, demanding a lawyer be present. A cold fish, that one. No emotion whatsoever when I brought up the murder of both Rhea and now Cher. For a friend, even a former one, she didn't seem to care much."

"You think she had something to do with their murders?" Emme probes.

"I don't know, at this point anything is possible. What I do know is David Hines's name is somehow connected to all of these cases and he's out there, probably feeling the pressure. I've pulled in the rest of my team and we're actively out looking for him, but until we find him…"

I notice Emme wrapping her arms around herself and curve my hand around the back of her neck.

"We'll be careful," I assure Luna.

"Good, because a desperate man is a dangerous one."

# CHAPTER
# NINETEEN

*Emme*

Already I'm going stir-crazy.

Normally, I'd love to have a couple of consecutive days to work on my house, but my heart isn't in it right now.

I've been on my knees for the last hour or two pulling a gazillion tacks from the subfloor with pliers. Honon and I ripped up the old carpet in the bedroom this morning and whoever put it down secured it to withstand a tornado. It doesn't help I've been sucking in drywall dust and fifty-some years of carpet odors the entire time.

Honon taped off the bathroom doorway with plastic while he sands down the bathroom walls, but the damn dust is so fine, it gets through anyway.

I need some fresh air.

Tossing the pliers on the ground, I get to my feet, groaning as I stretch my knees. Leaving Honon in the bathroom, I make my way to the kitchen to grab a glass of water. The clock on the stove shows it's almost noon. Paco should be here soon to finish up the new security system.

It's a beautiful day, so I take my water out on the back deck and walk up to the railing to take in the view. Once the inside of the house is done, I plan to do some work out here. I saw a picture on a DYI blog online, depicting a pergola-like structure made entirely of logs I'd like to replicate. Covered in vines it would provide a little oasis of shade in my otherwise mostly exposed yard. The logs would meld into the rustic landscape. I'm not much of a gardener—nor do I have much interest in it—but I thought it might be nice to create a patch of rock garden with indigenous plants that don't need to be babied.

The faint whine of an engine has me look up at the small ridge that runs parallel to Junction Lane along the back of my property. There must be some kind of trail up there because every so often I see hikers or the occasional ATV come by. I don't see anything now though, and I can't hear it anymore either. So I turn to go inside, reaching for the water glass I left on the railing when it splinters in my hand.

A sharp snap registers an instant later, but before I can react, wood splinters fly up as something hits the deck at my feet. Instinct has me duck down in a crouch and rush for the sliding glass door I'd left open. Something whizzes by me, hitting the siding.

*Shots?*

Just as I dive inside, the sliding glass door shatters behind me.

"Emme!"

Honon comes tearing out of the hallway, a gun in his hand as he races for the back door.

"Don't go out!" I manage to call after him as another shot hits the siding with a ping, but he's already gone from sight.

"Stay down!" I hear him yell from outside.

The next moment I hear a volley of shots fired, making my backyard sound like the O.K. Corral. I can't just sit here and do nothing, so I scramble to my feet and make a run for the shotgun I keep in the front hall closet. I'm not a fan of guns, but I'm also not an idiot. A woman living alone on the outskirts of town with nothing but wilderness behind her would be stupid not to have some protection.

I'm no marksman, and although I can hit a target at twenty-five yards, I'm pretty sure the shooter is a lot farther away than that. My buckshot rounds won't do much but I'm not about to sit around helpless when Honon is out there alone.

Instead of going out the back and into the line of fire, I duck out the front door. Keeping my eyes open in case there are more, I ease around the corner and between the house and the garage. The shots have stopped, the sudden quiet unsettling. I carefully poke my head around the rear, hoping and praying Honon isn't lying somewhere bleeding, but I can't see him.

From up on the ridge comes the high whine of an engine starting up before the sound fades into silence again. I assume that was the shooter getting away, but I'm not taking any chances and lift my shotgun as I step into the backyard.

There's no sign of Honon. I round the deck to see if he's on the other side when I hear something move behind me and swing around.

"Jesus, Wildcat." Honon steps out from the trees, one hand up defensively. "Put that damn thing down, will ya?"

I lower the barrel and wait for my heart to sink back down from my throat as I scan him for holes.

"Fuck, you're bleeding," he mutters, jogging up to me.

The blood never registered. It isn't until he takes the shotgun from my hand, I notice it dripping from between my fingers and down my arm.

"It's just glass," I comment as he flips my hand around to reveal what looks to be a few cuts in the palm of my hand and one on the side of my wrist.

He clamps his hand around my forearm and pulls me to the steps of the deck.

"What the hell is going on here?" Paco asks, appearing in the doorway where my expensive sliding door used to be. "Leaving the goddamn front door wide open," he grumbles before catching sight of us. "The fuck, Emme?"

"Get Luna on the phone and put her on speaker," Honon snaps before pulling me inside.

Then he turns and lifts me up on the counter next to the sink and runs the water.

"Paco, what's up?" I hear Luna's voice, just as sirens sound in the distance.

Someone must've called 911.

I feel oddly removed as I listen to Honon describe to Luna what happened. Paco is at the front door, his hands up by his shoulders as patrol cars pull up to my house, their lights flashing. I feel like I've landed in some kind of alternate reality.

This is not my life.

---

*Honon*

My damn blood is still roaring in my ears as I stuff a

large garbage bag with any of Emme's stuff I think she might need.

I haven't told her yet, but we're going to the clubhouse. I've already notified Ouray.

God, I wish I could've taken that bastard down. I wouldn't have hesitated a single second but, even for me, it's nearly impossible to hit a moving target at a good hundred and fifty yards or more with a 9mm hand gun. I tried to get closer but knew going after him was futile when I heard what surely was an ATV engine start up, plus I needed to check in on Emme.

That could've gone so wrong. I'm almost sick thinking about it.

Grabbing some toiletries from the bathroom, I stuff them in the trash bag before carrying it and my own bags out of the bedroom.

Emme is sitting on the couch when I walk in, staring at the blank screen of her TV. Out back I catch sight of Luna, who is on the deck, conferring with a couple of uniforms and Benedetti, who showed up half an hour ago. Paco is in the kitchen, leaning against the counter.

I drop the bags and head over to him.

"She's been sitting there, staring at nothing," he mumbles.

We'd gone over what happened three separate times. Once with the first uniform on the scene, then Luna when she got here, and we were asked to repeat it again for the chief. Emme recited her experience in the same almost monotone voice each time. I'm pretty sure she's in shock.

"I'm taking her to the clubhouse," I tell him. "Ouray is sending Shilah over with some plywood to board up the door, can you give him a hand?"

"Sure. I'll see if I can find a replacement for that one panel, or else order a new unit."

"Thanks."

I move to the back door and step outside.

"You done with us?"

Luna turns to look at me.

"For now, yeah. Why?"

"I'm taking her to the compound."

She glances past me inside, where I'm sure Emme is still staring at the TV. She's been a scrapper through everything that's led up to today, rolling with the punches, but I'm guessing getting shot at pushed her past capacity. She may well be at, or at least close to, her breaking point. I want her out of here before that happens.

Luna's eyes come back to me as she nods her understanding.

"I'll catch up with you there later."

"I can get a unit to follow you," Joe offers.

"No need," Luna answers before I can. "Barnes should be here any minute. He can escort them."

Benedetti flinches visibly at the implicated lack of trust in his department, but I appreciate Luna's caution.

By the time I have the bags in the back of the Jeep and head inside to get Emme, Agent Dylan Barnes arrives.

"Let's go, Wildcat," I tell Emme, taking her arm.

"Where are we going?" she wants to know, a little unsteady as she gets to her feet.

"Clubhouse."

"Okay," she concedes, way too meekly.

I figured she'd at least argue about not wanting to compromise the kids' safety, and the fact she doesn't shows how out of it she is.

Barnes follows close behind the two miles up the road to

the Arrow's Edge compound, but the only traffic we see is Shilah's truck with a large sheet of plywood strapped down in the back, heading in the opposite direction. When I turn up the driveway, Barnes stops his SUV at the bottom and waits until we drive through the gate.

At the clubhouse, I help Emme out of the Jeep and inside. There's no one at the bar, but some of the kids are doing homework at the big table and Mika is slouched on the couch, watching the replay of a Rockies game on the big screen. I don't see Malco, though.

"The kids are probably in the kitchen with Lisa, why don't you pop in there while I grab our stuff?"

Lisa is already poking her head out to see who came in and takes one look at Emme's pale face before she nods at me.

"Timing's great," she addresses Emme. "I just made a pot of tea. Malco is at the shop with Brick, he didn't wanna watch the game, but the baby's in here with me. She'll be glad to see ya."

As soon as she disappears inside, I turn on my heel and head back out to get the bags.

"Oh, you *are* here."

I back out of the Jeep and turn to find a truck stopped on the drive that runs all the way up to the shooting range along the outside of our fence. They look to be on their way out. Front and rear passenger windows are rolled down and I recognize a couple of DPD guys.

*Shit*. With everything going on, I forgot about today's drill.

I walk up to my side of the fence.

"Hey, guys. I'm so fucking sorry," I explain through the chain links. "I had an emergency and—"

"No worries. Your buddy, Lusio, was up there and let us

in to do some target practice instead. Said you'd make up for it."

"Yeah, man. Let me check the schedule and I'll shoot your boss a couple of possible dates. Sorry to make you drive up here again."

I give them a wave and walk back to the Jeep for the bags.

When I walk past Nosh's room, I glance in. The old man is in bed and Ouray is sitting in the recliner next to him. He looks up when I walk in.

"How is he?"

"Rough night." He jerks his chin in the direction of the new connecting door. "Wapi is catching a couple of hours. Emme okay?"

"Shaken. She's with Lisa." I hold up the bags. "Your room all right?"

"Spare room now," he corrects me with a grin. "Have at it." Then he turns serious again. "Kaga, Trunk, and Yuma will be here after dinner and by that time Paco and Shilah should be back too. We'll talk then."

I nod and head for the big bedroom, drop the bags on the king-sized bed, and quickly unpack. Both my stuff and Emme's fits easily in the large closet and I drop the toiletries on the counter in the bathroom. This room is like a goddamn hotel compared to the other bedrooms.

I find Emme at the kitchen table with Athena on her lap, giving her a bottle. *Damn.* My chest feels funny and I press the heel of my hand against my sternum.

Finn, Brick and Lisa's four-year-old grandson, is sitting across from them and is coloring with crayons. He looks up when I walk in.

"Honon!"

"Hey, buddy." I walk over and ruffle his blond hair. "Whatcha doing?"

"I drawed a horse, wanna see?"

"Drew," Lisa mumbles without looking away from the stove.

"Absolutely."

He flips a page in his sketchbook and points at what looks more like an alien arachnid than a horse, but I hum in approval.

"That's…uh…impressive, bud. Where'd you see a horse like that?"

"Trunk and Auntie Jamie taked me and River and Eden to a farm."

"Took."

I glance at Emme when I hear a soft snort, and catch her smiling.

"That's pretty cool, Finn. Did they have a lot of horses?"

"Just two, but they had a thousand pigs."

"One of the guys from Station 3 is a pig farmer, and apparently has a couple of horses too," Lisa explains.

"Hog, I know him," I tell her.

He's on the same crew as Trunk's brother-in-law, Evan.

"Right. Anyway," she continues. "Finn was invited to go with Trunk and Jamie to a pig roast at his farm last weekend. Now he wants a horse."

"Yes," the little boy confirms with a grin, despite Lisa's eye roll.

"Nana!" Lisa's granddaughter, Kiara, waltzes into the kitchen. "When's dinner?"

"Same time as every other day," is the dry response.

"Can we have pizza?"

Lisa steps back from the stove and gestures at the pots.

"This look like pizza to you?"

"I want pizza too!" Finn yells.

"See?" Kiara exclaims triumphantly.

Foreseeing this might take a while—I speak from experience—I catch Emme's eye and jerk my head toward the door.

"That's only the start of the zoo it'll be in here until feeding time," I warn her when she follows me out, the baby against her shoulder and her bandaged hand on Athena's back. "Want me to take her?"

She shakes her head.

"I've got her."

I lead her to the bedroom and let her go in ahead of me. She walks over to the bed while I close the door behind us.

"Bah! Ngh bah!" Athena squawks, patting Emme's cheek.

"Nothing wrong with her volume," she observes as the baby starts wiggling.

"That's not a bad thing here," I point out. "Only way to get heard sometimes."

I sit down on the other side of the bed and scoot up so my back is against the headboard.

"Put her on the bed and hop up, we'll block her in."

I pull the Jeep's keys from my pocket and give them to her. She's pretty steady sitting and seems fascinated with the shiny metal. Then I lift my head and catch Emme's eyes on me. I don't think she's really looked at me all afternoon.

"How are ya, Wildcat?"

I reach over Athena's head and brush a wayward strand of hair off Emme's forehead. Immediately her eyes well up and she blows out a shaky breath.

"I'm not gonna lie, I was scared shitless."

"So was I," I admit. "It's a common side effect of getting shot at."

She gives me a look, but I still get a little smile out of her.

"The thing is, that didn't scare me nearly as much as you running straight into the line of fire did."

Lifting up the baby with one arm, I scoot closer to Emme, and pull her against me with the other while settling Athena on my lap. Then I press a kiss to the side of Emme's head.

"You forget, I was trained for that stuff. I've been in dicey situations before."

"Yeah, and you have the holes in your body to show for it," she snaps.

She'd discovered the scar on my thigh as well. That one was from a round I caught almost five years ago in a shootout with a former brother of ours who'd kidnapped Sophia.

"I walked away every time," I remind her. "And it's not like I make a habit of it."

"Good, because at some point your luck may run out, and that would seriously suck."

Her words are almost flippant, but the emotion behind them isn't.

Damn, if that woman isn't hooked on me as badly as I am on her.

# CHAPTER
# TWENTY

*Emme*

As Honon predicted, dinner was mayhem.

At first, I thought the kids were simply excited about the start of the weekend, but during the course of dinner I found out this coming Thursday would be the last day of school before summer break. They'd be off for almost two-and-a-half months. That's a long time.

I glance over at Malco beside me. He's been even more withdrawn tonight than he already was. He barely managed a hello earlier when we were sitting down for dinner. Could be he's missing school with the younger kids' excited chatter about the fun things their teachers have planned.

Guess I have two and a half months to figure out school for him. That is, if we're out of this nightmare by then.

"Do you miss school?"

He shrugs his shoulders without looking at me.

"Are you okay?" I follow it up with.

This time I get a brief flash of his eyes. His, "Yeah," is barely audible.

I look up to find Honon observing us, raising an eyebrow at me. I shoot him an I-don't-know look.

At that moment Luna walks into the clubhouse and immediately Ouray gets to his feet.

"All right, crew. My office."

He leans down to give Luna a peck on the lips before the two start walking to the back.

"You too, Emme," he calls out over the scrape of chairs on the wooden floors, as the men start getting up to follow.

I put a hand on Malco's shoulder and bend down to whisper in his ear.

"Honon and I will be staying here. If you need me, or just want to talk, come find me, okay?"

He nods but keeps his eyes on his half-empty plate.

I join Honon, who is waiting for me and slings his arm over my shoulders, leaning in.

"What's up with the kid?" he asks as we start following the rest of the guys.

"Not sure. I thought he was starting to settle in a little, but if anything, he seems even more withdrawn. He says he's okay, but something feels off," I share.

"He may have picked up on rumblings around the clubhouse about what happened at your place. He may be worried," Honon suggests.

Could be, but even the possibility me being here is causing him more anxiety doesn't sit well with me.

"This has to end," I mumble when he steps aside to let me into the office where the others are already gathered.

"Let's see whether Luna has some news," he responds in a low voice before chasing one of the younger guys off the couch to clear a space for me. He takes a seat on the armrest beside me.

"We've gotta talk security, boys, but first I'm gonna let Luna fill you in."

"I'm sure everyone's heard by now what happened earlier this afternoon?"

At the responding nods and confirming grunts, she continues, "Right, so I don't have to explain why Emme will be staying here. You also know why it wouldn't be a good idea to ask the DPD to provide any kind of security, so it'll be up to us to stay vigilant."

An involuntary shiver runs through me. Honon must've noticed because he slips his warm hand under my hair, and curls his fingers around the back of my neck.

"We're pretty sure there was only one shooter because we found shell casings all concentrated in one location. We know he got in and out on an ATV and he used a hunting rifle but, luckily for Emme and Honon, is not a particularly good shot."

"This the same guy?" Kaga asks. "The one who tried to grab Emme?"

"David Hines. I have reason to think so," Luna confirms. "His left forearm is injured, but that could explain why his aim was off when he should've had a fairly easy shot."

"I don't get why he would try to grab me one day and kill me the next?"

I've mulled on this and it's the part that still doesn't make sense to me.

"You bested him twice," Ouray offers. "Sounds like the guy has a temper so that probably didn't sit well."

"Plus," Luna adds. "I asked his friend in custody whether he knows if Hines has an ATV and, apparently, he does. He stores it at another friend's place who lives on W. 28th Way."

"That's only a mile or so south of your place," Honon points out.

"Exactly," Luna confirms. "Barnes and I were just there. We caught the buddy coming home from work. He claims he hadn't seen Hines but pointed us to the shed at the back of his property where the ATV is stored. It was there, and it looks like it's the ATV used because we found a spent casing in the footwell matching the ones at the scene."

"Fucking little pissant. I should've aimed for his head instead of his arm."

Honon squeezes my neck as some of the guys chuckle at my outburst.

"Easy there, Wildcat," he mumbles.

"Unfortunately," Luna continues. "We haven't located him yet, but Barnes found out from one of his friends' neighbors he saw a maroon SUV parked in the driveway. He figured it was a rental because of the license plate."

Even I know, in Colorado most rental vehicles have a special, red license plate with the letters FLT, for fleet, on the side.

"Barnes is following up on that, but in the meantime he's still out there."

"Right, so for now we're keeping the gate padlocked night *and* day," Ouray takes over. "I want someone on the monitors twenty-four seven, so we'll rotate in four-hour shifts."

Groans go up around the room and I feel myself shrinking, but Ouray isn't done yet.

"And don't be slogging down coffee unless you wanna piss in a jar, because those eyes better stay glued to the screen at all fucking times."

"This is too much," I interrupt, feeling incredibly guilty. Maybe it's better if I pack up those kids and take off for Utah or New Mexico. "You've done so much already; I can't ask you to do that. I can—"

"Stay right where you are," Honon growls beside me.

"He's right. If you take off, we're gonna have to chase you down and that'll be a real pain in the ass. Now," Ouray gets back to business. "Paco already said he'll take the next shift. Who's up to take midnight to four?"

"I'll take it," Honon volunteers.

Within ten minutes, they have a rotation put together for the next seventy-two hours. I sure hope it doesn't take that long to track Hines down, because already I don't think I've ever felt this helpless.

"You'll get used to it," Luna mutters beside me as we walk into the clubhouse.

I scoff at that.

"I'm not sure I will. I'm not used to charity."

She darts me a sharp look and I feel instantly scolded.

"Has nothing to do with charity. It's family. Honon is ours, you're Honon's, and therefore you're ours too. It's not that hard."

Except when your own family cuts you out of their lives like you were some kind of festering abscess.

———

*Honon*

"Did something happen with Malco today?"

Brick looks up from his beer.

"Not that I know of. He spent the afternoon at the shop with me and nothing happened there. Why?"

"I don't know. He hasn't said a word to me tonight."

In fact, he didn't even react when I told him goodnight earlier when Lisa took the kids to her place.

"Brother, he hasn't talked to me at all and he sleeps under my roof. The world's gotta be a scary place for that boy right now. Imagine being nine and seeing what he's seen. He's probably just having an off day."

He's got a point. It fits with what I suggested to Emme earlier, about him overhearing something.

"Well…" I finish the dregs of my beer and set the bottle on the bar. "Let's hope tomorrow is better then. I'm going to grab an hour or two before I'm on the monitors."

"Yeah, I should turn in too. I've got four o'clock."

I call out a good night to Shilah and Lusio, who are sprawled out in front of the TV, in passing.

Emme went to bed at around eight thirty, right after Lisa took the kids. When I offered to go with her, she told me to finish my beer, that she'd probably have a bath and crash.

Seemed plausible enough after the day she had, but when I walk into the bedroom, I find the lights on and the TV set to some baking show. Emme is sitting up in bed, her eyes red-rimmed, looking as if she's been crying.

"Can't sleep?"

She shakes her head.

"Not anymore."

"Nightmare?"

I know all about nightmares. They started while I was still recovering at the U.S. military hospital near Landstuhl, Germany. They still plague me every so often.

Kicking off my boots, I turn off the lights, leaving the TV on, and lie down beside her.

"Come here."

I open my arms and she doesn't hesitate, snuggling up against my side.

"Wanna talk about it?"

I feel rather than see her shake her head.

"I'll pass."

"Fair enough." I press a kiss to her forehead. "Try to get some sleep, baby."

I cover her hand on my chest with mine and wait for her breathing to even out. Trying to stay alert, I watch grown men cry over deflated cream puffs and runny mousse, afraid I'd wake Emme if I tried to change the channel.

The alarm on my phone starts buzzing in my pocket, and I quickly reach a hand in to silence it before untangling myself from Emme without disturbing her too much. She rolls onto her side and curls up in the spot I just left. Turning off the TV, I grab my boots, flick the light on in the bathroom, and leave the door open a crack so it's not completely dark should she wake up in the night. Then I tiptoe out of the room, closing the door with a soft click, before putting on my boots.

Despite Ouray's warning, my first stop is the kitchen, where I brew a fresh pot of coffee. I'm gonna need it if I'm to keep my eyes open. Luckily, I have a bladder like a camel.

Paco is rubbing his hands over his face when I walk into the small office next to the kitchen, a few minutes later, with the largest travel mug I could find filled to the brim with the hot brew.

"Thank fuck," he grumbles, getting up to make room for me in front of the monitors.

Just as I sit down, I catch a flash of something at the edge of the view on one of the cameras. This one is mounted on the boys' dorm building on the other side of the drive to Brick and Lisa's cottage. It's aimed up the hill toward the range.

"What's that?"

"Probably a deer, I've seen a couple tonight in that area. I also spotted a mountain lion on camera six, maybe an hour ago. I've seen him on the trail cams a few times in the past month but near the shooting range. Looks like he's coming closer."

Camera six is aimed uphill as well, but a little farther from the compound and on the other side of the trail.

"We may need to contact Parks and Wildlife if it gets too close to the compound."

"Hmm. I'm going home and to bed. I'm fucking toast."

"I appreciate you, brother."

"Yeah, yeah." He waves me off and rubs his hands over his face again.

"You okay to drive?" I ask him. "You can always crash here."

"Nah. Mel likes me home. She sleeps better."

I want to bet it's the other way around and Paco is the one who needs his wife close for a good night's sleep. But I'm not going to call him out on his bullshit. I'm not one to talk. Having slept with Emme in my arms every night for the past week and a half, I wouldn't want it any other way either.

"See you in the morning," he says, clapping me on the shoulder.

"Night."

The next few hours crawl by and I struggle to keep my eyes open. I ended up closing the door so I could play some Fleetwood Mac to keep me awake and just resorted to rummaging through the desk in search of something to eat.

Paco is going to kill me when he finds out I jimmied the lock on the bottom drawer and discovered his cache of Snickers bars, which I've halved over the past forty-five minutes.

All I've seen on the screens are bugs, the occasional bird, and that glimpse of the deer, heading in the same direction Paco caught the mountain lion earlier. That may not be good news for the deer, which is the prime source of food for the cougars.

I'm already counting down the last twenty minutes of my shift when Wapi pokes his head in.

"What are you doing up?" I ask.

"Nosh woke up earlier, disoriented and combative when I tried to get him to pee in the bottle. Insisted on using the can. Not a lot of the man left, but I still almost put out my damn back carrying him in and out of the bathroom. Anyway, I was grabbing something to drink when I heard the music in here."

"Trying to stay awake," I tell him. "Ouray filled you in?"

"Yeah, how's Emme?"

"I hope still sleeping. She had a nightmare earlier."

"Not a surprise. Getting shot at gets to the best of us."

"Sure does," I agree.

"Before I go check in on Nosh, can I grab you something from the kitchen?"

"Nah, man. Brick should be here shortly to take over and I'll probably just crash for a few hours."

Just then I catch sight of someone crossing into view of a camera mounted on the roof of the clubhouse and aimed at the boys' dorm.

I'm halfway out of my seat when Wapi blurts, "That looks like Brick."

I lean closer to the screen, and squint my gritty eyes.

"Yeah, you're right. What the hell is he going to the dorm for?" I wonder out loud, watching as the lights inside the building turn on.

"A scuffle?"

The dorm houses all the boys we have in our care plus our two prospects, whose job is to mind the kids during the night. Maybe Wapi is right and a fight broke out. Brick might have heard the commotion on his way to the clubhouse. Wouldn't be the first time the kids try to work out their differences with their fists.

"There he is. He's heading here now," Wapi observes.

Something about the way Brick is moving has the hair on my neck stand on end.

"Do me a favor, keep an eye on the monitors for a sec."

I step out of the office at the same time Brick comes in the front door. The look on his face is grim.

"What's wrong?"

He stops and flexes his hands by his hips, before clenching them into fists, and when he speaks his voice is gruff.

"It's the boy…"

# CHAPTER
# TWENTY-ONE

*Honon*

"What do you mean, he's gone?"

Emme shoots upright in bed. She'd been fast asleep when I walked in.

God knows I didn't want to do this. For over an hour we've been scouring the grounds in the dark, hoping to find Malco since Brick reported him missing.

He'd gotten up for his shift at the monitors, decided to check on the kids before heading to the clubhouse, and discovered the boy's bed slept in but empty. He'd been nowhere in the cottage or the dorm, where Brick had gone to check, hoping maybe he'd gone there.

Lisa said he'd gone to bed at nine thirty, and Brick checked in on all the kids when he came in from the clubhouse, as he habitually does. They'd all been asleep in bed, or so he thought, until he noticed Malco's shoes missing from the front hall this morning. When he went to check his bedroom, the boy was gone.

Wapi got Lusio, Shilah, and Mika up and Brick got one

of the prospects to keep an eye on the monitors, while the rest of us headed out to search for Malco. We checked the grounds all the way to the fence lines, looked in all the nooks and crannies in and around the buildings—including Brick's shop—but found no sign of him.

Ouray and Luna—who were called in by Wapi—have maps of the property spread out on the dining table and are organizing a more methodical search. Yuma and Trunk live just down the road so they're already here, and Paco and Tse are on their way.

We're going to need all the help we can get. There's a lot of ground to cover beyond the fence and it'll be another forty-five minutes or so until sunrise.

There's no way I can keep this from Emme any longer, but I'm worried about what this will do to her.

"When Brick checked on him this morning, he wasn't in his bed. His shoes were gone and it looks like he may have grabbed some supplies."

Lisa discovered a few water bottles were gone from the pantry, as was a box of granola bars, a bunch of bananas, and a throw they had draped over the couch had disappeared. The fact he's smart enough to plan ahead is a small comfort.

"He left by himself?"

Panic has her voice pitched higher than normal as she struggles to get into her pants.

"Looks like it."

"Oh my God, the baby…"

"Is fine. Lisa kept the baby in their bedroom because she still wakes up at night for a bottle."

She briefly closes her eyes, and then finishes dressing.

"Why would he do that? Why would he run away? It just doesn't make sense."

She doesn't wait for an answer—not that I have one—and brushes past me out the door. I hustle to keep up with her as she storms down the hallway and into the clubhouse.

"Why is everyone just standing around?" she demands loudly when she catches sight of the group gathered around the table.

Every eye turns to her.

"Why aren't you out there looking for him?"

She darts past them on her way to the front door, where I just manage to catch up with her.

"Let me go!"

She struggles at the arm I have wrapped around her waist.

"Calm down," I try, but she keeps fighting me even as I lift her off her feet and turn her away from the door.

"Calm down?" she echoes. "He's by himself in the dark. What if David Hines is out there somewhere?"

Nothing I haven't thought myself, with the added danger of a mountain lion hanging around, but I wasn't planning on telling her that.

I carefully set her on her feet and turn her around, my hands resting on her shoulders.

"Emme, we've had eyes on those cameras all night. If Hines is out there, we would've seen him."

Suddenly her head snaps up and her eyes shoot fire.

"Then how come you didn't see Malco?"

*Fuck.*

I've been beating myself up over that since Brick came storming in.

"Wouldn't have seen him if he slipped out the back of the cottage, Emme," I explain. Even as I'm saying it, I remember the glimpse of what I thought was a deer ducking into the trees I saw as I was taking over the watch from Paco.

Could that've been Malco? It's hard to tell with the grainy black-and-white images from the night-vision cameras. If it was him, he's already been gone for over five hours. A lot can happen in that time.

"That's enough!" Ouray barks. "Not gonna do the boy much good with you two wasting time bickering. Let's get ourselves organized."

I follow Emme to the table where Luna is marking off sections and numbering them. Tse and Paco walk in while Ouray is giving instructions and dividing us up into groups. Lisa is handing out tumblers with coffee, urging Emme to take one.

"I wanna look up there," I indicate, pointing at the section Luna marked with the number eight.

It's an area northwest of the compound. The general direction Malco would have been going in if that quick glimpse on the monitor had in fact been him.

"Fine. Take Tse."

My brother comes to stand beside me and claps me on the shoulder.

"I've got my Maglite, rope, and a first aid kit in my pack," he says.

Good. I hadn't even thought of that but with the kind of terrain we're about to search, it's probably smart to be prepared. The area is rough, with gullies and a few sheer drops into a mountain runoff feeding into Junction Creek below. What is barely a trickle during summer and fall can swell dangerously in spring with the melting snow from the highest peaks.

"And grab a radio from the office," Ouray adds.

I turn to Emme and hook my hand behind her neck, pressing a hard kiss to her stubborn mouth.

"We'll find him."

Then I let go and am about to head for the door when she pipes up.

"Yes, we will. I'm coming with you."

"Wildcat…"

"I'm not sitting around twiddling my thumbs when I should be out looking," she insists.

I throw a pleading look at Lisa, who is standing behind her.

"Don't look at me," she sputters, shaking her head. "If I didn't have kids that need minding here, I'd be right behind her."

"These guys know the terrain, Emme. You'd probably be more of a holdup than a help," Ouray points out none too gently. "Those shoes won't get you far." He points at the Chucks on her feet.

Then he adds in a gentler tone, "Besides, we could use you here, monitoring the radio."

———

*Emme*

I've effectively been sidelined.

*Damned Ouray.*

It's becoming clear why the otherwise easygoing man is president of this club. He has a way of breaking you down before building you up again, as I just experienced in the flesh. Not once, but twice. Leaving you no choice but to comply or look like a stubborn fool.

"Eat something."

Lisa slides a plate with an omelet and toast on the desk in front of me.

"Thanks, but I'm not really hungry."

"Doesn't matter," she insists. "You need the energy. Don't need you fainting on me."

As she walks out, I once again press my lips together to keep from reacting to what feels like another admonishment. But she's got a point as well, so I pick up a piece of toast and take a bite, without taking my eyes off the monitors.

With all the guys—except Wapi—out looking, Luna took me into the office and gave me the map with her markings. She'd written down who was searching where and added the location of each of the security cameras and in which direction they're aimed. After showing me how to use the radio, she took off to pick up her own search for David Hines.

I try hard not to let panic get hold of me as the morning passes surprisingly fast. Groups check in with me from time to time before moving to a different section, and I mark each change down so I know at all times where everyone is.

I only heard from Tse once, about half an hour ago, to say they were halfway done with section eight and would check in again in a couple of hours. They'd taken the ATV up the trail to a ridge bordering the north side of the property, so they'd have to hike back to get it before moving on to the next section.

There have been occasional glimpses of the guys crossing into view of the cameras, and each time my heart would stop until I recognized who it was. I've even seen a deer and a couple of birds, but no sign of Malco. Of course, they only cover the area immediately bordering the compound, which has already been searched, but that doesn't stop me from keeping my gritty eyes glued to the monitors.

I almost jump a foot when I suddenly hear Wapi's voice behind me.

"Take a break."

"I can't, what if I miss—"

He taps me on the shoulder.

"I've got this. Take a break."

"What about Nosh?"

"He's sleeping. Come on, Emme. Make room."

He nudges me with his hip and I finally peel my eyes from the screens as I get up, feeling instant relief. Maybe I do need a little break.

I walk into the kitchen to find Lisa making a huge stack of sandwiches. Athena is sitting in the high chair, squawking for attention.

"She needs a bottle and probably a clean diaper after, if you don't mind," Lisa suggests with a glance over her shoulder. "I'm just trying to get these done."

I quickly get a bottle ready and lift the baby out of the high chair, settling her on my lap.

"It's so quiet, where are the other kids?" I ask her, I only saw a few of the older ones on the couch playing a video game.

"Brick has them at our place doing God knows what to keep them busy, but at least they're not underfoot here."

Makes sense.

Athena's little independent hands grab the bottle from

my hold, which makes me smile. Already she knows what she wants and isn't afraid to go for it.

I'm suddenly hit with a wave of sadness Rhea won't get to see her kids grow up, especially Athena, who is only just starting to develop her own personality. Along with the sadness comes the fear for Malco.

Glancing at the clock on the stove, I see it's almost one o'clock. He's been gone for at least nine hours, probably longer. It's hard to see him wandering around by himself, unless he's hiding, or hurt, but then surely they would've found him already, wouldn't they?

Mental images of him scared, or lying hurt somewhere, bombard me, but it's almost worse to consider the other alternative; that somehow, somebody got to him.

"Egg salad or ham and cheese?"

"Sorry?" I blink a few times to clear my maudlin thoughts.

"Do you want an egg salad sandwich or ham and cheese?" Lisa repeats.

I'm not sure I want either, but I know that won't be an acceptable answer for her so I pick.

"Egg salad, thank you."

"More coffee?" she asks, handing me the sandwich in a paper towel.

"You don't have to wait on me, Lisa. I'll just grab some water in a minute."

I dutifully eat the sandwich, barely tasting anything, but I'm instantly alert when I hear the door to the clubhouse slam shut. At the same time Athena tosses her empty bottle on the floor to indicate she's done.

"I'll get it," Lisa offers when I try to reach for it.

"Where can I find her diapers?" I ask, eager to see who came in.

"Her bag is in Ouray's office."

I get up, settle Athena on my arm, and walk into the clubhouse where I catch sight of Paco, who is about to go into the office next door.

"Anything?"

He shoots me a sympathetic smile.

"Not yet." He holds up a radio. "I'm just picking up an extra battery pack, it's dead."

"Oh."

For a second my hope soared and the instant disappointment brings tears to my eyes.

"We'll find him, Emme. We won't stop 'til we have him."

I force a smile and nod before turning on my heel and rush with the baby to Ouray's office. Closing the door, I rest my back against it and slowly let myself slide to the floor, the baby on my lap.

Then I allow the tears free.

It doesn't take long for Athena to get restless and start clambering off my lap onto the floor.

"Hang on, baby girl," I mumble, grabbing the bottom of my shirt to mop up my face.

Enough of that. Sitting here on the floor crying isn't going to do anyone any good, and this little one needs a change.

I get to my feet, snag Athena before she can crawl to the cords under Ouray's desk, and take her to the couch where Lisa left the diaper bag.

The baby is less than cooperative—I swear she's an octopus, and I haven't had time to become a pro at this yet, so it takes us a while—but eventually I manage to get her changed. Unsure where to leave the stinky diaper, I take her to dump it in the trash in our bathroom next door, and grab the opportunity to splash some water on my face.

"Emme! I think something's going on," I hear Wapi call when I'm on my way back.

Lisa, who must've heard, comes out of the kitchen and holds out her arms.

"I'll take her."

I hand over Athena, who protests loudly, and dart into the office next door. Wapi is pointing at one of the video feeds on the monitor showing the ATV carrying Honon rushing down the trail.

"Where is Tse?"

"No idea, but your man is flying. They must've found something."

*Or maybe someone is hurt.*

I rush out of the office and head straight outside, breaking into a run when I round the corner of the club-house. Then I hoof it up the trail, ignoring someone calling after me to hold up.

Something is wrong.

*I can feel it.*

# CHAPTER
# TWENTY-TWO

*Honon*

*Half an hour earlier.*

"I've got something."

I make my way to Tse, who's reaching down between two rocks and comes up with an empty water bottle. He shakes it.

"There's still a bit left," he indicates.

We're a few hundred yards from the base of the overlook and not far from the trail where we left the ATV. The ground here is rough, sloping up and littered with rocks and boulders, and vegetation is sparse.

Ten minutes or so ago we found a granola bar wrapper and a few tracks that sent us in this direction, but lost the trail since hitting this rock slope. Until now.

Tse had tried radioing in to get more eyes up here but the damn battery pack ran out. Should've grabbed an extra one when we left, but we'd been in a rush to get out here.

"He can't be that far," I suggest.

As it is, I'm surprised the boy got all the way out here.

"What the hell is the kid doing all the way out here?" Tse wants to know.

I may have an idea.

"I took him up to the overlook on the ATV last week."

I remember showing him the view of Durango down below and pointed out Junction Creek campground, maybe half a mile to the west, where we could just make out a few trailers parked between the trees.

"Could be he's trying to get to the campground," I wonder out loud.

"He'd have a hell of a time getting there," Tse points out. "Even if he did manage to climb up to the overlook from here. Why wouldn't he have stuck to the trail? That'd be a hell of a lot easier."

"The kid's smart, if he wants to avoid being found he'd stay away from the trail," I point out.

When I start walking to the rock wall, looking for a place he may have tried to climb up, I hear Tse's footsteps crunch on the gravel behind me.

The edge of the overlook is probably a good ninety feet up from where we are. Even though I can see a few routes up the rock face where there are enough outcroppings and ridges for hand and footholds, it's a long fucking way up. Especially for a nine-year-old kid with nothing but his bare hands and a pair of sneakers.

To my right is a narrow ledge about three feet off the ground. It would make a good starting point and I let my eyes track up the wall. About halfway to the top I see a second, larger ledge, this one jutting out farther from the wall.

"Tse!" I call out when I catch sight of what looks like fingers hanging motionless off the edge of the platform.

Something appears to be dripping off the tips, hitting the rock wall a few feet lower and creating a long dark streak running down.

"Jesus," Tse mutters when he sees what I'm pointing out. "We need to get up top, get an eye on him."

I'm transfixed on the slow drip I'm pretty sure is blood running down the pale rock, when Tse gives my shoulder a shove.

"Brother, dead bodies don't bleed, let's get a move on."

It gets me moving and I hustle after him, doing my best to keep my footing on the uneven terrain, heading for the ATV parked on the trail only a few hundred yards from here. Tse jumps on and starts it up while I climb on and takes off up the trail before my ass hits the seat.

"Fuck!" he curses loudly a few minutes later when we crest the plateau of the overlook.

Bringing the ATV to a halt, he points up ahead where I catch sight of a mountain lion pacing back and forth along the edge. The large animal stops and lifts its head in our direction briefly, before resuming his pacing, his attention on something below.

"He smells the blood."

I get off and pull my gun from the holster at the small of my back and aim it up, shooting a round in the air.

The cat freezes, but doesn't take off.

"He's not scaring easy," Tse observes.

"If it's the same guy Paco says has been hanging around the shooting range, he may already be too used to people and gunshots. Look. Is that blood on his muzzle?"

"Hang on."

Tse digs through his pack and comes up with small binoculars he puts to his eyes.

"Looks that way, and this big boy doesn't look like he's

backing away."

The possibility the blood on the animal is from Malco has me raise my gun and aim it at him.

"Risky, brother. We're talking well over a hundred yards here," Tse cautions, swinging his leg over the quad to stand beside me.

The cougar briefly glances over again.

"I can make the shot."

"Maybe at the shooting range on a stationary target. You miss or clip him; we have a pissed-off cat on our hands. The same if you try to get closer, he's wary of us already. We're gonna have to go for help anyway, you stay here, I'll go and bring back a rifle."

"No, I'll go," I volunteer, handing him my gun. "He comes at you don't stop shooting until he's down."

Then I hop on the ATV and spin it around, heading back down the mountain.

Emme is down there, waiting for word and I want to be the one telling her.

*Goddammit.*

Stubborn woman.

Her hair is flying out behind her and her face is red from exertion as she comes running up the trail toward me.

I stop the ATV and reach out just in time to catch her in my arms.

"Did you…find him?"

She barely gets the question out, panting heavily.

"Possibly, but we can't get to him. I need to get down to the clubhouse for help. Get on."

As I wait for her to get on behind me, I hear the sound of another quad. Up ahead Ouray comes into view, standing up behind the handlebars.

"Whatcha got?" he wants to know, pulling up

alongside.

"He may be on a ledge halfway up the cliff to the overlook." I hear Emme's shocked gasp behind me as her hands grab on to my sides. "We tried to confirm from up top but we can't get close. Fucking mountain lion is pacing back and forth along the ridge, feeling protective."

I know he understands what that means when he narrows his eyes slightly.

"I need my rifle, I need more guys, more rope, and we should get medical here."

"Tse?"

"He's keeping an eye out, and before you ask, battery on the radio died."

"Go, get what you need down below. I'll meet up with Tse."

Before I know what she's doing, Emme is off my vehicle and climbs on the back of Ouray's.

"Emme, come on, I'm taking you back to the clubhouse."

Her face is suddenly pale as a sheet, but her lips are pressed together in a stubborn line, and her eyes are determined.

"I need to be up there, and don't waste precious time arguing with me," she snaps, already grabbing hold of Ouray's vest.

"I've got her," he assures me as he aims his vehicle uphill.

"*Fuck!*"

I slam my fist on the handlebar in frustration before I take off in the opposite direction.

———

*Emme*

"Malco!" I yell as soon as I get off the quad.

"Quiet," Tse warns, grabbing onto my arm. "That animal is agitated enough as it is. What the hell are you doing here anyway, Emme?"

I don't bother answering when my eyes catch the fierce-looking animal on the edge of the cliff, his head turned this way.

I've lived here many years and although I have never seen a mountain lion before, I've heard the cautions in case of an encounter. Don't run, don't turn your back, but make yourself as big as you can, throw stones or branches, and make a lot of noise.

"Aren't you supposed to yell?" I suggest.

"Yeah, but this guy isn't scared," Tse points out. "Not even of a gunshot."

"Paco warned he'd spotted one around here for a while, getting closer to the compound," Ouray mentions. "Which is out of character too. They tend to avoid people."

"Can't you shoot him?" I try.

"Not at this distance," Ouray volunteers. "Honon should be here soon with his rifle."

There has to be a way to check on Malco, if he's on that ledge as Honon suspects.

Good God, what if he fell and is hurt? He could be dying while we're here doing absolutely nothing.

I feel Tse's hand tighten on my arm.

"Patience, Emme. We'll get to him."

"Can't we chase him off with the ATV?" I suggest, feeling more and more desperate.

"There have been cases of mountain lions attacking

people riding bikes and even ATVs," Ouray points out. "Be stupid to risk it."

My eyes are glued to the animal pacing back and forth, back and forth, until I'm about to come out of my skin. Then he stops suddenly and lifts his head at the sound of an engine approaching.

My relief is instant when Honon pulls up, a rifle slung over his shoulder. Lusio came with him, a long coil of rope slung across his chest, and a large, red emergency kit in his hand.

"Paco and Trunk are hooking up the small trailer behind the other quad, they should be right behind us," Lusio announces.

I meet Honon's eyes and he gives me an encouraging smile.

"Hang tight, Emme."

Then he walks about ten feet out from our little group and widens his stance, one leg in front of the other, before lifting the rifle to his shoulder. Beyond him the mountain lion is on full alert now, dropping his head down to the level of his shoulders as he slowly starts to move in this direction.

"Crazy fucker is coming," Tse mumbles the moment a loud shot sounds.

The animal stops abruptly, then turns and takes a few steps, before sagging through his legs.

I'm already running past Honon before the big cat's body hits the ground. I hear him cursing behind me but am focused on the ridge and slide to a stop right at the drop.

"Malco!"

Maybe thirty feet down I see him, lying on his back on a ledge, looking...broken. *So much blood*. I sink to my knees and lean forward, placing my hands on the edge and force myself to take stock. Unmistakable is the damage to his left arm, which looks almost mangled. His eyes are closed and I see blood on one side of his face, but I can't tell where it's coming from.

"Malco!"

"Fuck, Emme," I hear Honon behind me.

The next moment I feel him grab me from behind, a strong arm wrapping around my waist as he picks me off the ground and sets me on my feet.

"He moved." I point down to where I just thought I saw his foot move. "Look!"

I pull free and crouch back down on the edge.

"Malco! We're here, buddy. We're gonna get you up!"

Behind me I hear all kinds of activity while Ouray barks out orders, but I don't take my eyes off that foot, occasionally calling out to him.

"Emme, I need you to move. I'm going down to get him."

This time I let Honon pull me back and I watch from a distance as he takes my place on the edge and fastens the end of the rope around his waist and between his legs, like a makeshift harness. Then he looks me in the eyes, winks, and slowly rappels out of sight, trusting his brothers to hold on to the rope without question.

I turn my back and close my eyes, putting all my trust in him. But just in case, I shoot up a prayer to whatever superior being is willing to listen, to get both my guys out safe.

I'm afraid to look or move until I hear Honon call up, "He's alive!"

Then I jump into action and join the guys, taking a spot on the rope. When Ouray calls out at some point Honon has the boy secured, I put every muscle in my body into helping pull both of them up.

Malco is unconscious.

Honon had encased his left arm in an inflatable splint, wrapped a bandage around the boy's head, and then strapped him to the wooden board Trunk and Paco had brought up in the small trailer. He'd done everything to stabilize Malco before we hauled them up.

"I need you in the back with him, Emme," Ouray directs me. "Keep him as steady as you can."

That's how we ride back down to the clubhouse, me sitting in the trailer with Malco still strapped to the board between my legs so I could keep him from moving too much.

An ambulance is already waiting.

"Go with him," Honon urges, holding me as the EMTs move Malco onto a gurney. "I'm gonna be right behind you."

"Are you his mom?" the EMT asks when I get in the back of the ambulance.

He's already placing an IV in Malco's good arm.

"Yes," I answer without thinking.

"What happened?" he probes before I have a chance to correct myself.

"He fell and landed on a ledge halfway down a lookout. We think he was trying to get away from a mountain lion when he fell."

The guy lifts his head and looks at me.

"No shit? That would explain some of his injuries."

I suppress a shiver, thinking of the damage I saw to his arm.

"We had to shoot the animal so we could get to him."

"Wow."

Wow indeed.

None of it has caught up with me yet. It almost feels like

I'll wake up at any minute to discover this was all a dream.

I focus on the EMT as he works on Malco, trying to glean any information from his expression, or his actions.

"I'm not going to take this off," he tells me, pointing at the inflatable splint. "In addition to keeping the arm stable, it stops the blood loss. They'll take care of that when we get to Mercy where they have everything they need to address his injuries."

"Okay."

My voice sounds mechanical even to my own ears.

When we get to the hospital, the EMTs quickly help me out of the ambulance before pulling the stretcher out. They hurry him through the sliding doors and I jog along, trying to keep up.

"Ma'am? I need some information, ma'am."

I ignore the nurse calling out from behind the desk we pass.

But when we get to a set of wide swinging doors, the EMT who was in the back of the ambulance turns to me.

"I'm sorry, you're going to have to wait out here."

"But he's my responsibility."

He gives me a friendly smile. "I understand, but you've gotta trust the doctors to take care of him." Then they disappear through the doors.

*You've gotta trust…*

Suddenly I'm swaying on my feet and have to brace myself against the wall to stay upright.

"Ma'am?" the nurse sounds behind me.

Then I hear Honon's voice as I feel his strong body close in.

"I've got you, Emme."

I let go of the wall and lean back.

*He's got me.*

# CHAPTER
# TWENTY-THREE

*Honon*

"We're still waiting."

I glance through the narrow window next to the door into the waiting room where Emme is sitting, Sophia by her side. Trunk and Ouray left to pick up something to eat and I stepped out to take Lisa's call.

"It's been three hours."

"And it could be three more. The surgeon said there was no way to predict exactly how long it would take since they wouldn't be able to see the full extent of the damage until they had him on the table."

The doctor figures Malco tried to ward off the mountain lion with his arm when the animal grabbed hold, likely shaking the boy before he either fell, or was dropped off the edge. He had tissue damage from his jaw down his arm on the left side, a dislocated shoulder and fractured humerus, a gash on the back of his head—which he probably sustained when he fell—and a concussion.

Hard to believe, but the ER physician considered him

lucky, given what he'd gone through. There'd been no detectable damage to his skull or spine and no additional broken bones. First concern had been to repair the damage and try to preserve as much, if not all, of the use of his arm.

It took until earlier this morning to get a surgical team of specialists together to work on him.

"How is Emme holding up?"

"She's hanging in."

Lisa snorts. "That girl, she's tough. She's not gonna fall apart until she knows he's in the clear. Then you better be around to hold her together."

She's right, even yesterday when we just got here and she could barely keep her feet under her, she kept that chin up. She sat by his bedside all through the night, holding his hand and refusing to try and catch some sleep on the recliner. But there are cracks in her armor, especially this morning with nothing to do but wait.

"I'm not going anywhere," I assure Lisa.

"Good. Now, I was going to send Shilah to drop off some food. Anything else you need?"

"Ouray and Trunk went to pick up something, but if you wouldn't mind packing a change of clothes for Emme and me he can bring us?"

Both Emme and I were given scrubs to wear when the nurse last night saw our blood-stained clothes, but I'd feel better wearing my own stuff and I'm sure she would too.

"I'll do that right now."

"Appreciate it. Oh, and Lisa, one more thing, how is Nosh?"

"Believe it or not, he's up, although I'm not sure how long he'll last. Ate his breakfast at the kitchen table and is now watching *Dateline* in the recliner in his room. Yuma and Lissie are here with the kids."

"That's good."

At least it is for now. You often hear of people who are terminal having a brief resurgence right before the end. I hope this isn't that.

After ending the call with Lisa, I return to the waiting room, taking a seat on the other side of Emme.

"Everything okay?" she asks.

I'm about to relay what Lisa told me when Luna walks in, followed by Trunk and Ouray carrying takeout bags and coffees.

"Thought I'd check in but Ouray already told me there's no news," Luna starts. "Still, I figure while I'm here I may as well get you up to speed. We got some information on that maroon rental vehicle. We were able to trace it back to Enterprise and found Mandy Lewis's name is the only one listed on the rental agreement."

"She's up to her eyeballs in it," I point out.

"Oh yeah. We already figured that when the Hines family's lawyer showed up to the station when we were questioning Mandy. Problem is, looks like she's gone as well. There was no one at the townhouse and a neighbor reported seeing her get into a maroon SUV with two suitcases sometime yesterday." Luna pinches the bridge of her nose. "Problem is, with this investigation pulling us in different directions and DPD being understaffed, we weren't able to put twenty-four-hour surveillance on her."

"What about the older Hines?" I ask.

"Hiding behind his lawyer and they've been throwing up roadblock after roadblock. I can't get a judge to sign off on a search warrant without any evidence something illegal is going on at The Pink Petal. Not even Rhea's notes to you are considered enough since she doesn't indicate work or any person specifically."

"And the fact a second employee was murdered shortly after?"

She shakes her head.

"There's nothing to indicate that wasn't a tragic coincidence. Other than the victims knew each other, there are no similarities between the murders at all. Not in the method, and not in the execution," she explains. "It's hard to believe the same person who killed Rhea and was smart enough not to leave a single trace of himself behind in such a brutal scene, seems to have been so inept when trying to make Cher's murder look like a random killing."

"Unless they're not the same killer," Ouray suggests.

"Yes, but given what we know, what are the odds of that?"

She turns to Emme. "I'm sorry. I wish I could tell you we have the bastard, but we do have a BOLO out, a be-on-the-lookout order, for both David Hines and Mandy as well as the rental vehicle. I hope to have better news soon."

She gets up and leans over to Ouray for a quick kiss.

"I've gotta get back at it, but do me a favor, until we have this guy, everyone stay vigilant."

She's about to step out the door when she almost collides with a woman in surgical scrubs coming in.

"Are you all here for Malco Scala?"

Emme shoots to her feet and I get up as well, curving my hand around the back of her neck.

"Yes."

"Dr. Wolfson asked me to give you a quick interim update. Malco is doing well so far; we were able to set and pin the bone, repair the two major nerves, and reconnect the tendon between the biceps and the ulna in the forearm, as we explained earlier. Dr. Wolfson is now working with the plastic surgeon on trying to salvage as much of his muscle tissue as possible, and once that's done, they will start closing the skin."

She smiles reassuringly at Emme.

"The hard part is done, but it still may be another hour or two before he is moved to recovery. As soon as Dr. Wolfson is done, he'll come and speak to you himself."

As soon as the woman leaves, Emme swings around, planting her face in my chest. My arms curl around her and I feel her take in a few deep breaths.

Then she almost immediately straightens up, turns to face the room with a wobbly smile, and announces, "Let's eat."

———

*Emme*

"Hey, shouldn't you be at the restaurant?"

Sophia moves into the room and hands me a bottle of water before sitting down next to me.

"Mack and Chris have it under control," she answers, mirroring my low voice. "The first of the new hires started yesterday so we've beefed up the schedule. They have enough bodies."

"Are these the people who were laid off from that place on Florida Road?"

She nods. "I lucked out, found someone for kitchen support, an extra bartender, and a couple of servers. We'll see how they work out."

In the bed Malco shifts and moans softly. I wait to see if he's waking up, but then he seems to settle down again.

The nurse had warned he'd probably be sleepy because of the medications they have him on. In addition to pain medication, they're keeping him sedated and have him on intravenous antibiotics.

His arm is completely immobilized, and we were told he'd be in the hospital for at least a week to allow the nerves and tendons to start healing, and make sure he doesn't develop an infection.

I have no idea what I'm going to do, not just while he's in the hospital, but after. He'll need physical therapy, have follow-up specialist appointments, and I can't leave that for someone else to take care of.

According to Dr. Wolfson, the good news is with proper care, and sticking religiously to the PT, he has a good chance of regaining most if not all use of his left arm. The bad news is that could take anywhere from six months to a year.

"I hope they do," I tell Sophia. "Because I think I'm going to have to quit."

"I can't say I'm surprised." She smiles. "It's what I would do in your shoes. But I'm sad to see you go."

I nudge her with my elbow.

"I have a feeling we'll find other ways to stay in touch."

She's grinning when she turns to me. "Yeah? You and Honon? I've gotta admit, when you first told me he'd been helping you out, I couldn't see it, but now…I think it's sweet."

"Sweet is not an adjective that fits either Honon or myself, but whatever. I like him, okay? A lot. At this point I have no idea what the future is going to look like on any front, but I figure if my life is off the rails anyway, I've got nothing to lose giving this relationship thing a try. That is, if that's what he wants."

"He wants."

I snap my head around to find Honon standing in the doorway, a cocky smirk on his face.

"Aaand...that's my cue to go check on the kids," Sophia jokes as she gets to her feet. By the door she looks back at me. "When life spins out of control, grab on to all the good you can. I'll check in later."

With a wave she disappears down the hall.

"So..." Honon drawls, taking Sophia's seat beside me. "Nothing to lose, huh? Gotta say, you're making it hard to resist."

"Serves you right for listening in on conversations you weren't invited to. Besides," I add. "Weren't you having a shower?"

"I did. Don't I smell better?"

I roll my eyes at him, to which he grins and drapes an arm over my shoulders, tucking me close.

"You know Lisa packed a change of clothes for you too," he points out.

I look down at the plain blue scrubs I've had on for the past twenty-four hours or so, and have to admit I do feel a little grungy. But then I look at Malco, his face still so pale.

"I don't want to leave him."

"Just splash some water on your face and put on your own clothes. It'll take you two minutes and you'll feel so much better. I'll be here."

"Did she pack a toothbrush?"

Honon cocks his thumb at the bag he dropped by the door.

"It's all in there."

Thank God. My mouth tastes—and I'm sure smells—like the inside of a dumpster. All that coffee I've been drinking doesn't help.

"Okay, I won't be long."

He presses a kiss to the side of my head and lets me go.

Since Malco's room and the one next door share a bathroom, I walk into the ladies' room at the end of the hallway. There are two stalls but I pick the wheelchair accessible one because it has hooks. I hope no one comes in who needs to use it. Hanging the tote on a hook, I quickly strip out of the scrubs, dig into the bag, and pull out my clothes. A pair of my jeans, so well-worn they're soft like butter, my favorite slouchy long-sleeved T-shirt, a sports bra, and a pair of fresh underwear.

Comfort clothes. I could kiss Lisa.

I'm just shoving my feet back in my Chucks, and my phone in my pocket, when I hear the swoosh of the hall door falling shut. Embarrassed to be caught in the accessible stall, I hurriedly stuff the dirty clothes in the bag, fish my toothbrush out of the side pocket, and duck my head as I exit the stall.

"Where is it?"

My head snaps up and I'm once again staring down the barrel of a gun, but this time it's not a man holding it.

"Mandy?"

I drop the bag and shove my toothbrush up my sleeve.

"Where is it, Emme?"

"Where is what? I don't know what you're talking about."

My mind is working at warp speed. The bathroom isn't big, and Mandy is blocking the only way out. Even if I could somehow overpower her, I'd still have to get past her to get out the door.

Then there's Malco, only a few doors down the hallway. If the gun went off, God knows where a bullet might end up and Honon is not Superman, he can't stop bullets.

No, I can't risk it. I have to get her away from here somehow, before someone else walks in and this situation gets even more complicated.

"Don't bullshit me, you're not getting away this time. I know Rhea must've given you the key, Cher didn't have it and you're the only other person Rhea would trust."

She cocks the gun and my blood runs cold.

"You don't have to do this, Mandy."

The expression on her face is cold.

"I most definitely do. David had his chance but fucked it up. Twice. Now, for the last time, where is it?"

"It's at my house," I blurt out, just to say something.

"Nice try. We already looked, it's not there."

They looked through my house? When? And why did the alarm not go off?

"Fine. It's safe in the glove compartment of the Jeep."

Her eyes narrow on me. "I don't believe you."

I shrug, attempting to look indifferent.

"I can't help that. Unless you want me to make up another story? The key is in the glove compartment of the black Jeep parked right downstairs in the parking lot."

I know I'm playing with fire, mocking her, but I'm hoping she'll think it's easy enough to check. Anything to get her as far away from this floor as I can.

"You lie and it won't end well for the boy."

It's like a punch in the gut and the taste of bile burns my throat. God, the thought of anything happening to him after all he's already been through makes me nauseous.

Something must've shown on my face because Mandy smirks at me.

"You thought we didn't know? We've known for days you had her brats."

"I'm not lying," I state calmly, not responding to her taunt. "The key is in the Jeep."

"You have the keys?"

Fuck.

"No need. It's never locked," I bluff.

Somehow, I'll have to find a way to get the gun away from her before we get to the parking lot.

She steps aside to let me go first.

"Stairwell on the left," she orders, the barrel of the gun pressing in the small of my back when I push open the door.

I turn left, relieved when the door to the stairs is right there. The sooner we get away from Malco's room, the better.

The stairwell is empty, which is fortunate since I don't want to risk anyone else getting hurt when I try to make my move.

I start heading down the stairs, keeping one hand on the railing. Mandy stays two steps behind me. On the small landing I turn toward the next flight down and then take three steps down so I'm sure she's on the top tread.

Then I pretend to slip, spin around as I drop, and jab the handle of my toothbrush in the top of her foot. She yelps, pulls her leg out of the way, and is already teetering on one foot when I grab her gun hand and yank her off-balance.

With a loud scream, she topples forward, tumbling down the stairs before she lands with a hard smack on the next landing below.

# CHAPTER
# TWENTY-FOUR

*Honon*

"How is he?"

I'm surprised to see Lisa standing in the doorway.

"Pretty drugged up. Come in."

I watch her walk into the room. The normally stoic woman is visibly moved at the sight of the boy in the hospital bed.

"Where is the baby?"

"I left her with Lissie. I just had to come see him for myself."

"Brick with you?"

"Parking the car."

She strokes the back of her fingers down the exposed side of Malco's face, mumbling, "Poor child."

Then she glances at me.

"Where is Emme?"

"Gone to freshen up. She should be back any min—"

Before I can finish my sentence, the distant sound of a scream has the hair on my neck stand on end.

Lisa heard it too as her eyes widen.

"Close and block the door," I bark at her as I rush into the hallway.

Looking left, I see a nurse coming out of a room farther down, apparently alerted by the scream as well.

"Call security!" I yell out.

Then I turn right and run toward the bathrooms at the end of the hallway, pulling my gun from the holster. I shove open the door and catch sight of the bag in the middle of the floor.

"Emme!"

Both stalls are empty.

Right outside of the bathroom is the door to the stairwell and I burst through. I swing my gun right, covering the stairway going up but it's empty. Then I ease up on the railing, peeking down, and catch sight of someone lying on the second landing down. All I register is a leg wearing blue scrubs, and with my heart beating in my throat I pound down the steps, two at a time.

The fist squeezing my chest instantly releases when I see Emme sitting halfway down the next set of stairs, her back against the wall and her knees drawn up. In one shaking hand she's holding a gun, aimed up at me, and in the other a toothbrush.

"Hey, it's me." I lift my free hand while I tuck my gun away. "I'm gonna be pissed if you shoot me, Wildcat."

A sob bursts from her as she lowers the weapon. I immediately rush down to her and sit down one step higher, pulling her into my body.

"You're okay," I mumble as I take my first good look at the body on the landing below.

The woman looks like a nurse, but my gut tells me she's not. Either way, she's not moving.

"Mandy. She came after me in the bathroom," Emme starts talking. "She had a gun. I couldn't let her get to him."

Suddenly her body stiffens and she pushes away from me.

"I have to get to Malco—"

"He's safe, Lisa's with him, she's got the door blocked."

At least I hope she has, although anyone trying to get to the boy would have a hard time getting through Lisa.

"I-I think I killed her," Emme stutters, a shudder going through her body.

A door slams open somewhere below us, and footsteps come pounding up the stairs. Grabbing the gun Emme discarded on the step, I aim it down.

"Put down the gun!"

Two security guards, their weapons drawn, come into sight.

———

It took Luna showing up, flashing her credentials, to get control of the chaos.

I can't fault the two security guards for putting Emme and me in handcuffs. I'm sure the situation looked pretty damning from their perspective.

We were taken to a small office off the front lobby and held there until the cops showed up. When they tried to question us, we both mentioned FBI agent Luna Roosberg, and told them we'd talk to her. Emme asked several times if Mandy was alive, but they wouldn't—or maybe couldn't—answer. It wasn't until Officer Conley walked in, recognizing Emme and me, that the cuffs were removed, but they still wouldn't let us go.

"Thanks, fellas," Luna addresses the cops. "We've got it from here."

Then she urges us out of the office.

Once we're alone in the elevator, she turns to us.

"Sorry I didn't get here sooner, but I got held up in the parking lot. Apparently, Brick was looking for a spot and noticed a dark red SUV with rental plates, decided to block it in, and called me while holding the driver at gunpoint."

"Hines?" Emme asks.

"You've got it." Emme blows out an audible breath of relief while Luna continues, "By the time I got here, the cops had arrived and there was a bit of a standoff I had to get resolved. I sent Barnes straight up to Malco's room though. He says all is secure, so you can breathe easy."

When we get off the elevator the first thing I notice is Agent Barnes in the hallway, his back leaning against the wall next to the boy's room.

"She says she'll only unlock the door for you guys, her husband, or God himself," he explains with a sardonic grin when he catches sight of us.

"Lisa?" I tap on the door. "You can let us in."

No sooner have the words left my mouth when I hear some scraping on the other side of the door before it opens a crack. Lisa glances out. She zooms in on Barnes as she opens it wider. I notice one of the visitor's chairs right behind her. She must've braced it against the door.

"Nothing personal, but I had someone knocking earlier claiming to be a cop," she explains. "Wasn't letting him in either. No offense."

The agent responds with a grin.

"None taken."

Emme is already rushing to the boy's bedside, but he looks like he's still sleeping. Completely unaware.

Good.

I hold Luna back at the door.

"Any word on the woman? Mandy?" I ask, while keeping an eye on Emme.

Personally, I wouldn't lose a second of sleep if she didn't survive, but I'm afraid it would be hard for Emme to come to terms with.

"Unconscious but alive. That's all I know. Doctors are working on her under police watch." At my raised eyebrow she adds, "Benedetti is down there himself. What happened out there?"

"Haven't had a chance to get the full story yet. We haven't been alone and Emme wasn't sharing with the cops. I took her lead and enforced we'd only talk to you."

"Fair enough, let me see if I can find us an empty room."

But as soon as she asks Barnes to stay here with Lisa, Emme protests.

"I'm not leaving him."

Her tone invites no argument, then she walks to the farthest side of the room from the bed and waits for us to join her.

"A key?" Luna asks, when Emme finishes her account of events.

"That's what she said, that Cher didn't have it so I had to."

"Any idea what kind of key?"

Emme shrugs. "I have no idea, but I played along to get her as far away from Malco as possible."

"You did good," Luna tells her. "And she said it wasn't at your house?"

"Yeah. How would she know that?"

I haven't looked at the app for the alarm since Emme

was with me at the clubhouse, but I pull it out now. It shows as disarmed.

Immediately I call Paco.

"When you left Emme's place on Friday, did you set the alarm?" I barge right in when he answers his phone.

"No. I was afraid the plywood we put up wouldn't keep out a draft, potentially setting the motion sensors off. Emme wasn't going to be there anyway, so I figured I'd leave it until I had a chance to put in a new door. Why? Did something happen?"

"Not sure. Do me a favor? Run out there and check?"

"Tell him not to touch anything," Luna asks, putting a hand on my arm.

I relay the message and sign off.

"So, let's assume for a moment Mandy's right and Rhea somehow tried to get a key to you...it wasn't in anything that lawyer gave you, right?"

Emme shakes her head. "You saw the envelope yourself and emptied it out," she tells Luna. "Nothing other than the money and the notes."

"What else came from her?" I wonder out loud. "The blanket the baby was wrapped in. Her romper."

"The lab has already gone over those with a fine-tooth comb. I would've known if they'd found something."

"The boy's sneakers," Lisa pipes up from Malco's bedside.

When we all turn to her, she shrugs. "I remember Ezrah wanting a pair years ago. They've got a stash pouch."

"Stash pouch?" Emme asks.

Luna fills her in. "Back when weed was still illegal, potheads would hide their personal stash in a small pocket inside the tongue of their shoes."

I'm already checking under the bed and in his dresser. No shoes.

"Maybe they're still in the ER," Barnes suggests. "I'll go check."

Within ten minutes he's back, carrying a pair of worn sneakers in one hand and holding up a small copper key.

———

*Emme*

"Hey, buddy."

I smile at Malco as he blinks a few times.

Thank God he's been blissfully unaware.

At Luna's urging, we ended up moving to another room, under a different name, on the other side of the long hallway. She'd said it was only as a precaution, since she hadn't had a chance to interview either Hines or Mandy.

I'd been relieved to hear Mandy was alive. She's still in the ICU though, having sustained a serious head injury in the fall. When Luna popped in this morning, she'd mentioned she still hadn't regained consciousness.

Apparently, Hines had lawyered up right away and was refusing to talk.

Shortly after Luna left, Dr. Wolfson had come in and examined Malco. He seemed pleased and said they'd slowly be taking him off the sedatives, which is why he's waking up.

"Are you thirsty?"

The nurse left a cup with water and a straw on his

bedside table. I grab the cup and bend the straw to his chapped lips.

"Easy," I caution him when he starts sucking it down in big gulps. "Give your stomach a chance to get used to it."

Despite having had fluids administered through the IV the whole time, his mouth must be dry.

I let him take another sip before returning the cup to the bedside table.

"Am I…" His voice is hoarse and he starts again. "Am I in the hospital?"

"You are. Do you remember getting hurt?"

I watch him frown and then wince as he lifts his right hand to the bandages on his head.

"Be careful, okay?" I take his hand and place it back on the blanket, covering it with mine. "You fell and hit your head, and your arm is hurt too," I add.

He looks down at the injured arm they strapped to his chest.

"You have to keep it really still so it can heal, okay?"

"'Kay."

I hesitate telling him about the mountain lion. It was Trunk who warned us it's possible he won't remember everything right away. He explained sometimes after severe trauma the brain will temporarily block the memories, and if that were the case, it would be better for him to remember at his own pace.

"Athena?"

He suddenly looks worried.

"She's fine, honey," I assure him. "You'll get to see her soon. Do you want another sip?"

I grab for the cup but by the time I move the straw toward his mouth his eyes have closed.

The door opens and Honon walks in with some kind of insulated bag.

He got called down maybe fifteen minutes ago to meet Ouray, who was waiting in the lobby.

I'm going to have to thank that man when I have a chance. I found out from Honon last night when Malco was being moved, Ouray contacted a private security company he knows in Cedar Tree. I haven't actually seen anyone, but Honon explained that was the whole point since posting someone outside the door would give away our new location. He assured me we were well looked after. I surprised myself by taking his word for it.

I've changed, I'm no longer teetering on the edge of trust but find myself giving it freely.

At least to Honon.

"He was awake for a few minutes just now," I whisper, grinning up at him as he approaches the bed. "Not long, but he drank some water and asked about his sister."

"That's good news," he whispers back. Then he indicates the table on the other side of the room. "Let's sit over there and eat. Lisa sent food."

I fill him in while he pulls out containers of food and plastic cutlery.

"So did Ouray have any news?" I ask, digging into the hearty stew.

I hum at the rich flavors, a relief from the bland cafeteria food.

"He talked to Luna. She finally figured out what the key is for. A security box at the First National Bank in Cortez. It's where Rhea had one of her investment accounts. Luna was able to get hold of the bank manager, explained the situation, and he was able to confirm Rhea had a security box in her name, but wouldn't provide her more information without proof of death and the presence of the executor of the will."

"That's Nick Flynn."

"Exactly. So tomorrow morning, you, Flynn, and Luna have a meeting in Cortez at nine."

My eyes immediately fly to the bed.

"I don't want to leave him."

Honon reaches out and covers my hand with his.

"I know, Ouray is going to ask Lisa to sit with him."

I shake my head. I love Lisa, especially after the way she guarded Malco yesterday, but I'd feel much better if Honon stayed with the boy.

"I want you to stay."

He lifts my hand to his lips.

"I can't let you go to Cortez without me, Wildcat."

# CHAPTER
# TWENTY-FIVE

*Honon*

"Why is he looking at you funny?"

I glance over my shoulder at the bed, but as soon as Malco sees me looking, he closes his eyes. I've caught him doing the same thing a few times last night and this morning.

"I don't know," I tell Lisa.

We're standing by the door, waiting for Emme to finish brushing her teeth. Luckily this hospital room has a private bathroom so she doesn't have to go far.

"He hasn't said much. Nothing to me, but not even to Emme. He has asked about his sister a few times."

Lisa holds up her phone.

"I took some pictures of her like you asked. I'll show him."

I'd messaged her last night to take a few snapshots when Malco asked about the baby again, hoping maybe that would ease his worry about Athena.

The door to the bathroom opens and Emme steps out.

"Hey, Lisa."

She walks up to the other woman and gives her a spontaneous hug. I bite down a grin when I catch Lisa's surprised face. She's not really a hugger, but then Emme doesn't really strike me as one either. When I glance over to Malco, I notice his eyes are open again and he's watching the interaction between the two women.

"We should go," Emme announces. "I don't want to keep Luna waiting."

We're supposed to meet her in the lobby.

"See you soon, buddy," she says to the boy. "We won't be long."

He doesn't say a word.

She grabs her backpack, thanks Lisa, and follows me to the elevator.

Downstairs in the lobby there's no sign of Luna yet so we wait. A few minutes later I see her stalking toward us from a different part of the hospital. Her face looks grim.

"Change of plans," she announces. "I got a call early this morning, Mandy Lewis woke up and wanted to talk, so I came straight here. Unfortunately, by the time I got here she was dead."

She immediately turns to Emme who gasps.

"Oh no…"

"I'm not sure what happened yet. Her condition was improving, she was talking. It doesn't make sense. The officer stationed by her door had just arrived, relieving another, and said the only person who went in the room had been a nurse. Unfortunately, this all happened in the middle of a shift-change and the previous shift has already left. I'm afraid I'll be tied up here for a while, and Barnes has his hands full executing the search warrant on The Pink Petal we finally got signed."

"You want to reschedule?" I ask.

Luna shakes her head. "No. I need to know what's in that safety deposit box even more now. If it's that important to Hines, I'm hoping it can give me some of the answers I need."

"Fair enough."

"Ouray was sending Paco to tail you, just in case. He should be outside waiting. And call me as soon as you have something."

She hands Emme the key, who seems quiet when we walk out to the parking lot. I have an idea what might be going through her head.

"This isn't on you."

She swerves her head to me. "Like hell it isn't. Mandy is dead because of me."

"We don't know that. Sounds like Luna may have some suspicions as well. Who knows? Maybe Hines had her killed before she could talk."

"That's a bit of a stretch, he's in custody."

"You'd be surprised what can be arranged from jail. Either way," I add. "You did what you had to do to keep yourself and those kids safe, the woman had a gun on you."

Paco is already waiting by the Jeep, sitting sideways on his bike.

"Ready?" he asks, swinging his leg over when we walk up.

"Let's get this over with," Emme suggests, climbing into the passenger seat.

"Appreciate you, brother," I mutter at Paco in passing as I get behind the wheel.

It's not until we leave Durango behind us Emme speaks up.

"Do you think David Hines could be Athena's father?"

I glance in my rearview mirror to make sure Paco is still following.

"Technically, he's not a married man yet, but I guess it's possible. The father could be a possibility too."

"Seems odd, though," she muses. "She used the term 'authorities' in her note. That suggests law enforcement."

"Yeah, but it could mean anyone in a position of power, really."

"Like who?"

"I don't know, elected officials, judges, politicians." I glance over at her. "And wealthy business leaders."

"I guess," she concedes, but I can tell she's not convinced.

We've just passed the rest area we pulled into last time we were out this way when a large propane truck pulls out of a drive and into the lane in front of me, forcing me to slow down. I check the rearview mirror and see a pickup truck directly behind me. Asshole is obviously in a hurry as he rides up on my tail before veering into the passing lane at the last minute.

I glance out my side window as the truck speeds by but get only a quick glimpse of the driver. Not that it tells me much, other than his windows are tinted too dark to be legal and he's wearing a hoodie. Probably some punk kid with more money than sense. Or maybe he has parents with money.

Checking my mirrors so I can get around this damn propane truck as well, I realize Paco isn't behind me. I slow down even more and keep my eyes peeled for him.

"What's wrong?" Emme wants to know.

"Do me a favor, dial Paco on my phone. He's on speed dial."

He picks up on the first ring.

"Hit a snafu. Some son of a bitch cut me off. Bike hit the gravel on the shoulder and I wiped out."

"Shit. Are you okay? Let me see if I can find a place to turn around." Up ahead I see a sign for the Montezuma County Fairgrounds. "I'm coming up on the fairgrounds, I can turn in there."

"Nah, you're almost there. Keep going. I'm fine, just a few scrapes but my bike is a mess. I'm gonna make some phone calls. Touch base when you're done at the bank and we'll see where we're at."

"You sure?"

"Yeah. Go do your thing."

I end up staying behind the propane truck into Cortez, where I turn into the plaza housing the First National Bank. Nick Flynn is just getting out of his vehicle as we pull into the parking spot next to him.

Emme starts getting out when I stop her with a hand on her shoulder. She turns to face me and I lean over the console to give her a quick peck on the lips.

"Hey, stick close, okay? Let me get you out."

"I'm sorry," the guy starts apologizing the moment I get Emme out of the Jeep. "There was no safety deposit box listed on any of the paperwork. Otherwise, I would've suggested handling that last time you were in town."

"You couldn't have known."

She smiles at him but takes my hand as we walk into the bank.

It feels damn good.

———

*Emme*

"Ms. Lightfoot? If you'd follow me?"

I glance over my shoulder at Honon and the lawyer, who were asked to wait in the manager's office. Honon gives me a nod before I follow the bank manager to the vault.

The man had been clearly suspicious, asking me everything but the color of my damn underwear before he had me hand over my identification so he could make copies. Then he handed over a stack of paperwork, which I had Nick look over before I signed.

I'm not sure what I expected, but after he opens the imposing door, what lies beyond is a bit of a disappointment. Maybe I've watched too many movies, but the narrow, galley-like space beyond—rows of small numbered lockers on either side and a long, slim, stainless-steel table in the center—is anticlimactic.

He slides a key into one of the keyholes next to the number twenty-seven and indicates for me to do the same in the other. Then he motions me aside, and slides out a metal drawer he carries to the table.

"Call me when you're ready."

I wait for him to walk out and stop in the doorway, leaving his back turned to me.

Then I slide the lid of the drawer back.

For a second, it looks like it's empty and my heart sinks, but then I lift the lid off altogether. In the far-left corner I spot a metal thumb-drive. It's small, not much longer than the actual USB plug. I roll it around in the palm of my hand but there aren't any marks on it.

Since I had to leave my backpack with Honon, I slip the drive in my pocket and replace the lid on the drawer.

"I'm done."

We return to the manager's office where I sign more papers to terminate the safety deposit box rental agreement. Then the man tries to sell me on some other bank services I decline before we finally walk out of there.

"I appreciate your help," I tell Nick, shaking his hand.

"Wasn't a big deal. Let me know if you need help with anything else. I don't know if you plan to sell her trailer home, but I can certainly help with that when you're ready."

I hadn't even thought of that. I guess it would make sense, eventually.

"Thanks."

Honon stands beside me on the curb as we watch him back out and drive off with a wave.

"So?" He nudges me. "Was it empty?"

"Not exactly, but let's get in the car first."

I've already come to the conclusion the key Mandy was talking about was probably the thumb-drive rather than the bank key.

Once inside, I show Honon the drive.

"Information. I wanna bet what's on there is going to pull the rug from under the Hines family," he suggests.

I dig my phone out of my backpack.

"Let me give Luna a quick call."

She answers right away and I put her on speaker.

"And?"

"It's a USB key."

"The key they were looking for. Are you on your way back?"

"About to leave, why?"

"I'm going to give our tech expert, Jasper Greene, a heads-up. If you wouldn't mind dropping the key off at the FBI office on Rock Point Drive on your way into town? Honon knows where it is."

"Yup, I do," he answers.

"Great. I'll make sure Greene is waiting. He'll be able to extract any information stored on there safely."

She ends the call before I can ask how things are there.

"If there were any problems at the hospital, she would've told you," Honon assures me.

A little freaky how this man seems able to read my mind.

He starts up the Jeep and backs out, before pulling onto the road.

"By the way, I called Paco while you were in the vault. He was expecting Shilah any minute with the truck. He said they'd wait at the fairgrounds and follow us back to town."

"Is he okay?"

"Yeah. Seems to be. I think he's more pissed about his bike than anything else."

"I feel responsible."

Honon glances at me and shakes his head.

"If you have any flaw, it'd be that one; your overinflated sense of responsibility."

I shoot him a dirty look.

"I'm sorry, was there a compliment in there somewhere? I think I missed it."

He flashes me those damn dimples and picks up my hand, pressing his lips to the pulse in my wrist, which is already speeding up.

"Sure is. You've gotta listen better."

"There's nothing wrong with my—"

Honon's ringtone interrupts me.

"Mind answering that for me? Looks like it's Lisa."

God, I hope nothing is wrong.

I grab his phone from the console and put it on speaker.

"Lisa?"

"Honon there?"

"I'm listening," he confirms.

"The boy's fine. He's napping and I ducked into the bathroom. We had a chat—"

"He was talking to you?" I interrupt her.

"Took some doing. Got him talking about his sister first, then the club, and then he suddenly asked if you were a good person."

"Who, me?" I ask.

"No, Honon. Said when he was helping Brick in the garage, he saw you outside talking to someone who's not a good man."

I glance at Honon who looks confused.

"When was this?" he wants to know.

"The day Emme was shot at. Friday?" Lisa supplies.

"Who could he have seen you talking to?" I ask.

"Hang on one sec," Honon says, slowing down the Jeep. "Emme, roll down your window and stick your arm out? The guys are waiting up ahead. They'll pull in behind us."

Once we pass the fairgrounds, Honon speeds up again.

"Who was I talking to? Fuck!" he suddenly bursts out, slamming the heel of his hand on the steering wheel. "The DPD group. I was supposed to run them through a drill at the range. Lisa, I've gotta go, I've gotta get hold of Luna."

I end the call and am about to dial Luna for him when a bang reverberates inside the vehicle. It's immediately followed by a loud slapping sound.

"What the hell is that?"

———

*Honon*

"Goddammit."

I lift my foot off the gas as I try to keep the Jeep from swaying all over the fucking road.

"It's a blowout," I tell Emme. "I'm gonna pull off the road here."

There's all kinds of traffic on this road and not a lot of room on the shoulder, so I turn onto a dirt road that leads to an old barn.

I've barely rolled to a stop when a black pickup stops right behind me.

"What the hell?"

Emme swings her head around.

"Who is that?"

I'm already reaching for the gun behind my back, because that truck does not belong to the club, and my tire didn't just blow out.

"Get down, Emme, all the way down. And stay down, no matter what happens."

I watch him get out of the truck, hoodie tucked low over his head, a rifle in his hands which he has aimed at me. I swear it's the fucking guy who almost rear-ended me earlier this morning, and I'm starting to think he's probably the same idiot who ran Paco off the road.

The only difference is, I now know he's not just some punk-ass kid. I also know neither Emme or I are getting out of this alive unless I stop him first.

Suddenly he ducks behind the Jeep and I take my chance, slipping out of the Jeep and immediately dropping to the ground. I don't hesitate, the moment I catch sight of his boots moving on the passenger's side of the Jeep, I aim for his ankles.

He screams and I see him land on his knees. Then I scramble to my feet and rush around to the other side, just in time to see the passenger door fly open, hitting him squarely in the head.

Emme jumps out right after, dives for the rifle in his limp hand, and aims it right at his head.

Fucking stubborn woman.

"Partying without us?"

Behind her Shilah and Paco come jogging up.

"Whoa, is that Conley?"

# CHAPTER
# TWENTY-SIX

*Emme*

I breathe a sigh of relief when we pull up outside Mercy Hospital a few hours later than anticipated.

"I'm going to run this over to the office." Luna holds up the thumb-drive I gave her. "Hopefully, it'll provide some answers to figure out this mess. I'll be in touch."

"Thanks, Luna," I tell her before getting out of the SUV. "I was getting a little nervous back there."

She glances over her shoulder at me and grins.

"From what I hear, you held your own again. First a toothbrush and now a car door. I've gotta say, you're creative with your weaponry."

Honon, who is standing in the open door beside me, grunts and motions for me to get out. As soon as Luna pulls away, he tucks me under his arm and marches me inside.

I'm guessing he's still ticked I didn't stay down.

The situation had been a little tense since state police patrolling the highway noticed the vehicles and decided to investigate. That resulted in a standoff with us held at gunpoint while the local sheriff's department and EMTs were called in. I guess it's not every day they come across an injured off-duty law enforcement officer and a bunch of bikers and are asked to believe the cop is the bad guy. Especially since said cop had come to and was telling them otherwise.

Honon was put in the back of a cruiser while Paco, Shilah, and I were handcuffed while trying to explain what went down.

Luckily, Honon had already called Luna before the state police cruiser appeared and she and Barnes showed up before the ambulance could take off with Conley. Barnes went with the ambulance while Luna had to throw her weight around to get the local sheriff—who wasn't too pleased the feds were sidelining him on his own turf—to release us.

Paco and Shilah stayed behind to replace the tire on the Jeep, while Luna drove us back to town.

"I'm so sorry we took so long," I tell Lisa when we walk into the room.

Malco is sitting up in bed, eating what looks like Jell-O. His spoon freezes halfway to his mouth when he catches sight of Honon coming in behind me. His face flushes a bright red.

"It's over, kiddo," Honon announces, walking up to the bed. "They caught the bad guy. You saw me talking to him, didn't you?"

Malco nods.

"Right, and you didn't know if you could trust me."

Another nod.

"I should get going," Lisa decides. "Before you know it the kids'll be back from school."

"When does summer break start?" Honon wants to know.

"Thursday is the last day of school. Half day. By noon the noise level in the clubhouse will be off the charts," she complains.

Honon chuckles, "You love it and you know it."

She ignores him and walks up to Malco.

"You're safe now, boy. Your little sister's safe. You got people who have your back, no matter what. Time to start talking."

I get a lump in my throat when I watch the gruff woman bend over and brush a kiss to his forehead. With a wave over her shoulder for us, she walks out of the room.

"Am I going to jail?"

My head snaps around to the bed.

"What?" Honon is the first to respond.

"Why would you think that?" I ask.

He glances at me from under his lashes before focusing his eyes on Honon.

"I hit him. He was yelling at my mom and hurting her. Mom told me I had to stay in my room, but I could hear her screaming, so I grabbed my baseball bat and opened the door."

Goosebumps break out over my entire body. That poor kid.

Moving the bedside table out of the way, I perch myself on the edge of the bed and take his right hand in mine.

"Mom was on the floor, she had blood on her face, and he was sitting on her, squeezing her throat. I hit him with the bat as hard as I could and he fell over."

It's like a dam breaking, the flow of words coming faster and faster as he purges what he's been holding on to all this time.

"Mom told me to take the baby and run. I didn't want to, but then Athena started crying and Mom said I had to get her safe like she told me to. He wasn't moving and I thought I killed him. I was scared so I grabbed the baby and the letter Mom told me to give you, and ran."

"You did the right thing, Malco," Honon tells him, patting the boy's leg.

I can't trust myself to speak, having a hard enough time holding on to my tears as I watch Malco's run down his face.

"I didn't wanna leave her," he sobs.

"I know, kiddo," Honon rumbles in a soothing voice. "But you had to take care of your sister because she's too small to take care of herself. Your mom told you to bring her to Emme at the restaurant?"

Malco nods.

"But it was dark and there were no lights on, and I was worried about my mom so I wrapped Athena tight in the blanket and put her in the box with the letter. Then I went back."

Then his eyes come to me. "I knew you would find her. Mom said."

I'm pretty sure I don't deserve his blind trust in me, but I'm so glad it was me who was scheduled to come in early that morning.

"So, you went back?" Honon prompts.

He nods. "I wanted to help her; she was hurt bad. But when I got there it was just Mom on the floor, she wasn't breathing. I thought he was gone but then he came out of the bathroom wearing a white suit, and I ran. He came after me. I didn't know what to do but I couldn't go back to the restaurant."

"So you went to hide at the fire station. That was very smart of you," I tell him.

"Hey, Malco," Honon draws his attention. "Who was the man?"

"Mom's old boyfriend. I saw him sneaking in a few times in the middle of the night when I was supposed to be sleeping, but that was a long time ago, even before the baby came. I didn't tell Mom and I think he stopped coming, but he was there that night, hurting her."

The married man she'd been seeing.

"And then I saw him again, talking to you," he tells Honon in a shaky voice. "I thought maybe he'd come looking for me and was afraid you'd told him where I was, so I snuck out and ran."

His tears start flowing in earnest and I can see a shiver running through his body. Maybe he's remembering what happened after.

I lean in and cup his face in my hands, forcing him to look at me.

"Listen to me. You're not in any kind of trouble. I'm proud of you for being such an awesome big brother but I want you to know, from here on in, you don't have to worry about being safe anymore. I will be making sure you are."

I glance at Honon.

"*We* will," he amends.

———

*Honon*

Joe Benedetti looks like shit.

He's sitting at the conference table in the FBI office when Emme and I walk in, flanked by Special Agent in Charge, Damian Gomez, and Keith Blackfoot, former detective but now a consultant for the Durango PD. Also at the table are Agents Barnes and Greene, and Ouray.

Luna just showed us in.

"Have a seat," she directs.

Lisa and Brick had shown up at the hospital with the baby this morning, with Luna in tow. I'd called her yesterday to pass on what Malco told us but hadn't heard back since. She asked us to step into the hallway, mentioned they'd made some progress, and invited us to the briefing. Brick and Lisa had offered to stay with Malco, so we followed her here.

"Let me start by saying that first thing this morning we executed warrants for the arrests of both Donald J. Hines and Benjamin Conley," Luna starts. "We recovered evidence from the thumb-drive Emme retrieved from the safety deposit box yesterday. It contained pictures, voice recordings, and some documents showing Hines used The Pink Petal club as a front to run a high-stakes prostitution scheme. We still have a lot of loose ends to tie up, but it's clear he targeted Johns who had a lot to lose, either financially, by way of reputation, or both. He would organize all-inclusive retreats—like the one he returned from right after Rhea was murdered—at luxury private estates somewhere in Central America he would rent and invite some of those individuals to. They'd pay a set amount for a weekend or week of unlimited partying with a variety of young women Hines would fly out. The real bill was served after, when Hines would blackmail them with photos and video footage from the cameras he'd rigged the entire house with."

"Holy shit," Emme blurts out beside me. "Let me guess, his son was involved in the scheme?"

"David Hines *and* his intended," Jasper Green elaborates. "It looks like he and Mandy managed and recruited for Daddy Dearest. Like Luna said, we'll need more time to build the case, but at this point we have both father and son on those charges and more will be added, I'm sure."

"What about Cher's murder?" Emme asks.

"That would be one of those potential added charges," Luna suggests. "But we still have Conley to look at."

"Clearly, he's the one who killed Rhea, but you think he has something to do with the other one?"

I can't really see what his motive would be to kill the other woman.

"Since analyzing the evidence and David Hines started talking yesterday, yes," SAC Gomez takes over. "One of the things we picked up in the search at the club was a file of pictures. One of which was of Conley engaged in a sexual act with Rhea. So, we know Hines senior probably had his hooks in him. Also, there's Mandy Lewis's death, which we suspect may be murder as well. When David found out she was gone, he was quickly willing to point the finger at Conley, who happened to be her overnight guard. We're waiting for autopsy results to confirm foul play but we're pretty sure those will indicate some kind of substance in her blood."

"And that will be on me," Joe Benedetti says. "You asked for my most trusted officers and I picked him."

"He would've been at the top of the list of my picks too," Keith Blackstone contributes. "He's been on the force for almost fifteen years, is good at what he does, and is studying for his detective badge. Anyone would've put him on that list."

Joe rubs a hand over his face.

"Christ, the guy got married a few years back, just had a baby last year."

"He must've started seeing Rhea around the time his wife was pregnant," Emme suggests.

"I have a working theory based on what we know," Luna says. "I think Conley made Rhea promises he couldn't keep, and either he cut her loose, or she him, when she got pregnant. It fits the timeline. What if she stumbled on this scheme of Hines's when she was put to work in the office. Think about it, why would a guy like Hines offer her alternative employment in the office after she was too pregnant to dance? It's clear Hines knew of the affair, and probably thought it might be handy to have someone in law enforcement in his pocket. So, he kept Rhea around as a silent threat. It would've made Conley sweat, knowing it could ruin his marriage and end his career."

"Why kill Rhea, though?" I wonder out loud.

"I think she may have approached Conley when she started uncovering some of the stuff that was going on at the club, not realizing he was already well aware. Maybe he warned Hines about it, who then told him to take care of her. Or, it's possible Conley himself wanted to get rid of the threat she posed. The fact he had what was probably a Tyvek suit with him indicates he wasn't planning on leaving any trace of himself behind. He didn't count on the boy seeing him."

"So, he had to eliminate Malco, and you think he was the one to kill Cher and Mandy as well?" Emme questions.

"According to David Hines he was, and was also the one who sent David after you."

"Why me?"

"Maybe Rhea mentioned you to him before you two stopped talking," I suggest.

"We can spend all day guessing at what happened, but we have some pressing issues we need to deal with," SAC Gomez interjects. "Given what we already know, this case is going to have a lot of bones rattling in a lot of closets. Even the arrest of father and son Hines will be enough to make a good number of prominent Durango citizens very, very nervous. Add to that the fact one of Durango's finest turns out to be a murderer, and you have absolute mayhem. Mostly so for Benedetti, who will be the focus of attention from all sides. So…"

He gets to his feet and starts pacing.

"We're pulling in extra agents to help with the ongoing investigation and I'm arranging to have both David and Don Hines moved to a federal facility. Blackmail and extortion are federal crimes and given the influence of some of their victims, it's best to move them out of this county. That gives Benedetti his hands free to deal with Conley and his department. But…"

He glances at everyone around the table.

"That'll only work if we keep a lid on things. If the press gets hold of this, they'll be up our asses for answers, but we're used to it. Can't comment on an ongoing case is the only answer they'll get. If media approaches anyone else, you say nothing at all. Also—and I'm sure I don't have to explain this, but—no talking about the case with friends, family, or anyone else. And make sure anyone who needs to know this does."

"Goes without saying," Ouray comments for the first time. "And if I may, I'd strongly suggest keeping the fact Emme has custody of those kids under wraps. I'd also not repeat outside of this room the suggestion Conley, a murderer, could possibly be the father of that baby girl. That boy is already scarred for life, no reason to burden his sister as well."

"Won't leave the room," Gomez agrees.

Benedetti looks at Emme and smiles for the first time.

"They won't hear it from me, and should Conley bring up the possibility of paternity at any time, I promise I'll strongly disavow him of going there."

Emme leans her head against my shoulder when we walk out of there not long after.

When we get to the Jeep—which has a shiny new tire—I kiss her lightly on the lips before opening her door for her.

"Relieved?" I ask her when I get behind the wheel.

"Yeah. I'm going to have to get used to not looking over my shoulder anymore. But it's also kinda scary, because going forward means dealing with my new reality."

"You'll handle it, like you handle everything else life throws at you." I dart her a glance. "You'll also not be alone. You've got the entire club at your back."

I was going to say, you've got me, but figured I should probably give her a chance to breathe.

She puts her head back and closes her eyes.

Then she mutters, "I love your president."

Excuse me?

Maybe I should've made my intentions clear after all.

"The man's taken, Wildcat. But hey, you've got me."

# CHAPTER
# TWENTY-SEVEN

*Emme*

"Malco, there's something I need to talk to you about."

The boy looks up at me as he shuffles back from the bathroom to his bed.

He's been up and about for a few days now, and is being released this afternoon. Lisa sent over some clean clothes for him yesterday, and I've already helped him dress. It was a little awkward—we ended up leaving his injured arm inside the shirt with the unused sleeved tucked in as well—but Lisa had the foresight to send over a pair of sweats that he could pull up with one hand. He's ready to go, but we're just waiting for the paperwork.

Malco was lucky and didn't develop any infections, but he's facing at least two more surgeries in the next year. One to remove the screws and plate they placed to keep the bones properly aligned while healing, and at least one more by the plastic surgeon, provided all continues to go well in his recovery. A lot of that will depend on how he does with his physical therapy.

I wait for him to climb back on his bed before I continue.

"We haven't talked about this yet but I need to make funeral arrangements for your mom, and I would really like your help."

Last time Trunk was here for a visit, I stepped out with him to ask advice on how to broach the subject. He suggested being straightforward, not to try and soften the topic by talking in euphemisms because it would only be confusing. He also advised me to involve Malco, let him make some simple choices, like favorite flowers, favorite music, things of that nature, so his mom's funeral can be meaningful to him. He felt perhaps that might go toward alleviating some of his feelings of guilt around not looking after his mother. Giving him the sense of looking after her now.

"Funeral?"

"Yes, honey."

"I thought she would already be gone."

I reach for his free hand and take it loosely in mine.

"Well, her spirit is gone, but her body is still at the funeral home. It can't stay there forever, so it's our job to come up with a way to say goodbye to her body that we think she would have wanted. The best way to do that is to think about things she loved."

"Us," he suggests immediately. "Mom loved Athena and me best. She always said."

Oh good Lord, this is going to be hard.

Already I'm regretting following Trunk's recommendation to have this conversation one-on-one. He felt it might be easier for Malco to respond if there weren't more eyes on him and he may be right, but I would've welcomed Honon's steady presence right now. He left an hour or so ago to run some errands and is waiting for my call we're ready to be picked up.

It's taken me this long to work up the courage to broach the subject.

I take a deep breath in and forge ahead.

"Absolutely. You and your sister are the two most important people. So maybe there is a favorite picture of your mom and you guys we can put on your mom's coffin so everyone can see how much she loved you. We could make extra copies so you and Athena have the same picture to remind you how special she was."

He listens intently, nodding. There have been a few tears these past couple of days, but he's never invited any talk about his mother and I've been hesitant to bring her up. I guess Trunk was right; giving him a purpose, a direction for his grief, may be good for him.

"Then I was thinking she probably liked flowers, right?"

He nods again, this time with a little more enthusiasm.

"She likes the purple flowers on the bush in our front yard. She says they smell nice."

I'm scrambling to think of purple flowers that grow on a bush, my botanic knowledge is limited.

"You mean lilacs? With lots of little blooms on one stem?"

"Yes, those ones. They have them in white too, but Mom says the purple ones smell better."

It doesn't escape my notice he's reverted back to the present tense when talking about Rhea, but I guess that's to be expected.

"Lilacs it is." I hope they're still in bloom. "And what about music? Is there a song she liked we could play at her funeral?"

He seems to be thinking hard on that one.

"This Little Light of Mine," he finally decides on. "I remember her singing that when I was little and now when Athena is a little fussy. I think Athena would like that."

"Perfect. Sounds like we have a good plan."

The only thing I have to figure out now is whether she'd want to be buried or cremated, but that's not something I feel comfortable bringing up.

Malco lies back against the pillows and closes his eyes. Poor kid, I wish I could hug him, but that may be more about my need to give comfort than his to receive it.

Funny, I'd probably have been the last one to think I had a maternal bone in my body and here I am, feeling all my maternal instincts roar to life.

A few moments later, the door opens and a nurse walks in with Malco's discharge papers.

Fifteen minutes after that, I'm standing outside with Malco in a wheelchair when Honon pulls up in the Jeep.

He grins at the boy as he walks up.

"You ready to ditch this joint?"

He gets the tiniest little smile in return. "Yeah."

Honon helps him into the back seat on the driver's side.

"It's easier on this side to put on your seat belt so it doesn't put pressure on your arm," he explains. "You can probably do it yourself."

He patiently waits for Malco to figure it out on his own where I would've probably jumped in and done it for him. Another reason to appreciate the man and his natural way with children. Not a quality I would have attributed to him before, but then, there are a lot of things about Honon that have surprised me in recent weeks.

I turn to look at him when he gets behind the wheel and shoot him a grateful smile. I get dimples in return and a quick kiss he presses on my knuckles before putting the Jeep in gear with my hand under his.

"Where are we going?" Malco asks from the back seat.

"Back to the clubhouse," Honon responds. "For now. At least until Emme's house is ready."

"Are you gonna live there too?" he wants to know.

I'd be lying if I said I hadn't been thinking about it. Part of me screams yes, but another side of me—the more conservative side, if there is such a thing—is worried it's way too fast. I mean, we've forged this connection under pretty strenuous circumstances. We haven't even been on a single date. Then again, during that same short period, he's been able to do what no other man has managed; earn not only my trust but my heart as well.

Over the past weeks, I've gone from mild interest to falling in love.

Honon gives my hand a squeeze before he answers Malco.

"Let's play that by ear, kiddo. First concern is getting you guys settled in."

Of course, he'd be the sensible one.

For just a second, I'm a little disappointed by his evasive answer, but then I remind myself he's not going anywhere. I have no reason to doubt him when he says things like; you've got me. Besides, there's no need to rush things, there's plenty of decisions needing more immediate attention.

"Emme?" Malco says a few moments later.

"Yeah, honey."

"Can we give Mom a gravestone so I can take Athena to see her when she's older?"

Oh man, my heart is getting a workout.

I swallow a few times until I'm confident my voice is steady.

"You bet we can, sweetheart."

––––––

*Honon*

"Done."

I glance over at Paco, who sidles up next to me at the bar.

"Yeah?"

He nods as he motions to one of the prospects to hand him a beer.

"Got the door in and have the alarm wired up again. Tse wants to head back tomorrow morning to wipe down the grout, but other than that, she's ready to go."

I'm pretty sure Emme's gonna have a shit fit initially, but she's going to just have to take it. She'll have her hands full with the kids, and ongoing renovations with associated dust and fumes in a house with a baby doesn't seem like a smart move.

When I heard Malco would be in the hospital for at least a week, I figured it could be done. I got the guys to help and used the excuse of having to run errands or meeting someone up at the range so I could put in some time myself.

I'd hoped to be able to bring them straight home from the hospital but the new door didn't arrive until earlier this afternoon, and I wanted it all done. It worked out fine, because Lisa had planned a barbecue to celebrate both the beginning of summer for the kids as well as Malco's home-coming. Emme didn't even question going back to the club-house, but then again, she thought her house was still a mess.

I clap Paco on the shoulder.

"Appreciate you, brother."

"Nothing compared to the hundred plus hours you probably spent building my house. Which reminds me," he adds. "Mel says as soon as the boy feels up to it, he should come over to hang out with Mason. We've added a few platforms in trees close to the treehouse. They're connected with plank and rope bridges, it's pretty cool."

Mason is Mel and Paco's adopted son, and we built him a treehouse at the back of Paco's mountain property a few years back.

"I'll talk to Emme."

I realize how domesticated that sounds when Paco grins and punches me in the shoulder.

"Fuck, man. Got yourself an instant family."

I have to laugh at that.

"Following in y'all's footsteps. Other than Kaga—who got married when he was barely out of fucking diapers—every one of you started out with a ready-made family."

It's true, most of us may have gotten a late start, but it looks like we made up for time lost by not only hooking a good woman, but getting at least one bonus kid included.

"True, guess he taught us well."

His eyes wander to Nosh, who is sitting on the porch with Ouray, supervising him while he grills. Every so often his old eyes drift to a couple of the boys playing basketball on the half-court we built next to the garage. I was surprised to find him up when we got here a little while ago. He even seemed more lucid, actually recognizing me.

The boy in me hoped he miraculously recovered, but the man knows he's living on borrowed time. Still, it's good to see glimpses of the old Nosh enjoying the family he built.

"Hey."

Emme walks up on my other side and puts her hand on my arm before lifting up on her toes to offer me her lips. An offer I'm not about to refuse.

"Did you see Malco?"

I glance over her head to find the boy on the couch, surrounded by a bunch of kids, wildly gesturing with his free arm.

"Somebody's coming out of his shell," I observe.

"One of the older kids asked him about the mountain lion. Apparently, his memory is back because he's giving them a detailed account." She fakes a shiver. "More than I ever wanted to know, but I guess it's a good thing he's talking about it."

I chuckle. "It's gonna dramatically increase his standing in the clubhouse. And I wanna bet one day he'll wear those battle scars like badges of honor."

Emme shakes her head.

"Some things I'll never understand about men."

"Are you kidding?" Paco pipes up. "We're open books compared to you ladies."

"Exactly. We're easy," Ouray adds, sliding behind the bar to grab refreshments. "Beer?"

"Please, and that's what you'd like us to believe, you're the less complicated sex, but I beg to differ," Emme returns.

"Tell him, sister," Lisa chirps as she hands the baby to Emme. "She needs a diaper change."

"I've got it."

I slide off the stool and pluck Athena from Emme's arms.

"Hey, leaving your girl to fend for herself?" Ouray taunts me.

"Against you guys? Yup," I toss over my shoulder as I head toward the back. "My *woman* can handle you both blindfolded with her hands tied behind her back."

Ignoring their heckling, I walk into Ouray's office and put the baby down on the couch.

"You're not complicated, are you? All you want is to play and eat and sleep, maybe the occasional clean diaper."

"Gah-bah!"

Lightning fast she rolls on her stomach the moment I peel the diaper off her, and pulls her legs up under her.

"Hey, Peanut. Where are you off to?"

I pick her up and try to lay her on her back.

"Stay still, would ya? You're gonna give me a bad rap."

To keep her distracted long enough to give her butt a wipe and slap on a clean diaper, I blow raspberries against her belly. Her little hands grab at my hair and she squeals loudly.

When I lift my head, I notice Nosh standing on the other side of the coffee table, watching us.

*"You're good with her,"* he signs. *"Always were good with the little ones. Momma swore you'd make a great dad one day. Glad I'll get to tell her she was right."*

I'm dumbfounded as I watch him shuffle out the door. What the hell just happened?

"A-gah," Athena gurgles and I return my attention to her.

I'm met with an—almost—toothless smile. In the bottom front a proud little white ridge is visible poking from her gums.

Snatching her up in my arms, I rush into the clubhouse, calling out, "Emme! The baby cut her first tooth!"

"Let me see?" Malco jumps up from the couch and hurries over. "I can't see, Athena, open your mouth."

"Blow raspberries, see if you can get her to smile."

The kid makes goofy faces at his sister, coaxing her to open her mouth, when I glance up to see Emme walking toward us, a lopsided grin on her face. Behind her I catch sight of Ouray and Paco, shaking their heads and undoubtedly laughing at my expense, but I don't give a fuck. Let them laugh. I'm feeling pretty damn good right now.

"I see it! Hey, guys, my baby sister got a tooth!" the boy yells excitedly, heading back to the couch.

Pumped up at his newfound fame, I'd guess. I'm sure there'll be hard times for him yet, but it's good to get a peek at his real personality.

"You know…" Emme purrs, wrapping her arms around my waist, the baby squirming between us. "You being all kinds of cute with the kids is a real turn-on."

My body responds in predictable ways.

"Watch it, I'm holding a baby," I warn her. "Not fair for you to tempt me when I can't pick you up and toss you over my shoulder."

"Hmmm," she teases with a grin. "But since Lisa already suggested she keep the baby and Malco at her place as long as we're here, I'm thinking maybe you'll get your chance tonight."

I look over her head toward the bar.

"Hey, Ouray! When's the meat gonna be done?"

# CHAPTER
# TWENTY-EIGHT

*Emme*

"So fucking gorgeous."

His gaze travels lazily down my body as he sits on his knees in bed beside me.

I'm only too aware of its many flaws, but there isn't a part of me Honon misses as his hand follows the path of his eyes. His intense scrutiny and thorough exploration make me feel as gorgeous as he says I am.

Who am I to argue? Beauty is all I see when I touch him. Every imperfection just a facet of a uniquely magnificent whole. Why question when he sees the same in me?

His finger dips in my belly button, turning even that part of me into an erogenous zone. I inadvertently roll my hips.

"Uh-uh...no moving. You said you were up to the challenge."

I almost jumped him the moment we walked into the bedroom last night, our lovemaking wild and frenzied. Since finding Malco on that ledge a week ago, simple touches and brief kisses have been enough to sustain me, but that didn't last long with the promise of privacy.

This morning, Honon woke me up when he pulled the sheet down my body excruciatingly slowly. At the first touch of his hand on my skin, I reached for him but he stopped me, laughing. Accusing me of having no patience, which I vehemently disagreed with. So, he bet me I wouldn't be able to keep still if he touched me. Of course I had to prove him wrong.

It's barely been a minute and already I'm failing, dammit.

"I am," I bluff, jerking my chin up.

He thinks it's funny, grinning as he lightly brushes the rough pad of his finger around my belly button. It feels like a light electrical current skims over my skin and I have to grind my teeth in an effort not to move.

"Besides, you never said how long."

"Another five minutes. Maybe I should put a wager on that challenge," he drawls, slowly torturing me with his touch. "Sexual favors come to mind first, but you can't keep your hands off me anyway."

This time I growl. He raises an eyebrow at me.

"You didn't say anything about being quiet," I snap.

In response, he stretches out beside me, propped up on an elbow, and softly blows air at my pebbled nipples as he slides his hand down my belly.

Closing my eyes, I try to concentrate on breathing when his fingertips brush the patch of curls I haven't trimmed in too long. He doesn't seem to care about that either. When he slips his hand between my legs and I suddenly feel the rough, wet brush of his tongue against my nipple, I moan deeply, my muscles starting to tremble under the dual assault.

His ministrations are unhurried and I'm having a hard time sticking to my guns as time ticks by.

"Honon…" I plead.

"Two minutes left, Wildcat," he mumbles against my skin.

It's on my lips to tell him he's evil but when he drags a finger between my lips and with target precision finds my clit, I'm rendered speechless. Already hypersensitized, a few strokes and circles with the pad of a finger is enough to have me hurdling toward climax.

"Hold that thought," he whispers, abruptly withdrawing his touch.

The next moment he's between my legs, the blunt head of his cock pressing inside. His excruciatingly slow progress has me grab hold of his fine ass, dig my fingers into his glutes, and force him deep inside.

I'm done holding still.

———

"Do you have a moment?"

Luna stops us on our way out the door.

Honon suggested we head over to my place to do an inventory of what yet has to be done to get it ready. My guesstimate is two weeks, if I spend all my time working and Honon helps out when he can. It would also give me time to figure out what I'm going to do for income in a way that is feasible, considering I have the care of a six-month old and her older brother.

It was all a bit too much to really process when we were still in survival mode, but now the threat is gone, reality is taking a foothold and scaring the crap out of me.

I did a quick calculation and with what is currently in

my bank accounts, I can probably last about six months if I'm really careful. I could tap into my 401k to last a little longer but that comes with fees and penalties, plus I'll get dinged come tax time as well.

I haven't even considered funeral costs and hospital bills in this. I suppose I could use some of Rhea's cash still in Ouray's safe to finance her funeral, but I want to keep the rest to make sure the kids have everything they need.

There's so much to figure out yet; what to do with her trailer home, how to handle the contents, I need a new vehicle so I can safely transport the kids. There's health and dental insurance for the kids. Figuring out school for Malco. There's so much, it's absolutely overwhelming me all of a sudden.

"Are you coming?"

I look up to see Honon halfway to the back of the clubhouse. Luna's already disappeared.

"Yeah, of course."

I shake my head to clear it of the almost paralyzing mental list and follow him to the office. Ouray is sitting behind his desk and Luna is perched on its edge. Honon takes a seat on the couch and pulls me down beside him.

"Quick update," she starts. "I was able to interview Conley, as well as Don Hines and his son over the past few days. Senior is still not answering questions on the advice of his lawyer, but I was able to play Conley and David Hines off each other. Both were pointing a finger at the other for the murders, which worked well for me. I was able to get enough information from each to piece a workable timeline together. I'm inclined to believe Hines, looking at evidence and timeline, his story makes the most sense."

"I'm hoping I'll eventually get a confession out of Conley, but that might never happen."

"You never know," Ouray inserts. "The guy's life as it was is already over. Whatever he had to lose is gone; career, family, I'm sure friends."

"We'll see," his wife responds, before continuing. "Phone records show Rhea contacted Conley about a month before she was killed. Presumably to ask his help or advice on the blackmail scheme she'd stumbled onto. Conley probably knew it was a matter of time before she'd discover he had fallen victim to that scheme as well. He probably told her to back off and he'd take care of it. There was one more call from her to his number a week before she died. He probably realized she wasn't going to give up."

"He killed her," I volunteer.

"Yes, and he might've gotten away with it. In fact, I suspect he would've done more than just kill *her*, if the boy hadn't knocked him out, giving him and the baby a chance to escape."

The implication of what she says sends chills down my spine.

"Conley probably knew who you were and although your altercation with David Hines may have been a coincidence, I don't think Officer Conley showing up the day after Rhea's murder to follow up on it was. I think he recognized your name and hoped to find the boy with you. According to David Hines, they collaborated to find the USB-key with information Rhea had mentioned to Conley. Hines admitted he talked to Cher, and shot at you—although he claims that was only to scare you—but that's all he is willing to confess to."

"It's likely Conley committed all three murders and I

might never have come to that conclusion if he hadn't overplayed his hand killing Mandy. I think by then he was desperately trying to plug holes, and with David already in jail and then Mandy in custody, it was only a matter of time before his name would come up."

I shake my head.

"Unreal. This whole thing is so unreal. I mean, I know things happen and people do bad shit, but especially Conley, he's a family man. Someone who spent most of his adult life upholding the law. How does it get to this? All because he cheated on his wife?"

"That was only his first in a series of really bad choices," Ouray comments. "It's how some good people turn bad, with a single step in the wrong direction."

———

*Honon*

"Is that Tse's truck?" Emme asks as I turn up her drive.

"I asked him to pop by. He's got experience and I figured he might be able to make some suggestions to expedite the work."

Her annoyed grunt doesn't bode well for the surprise we have in store. So damn independent.

"You've got some 'splaining to do," Tse calls out Emme in a surprisingly accurate impersonation of Desi Arnaz when we exit the Jeep.

"What are you talking about?" she returns.

"I had a peek in your garage and discovered you've been holding out on me. I recognized the work right away. I can't believe you never told me you own Twisted Rod Designs. I thought I was your friend, your best friend's husband. What gives?"

I bulge my eyes at Tse, he could've waited a damn minute before springing that on her.

I hadn't even thought of her stuff in the garage when I let the guys in to get at the building supplies. When Tse discovered the panel she's working on, he knew right away what he was looking at. I told him it was Emme's secret to share, not mine, but I didn't think he'd jump on her right off the bat.

As expected, rather than acknowledge, Emme goes on the defensive.

"What were you doing snooping around my garage anyway? How did you even get in? Because I know I keep it locked, and my stuff is well covered under a tarp."

He's not only going to blow the surprise, but has already reduced the chance of it being a happy one.

"Why don't you guys argue about it later, okay? Let's get inside and get this done."

Emme notices the sliding door right away when she walks in.

"How…?"

"Paco. He couldn't get a new slider, so ordered a new door and installed it yesterday," I explain.

"I would've been capable of doing it. I did it the first time."

She jerks that stubborn little chin an inch higher. I'm starting to understand she's not just stubborn, she's worried about being underestimated.

"I know that, hell, anyone who looks at the quality work you've already done to this place can tell you know what you're doing." I put my hands on her shoulders and give her a little shake. "Gotta let go of that chip on your shoulder, Emme. Some people lend a hand for the simple reason they want to. Nothing else. Not because they think you're not up to it, or have some kind of misogynistic attitude, or hidden agenda. Retract your claws."

She looks at Tse and then back at me, narrowing her eyes.

"Why do I get the feeling there's more?"

Not waiting for an answer, she turns on her heel and heads straight for the main bedroom. A muffled curse filters down the hall.

"She's hard to please," Tse concludes incorrectly.

"No, you're wrong about that. The opposite is true, when she trusts the motivation behind it. It's trust that doesn't come easy for her."

"Are you telling me she trusts you?" Tse questions with a sardonic eyebrow raised.

"Yeah, she does, but I had to work for it. Well worth it, though," I add with a grin before following Emme down the hall.

I find her sitting on the brand-new toilet, her elbows on her knees and her face in her hands. Walking up to her, I put my hand on the back of her head. The fact she doesn't shake me off is encouraging, so I crouch down in front of her.

"I was gonna do this in stages, because I can't afford doing it all at once," she mumbles behind her hands. "I have so many added expenses coming my way, more than I know what to do with, so I'd planned to abandon this project. I was gonna use the main bathroom, make room for the kids in the spare bedrooms, and at least give those a fresh coat of paint. I can't afford all this, and I haven't even figured out how I'm gonna—"

"Hush," I shush her, pulling her hands away from her face. "Here's the thing. I'm gonna live here with you. Maybe not right away—that's up to you—but I will eventually, so I'm buying in. This seemed like a good way to make a start with that."

"But new floors in the bedroom, as well as paint on the walls, all the tiling and hardware and…everything else, that's a lot of money."

"Good thing I have plenty of it," I confess, brushing the pads of my thumbs under her eyes. "I've never once in my life had to pay for room and board, Emme. That was covered by the club or the U.S. Army. Seriously, business has been good for the Arrow's Edge MC over the years, and I've been socking a fair amount of money away. I haven't had anything to spend it on until now. Best reason to spend money is to invest in the future, yeah?"

"But what if—"

I shake my head.

"Not gonna worry about what-ifs. In fact, I'm not worried at all. I spent half my life figuring out what I wanted. Now I have the promise of that in my hand, I'm not gonna mess it up or let it go. This is something I intend to spend the next half of my life enjoying the fuck out of."

She shoots me a watery smile and looks around, scrutinizing the space.

"I see you pilfered the files on my computer," she points out, noting the tiles, vanity, and hardware she picked.

"Sure did," I admit without shame. "I guessed at the kids' rooms, but we can always change the color if I picked wrong."

"You did the other rooms too?"

"It was a combined effort. Paco, Tse, and I work well together."

My knees creak when I get to my feet. Emme gets up too and starts out of the bathroom. I follow her to the rooms on the other end of the hall, where I picked what the paint can said is a sage green for Malco, and a pale violet for the baby. Other than the walls, the baseboards, and the flooring, the rooms are empty.

"I love it," Emme murmurs, running her fingers over the soft color on Athena's walls. "These colors are perfect."

"I left the rooms empty until we figure out what to haul over from their old bedrooms."

She swivels around, putting her hands on my chest and lifting her face up.

"Thank you. I thought about getting mad, but the truth is, it's such a relief. Now I can start tackling all the other things that need to get sorted."

I cover one of her hands with mine and curl my fingers around it.

"*We,*" I correct her. "We'll tackle them. You and me. Team Wildcat."

She snickers at that.

"Love you, Emmeline Lightfoot. For so many fucking reasons I don't even know where to start, but if you'll have me, I'll spend our future spelling them out for you."

I pull her hand to my mouth and kiss her pulse. She watches my every move with a shimmer in her eyes.

"I'll have you, Honon. I'd be nuts not to, seeing as you're not only a pro with the kids, you look hella sexy doing it. You also happen to be the one person in the world I trust blindly, when others have only gotten an edge of my trust, if any. Always had a hard time imagining a future with anyone, until you."

She lifts up on her toes and brushes my lips.

"Oh, I almost forgot; I love you back, Hank Wicks."

This time I initiate the kiss and it's not just a brush.

We're interrupted when heavy footsteps come down the hallway and Tse pokes his head in the room. The look on his face has my heart drop.

"We've gotta go."

# CHAPTER
# TWENTY-NINE

*Emme*

Nosh died peacefully in his sleep this morning.

A heavy pall has hung over the clubhouse these past two days since Tse came to tell us he wasn't doing well.

A doctor I hadn't met before was already there when we arrived, administering some medication that would allow Nosh—who'd become agitated and had been in some discomfort—to rest more easily.

Even though he was no longer aware of his surroundings, the entire club gathered over the course of the day. The clubhouse was full of Nosh's family, taking turns to sit with him as he slowly left this life. while the others would gather around the bar, recalling memories and sharing anecdotes.

I helped out as much as I could in the kitchen and with the kids, keeping a sharp eye on Malco, who seemed understandably subdued. Too much death for a child his age. He may not have known Nosh, but it was clear, even to him, how much the old man meant to the club. He paid particular attention to Honon, who'd been uncharacteristically quiet and withdrawn.

He didn't come to bed either night. I don't think many of the others slept much either. A sign of respect to the Arrow's Edge MC founding father, he was never alone as the whole club watched over him as he took his final journey. We all followed the stretcher out the door a little while ago when the people from Hook Funeral Home came to collect him. All the men got on their bikes to escort the white van into town.

I cried. I didn't really know the man, never had a chance to interact with him, but I know what he meant to Honon. I've been deeply moved by the display of loyalty and love in this family.

It's why I'm sitting at a picnic table outside the clubhouse, dialing a number I haven't forgotten, despite the many years since I've used it.

"Lightfoot residence," I hear my mother's cultured voice answer.

She sounds a little older, a light wobble in her voice I swear wasn't there before. Suddenly I don't know what to say.

"Hello?"

"It's Emmeline," I finally manage.

My parents hated it when I used Emme in school and college, and always persisted calling me by my given name.

"Emmeline? Is this some kind of joke?"

"No joke, Mom. It's me."

A heavy silence falls and I can virtually hear the wheels turning.

She doesn't disappoint.

"Did you get yourself in trouble? Because if you're calling—"

"Mom," I cut her off. "Of the handful of times I've called to check in over the years, how often have I asked for help or money or anything?"

She stays silent.

"Exactly," I continue. "Zero times. Trust me, I know better than to ask. The reason for my call—like the other times when I've called you—is to check in to see how you and Dad are doing."

"We're fine," she responds after a pause. "Your father spends his retirement golfing and I'm staying busy with the gardening club and am planning a Rhine cruise for the fall. We're both healthy."

It's like she's reciting a grocery list, without any emotion or inflection. Nothing much has changed.

"That's nice, Mom. Glad Dad's enjoying his retirement and you're planning something fun."

I hear her clear her throat.

"And how about you? Are you still working at that gentlemen's club? And living in that trailer park?"

*Jesus*, has it been that long since I spoke to her? Although I now recall that conversation had been a particularly bad one. I remember thinking at the time it would be the last time I subjected myself to that. It was always me calling after all, neither of them has ever called me in the past twenty years. When my parents said they washed their hands of me, they weren't kidding.

Over the years, I've never hidden what I did or where I lived. I wasn't ashamed to work any kind of job as long as it kept a roof over my head and, hopefully, allowed me some savings for my dream. That included living in a trailer and dancing in a club. I've been honest with my parents, even though I knew they'd disapprove. Not so much as an act of rebellion but because lying to them would demean me, and I wasn't willing to sell my soul for their approval.

"No, I haven't for a few years. I bought a house a few years back, an older place, but nice. On the mountain. I've been working on it bit by bit, updating and upgrading."

"*You* bought it?"

Her disbelief is evident.

"Yeah, Mom, by myself. I worked hard, saved everything I could, and bought it when I had enough put together."

"Well…good for you then, I guess."

Her sour comment isn't exactly a pat on the back, not that I was looking for it, and it's also not unexpected. I think my mother convinced herself one day I'd come crawling back with my tail between my legs and would conform to her life vision for me. This does not fit that picture.

I'd contemplated telling her about Malco and Athena, and also about Honon. Maybe I would've had this conversation gone down differently. I may still tell her the next time I feel the need to check in but not today.

I hear the rumble of motorcycles and see the first of the bikes turn up the drive to the compound.

"I have to go, Mom. Again, I'm glad you and Dad are doing well and I hope you enjoy your trip to Europe. Give my best to Dad."

I hang up before she has a chance to respond.

My eyes focus on Honon as he rolls his bike to a stop and pulls it on the kickstand before getting off. He's putting his helmet in the seat when I walk up.

"Hey."

I step in and slide my arm around his waist. He bends

down and kisses the top of my head as I walk with him into the clubhouse.

Honon steers me toward the bar where he asks Ouray for two beers and hands me one. He looks like shit, and I wish there was something I could do to make it better, but I know I can't.

"Honon?"

We turn around simultaneously to find Malco standing behind us.

"Yeah, Malco."

"I'm sorry he died."

*Good grief*, this kid.

Honon manages a smile for him.

"So am I, kiddo. He took care of me when I was a kid. Looks like we both lost someone special, huh?"

He nods with a serious expression on his face.

"Is he getting a funeral too?"

"He will," Honon answers. "Not sure when though. Why?"

"Well…I was thinking, Mom needs a funeral too, maybe we can do them together. That way they won't be alone."

Honon's face freezes, then suddenly he's brushing past the boy and stalks to the back. Everyone in the clubhouse is suddenly silent.

"Did I do something wrong?" Malco asks, near tears.

I shake my head, unable to speak.

"No, buddy," Ouray answers, leaning over the bar. "You didn't do anything wrong. I think Honon liked your idea. I kinda like it too. Why don't you go back with the kids and let me see what we can do, okay?"

As soon as Malco heads back to the group of boys in the living area, he turns to me.

"You're up, Emme. Go see to him."

I find him in the bedroom, sitting on the far edge of the bed, his back turned to me and his shoulders hunched. Kicking off my shoes, I climb up and make my way over, wrapping my arms around him as I press myself against his back.

"Fucking kid is still trying to look after his mother," he says in a hoarse voice.

"I know," I mumble against his shirt.

His body starts shaking in my arms and I hold on for dear life.

————

*Honon*

Never thought I'd be sitting at a funeral trying to keep from laughing.

When we made the arrangements, we decided to keep the funeral to family only which, in our case, still means the damn room at the cemetery is packed. Yuma suggested it after Ouray mentioned Malco's request.

*"Pretty sure Nosh would've been fine with it. He never cared much about being the center of attention."*

So here we are, a room full of bikers and their families, two caskets up front—one with a large arrangement of mostly lilacs and a framed picture, the other with Nosh's vest and helmet—listening to a recording of a children's choir sing "This Little Light of Mine."

I glance over at Yuma beside me. He has his head ducked down and his shoulders are shaking suspiciously.

"Seems appropriate for the old man," he mutters under his breath.

I hear a snicker from the other side of him. When I lean over, I see Lissie with a tissue pressed against her face. I almost lose it, but then I turn to my other side where Emme has an unusually quiet Athena on her lap and is just pulling Malco into her side. The urge to laugh disappears instantly.

"Let me take her," I whisper, moving the baby to my lap.

She shoots me a grateful smile before wrapping her other arm around the boy as well.

The service is short. Nosh wouldn't have wanted the fuss, and I'm sure Rhea would've wanted what's best for her kids, which is not to have it drag on too long.

We managed to get a plot for Rhea, only two rows down from where Nosh is about to be buried next to Momma.

Emme has taken the kids in the Jeep and is on her way back to the clubhouse, along with the others. It's just the brothers here now, to give our last respects.

Ouray pulls a bottle of bourbon from his pocket, and Kaga reaches into his, coming up with a stack of plastic shot glasses. The shots are passed around and Ouray sets the last one on the casket, suspended over the grave.

No words are spoken as we all raise a last glass with the old man and toss the shots back, I do two, taking care of Yuma's as well.

Then Ouray nods at the funeral director who presses a button on the mechanism and slowly lowers Nosh to lie once more beside the love of his life.

———

"Wanna take a ride with me, kiddo?"

Malco turns away from the window and looks at me.

He's been sitting there, staring outside, since I got back to the clubhouse. Emme is just putting the baby down in our bedroom, where it's quiet since the clubhouse is crowded and the volume high. Which made the solitary boy stand out even more.

"On your bike?"

I chuckle. "Nice try, kid. You need to be tall enough to reach the pegs and have two healthy arms first. Won't be long though." I ruffle his hair. "But...do you think you'd be able to manage one side of the handlebars of the ATV if I hold the other side?"

The boy's head is about to fall off his body, he's nodding it so hard. But that smile...fuck me, that smile hits me square in the gut.

"Okay, you go tell Emme. She's in the bedroom trying to get your sister to take a nap, so don't go barging in. I'll grab us some food to take."

I duck into the kitchen where Lisa and Shilah are piling sandwiches on large trays.

"Can I steal some of those?"

"Can you not wait like everyone else?" Lisa fires back, banging an empty tray on the counter.

"It's for Malco, I'm taking him for some fresh air."

It's blackmail and I know it. So does Lisa, who glares at me from under her eyebrows.

Then she marches into the pantry, comes out with a cooler bag, and starts packing sandwiches, a couple of apples, and a few drinks.

"Unless you're here to be useful, get out of my kitchen," she orders, handing me the bag. "And be gentle with that boy," she calls after me.

Malco is already waiting by the door, Emme by his side.

"What's this about you letting him drive the ATV?"

"More like help me steer," I answer her dryly. "I'll be holding on the handlebars and him. Don't worry."

"Okay, but we've just spent a week in the hospital and I really don't want to go back there."

I hook her behind the neck and kiss her softly on the lips.

"I'll be careful."

"Can we go now?"

Five minutes later, we're heading up the trail, Malco in front, proud as punch as we ride past a few older kids coming out of the dorm. I let go of one side of the handlebars, curling that arm around his waist.

"Your turn, kiddo."

He grabs on and as we race up the mountain, I hear him laugh out loud for the first time. Beautiful.

Right there I make a silent vow to make sure this kid has plenty to laugh at from now on.

# CHAPTER
# THIRTY

*Emme*

"I don't feel right getting rid of her stuff."

Honon puts his hand on my neck.

"Then don't."

I'm staring at the contents of Rhea's kitchen cabinets piled up on the counter.

It wasn't easy walking into a place where something so horrific happened, but better me than a nine-year-old boy who lived through it. I don't know what I was expecting but thank God the place had been cleaned. Not sure who arranged for that but I'm guessing it was probably Honon, or he would never have let me walk inside.

The idea had been to simply pack up the contents of the children's rooms, move it to my place, and set their new bedrooms up the same way before we physically move there. Athena may not know the difference but her big brother will.

Honon suggested if we were going to pack up the kids' stuff anyway, we might as well empty the rest of the home as well. Get it done all at once. A good idea, but harder than I thought. I've only just started in the kitchen and am agonizing over every little thing. I feel like I'm making decisions that aren't really mine to make.

"What then? Leave it for whoever buys this place?"

"No, but we've got a few other options. We can rent a storage unit, see if there's room in one of the buildings at the compound, or we get one of those moving containers dropped off on the far side of the garage, where it's not in your face all the time. Then we pack up everything that isn't broken or perishable, slap a label on it, and put it away until Malco is ready and willing to make decisions with you."

The weight of responsibility I felt heavy on my shoulders immediately lifts.

"Container at the house, that way we can take our sweet time," I suggest.

"Done. There's a place on the south side of town, I'll call Tse, maybe he and Wapi can swing by there on their way back and see if there's a way they can drop one off today."

The guys already loaded up Malco's room and are hauling it over to my place. Sophia came along as well and is sorting through and packing up Rhea's bedroom.

I was glad she offered, because I'm still a bit raw after the funerals a few days ago. I guess that's what happens when you finally allow yourself to actually feel. It's as wonderful as it can be painful.

Decision made, I feel a lot better and by the time Tse and Wapi come back, the kitchen is all packed up and Honon is helping me work my way through the living room.

"Emme, before I forget," Tse says, walking through with Athena's crib mattress. "I have a meeting with a new client next Tuesday, looking to open up her living space. She wants a new spiral staircase to the second level to be a prominent feature, so I told her to check out your website. She likes your work and wants to talk to you."

Excitement has butterflies flapping around my stomach, but immediately reality sets in. The kids will be with me and I planned to spend some time with them to help them settle into their new life with me. I haven't even figured out what to do for childcare when I do start working again. I'm not sure I can have that set up before next Tuesday and I don't want to ask Lisa, she's already done so much I don't even know how to begin to thank her for that.

"I'd love to, but—"

"No buts," Honon jumps in. "I've got the kids covered."

How the hell does he always seem to know what I'm thinking?

"Get out of my head," I snap at him, but he just grins.

"Great." Tse claps his hands together. "I'll let my client know."

It's like I'm not even in the room, bunch of bulldozers making decisions for me. It doesn't keep me from wearing a smile the rest of the day though.

When we roll up to my place with the last load, I let the guys haul the big stuff to the container Tse managed to get delivered this afternoon, while Sophia and I grab the few boxes of things I want in the house.

"By the way," she mentions when we walk inside. "I've started putting a few things aside I've kept from the twins I know you're going to need for the baby in the very near future. I'll bring them over when you're settled in. I don't think you'll need to buy much more than perhaps diapers. Lissie and Jamie each have a girl as well, so I'm sure they'll have things they can lend you."

She sets the box on the kitchen island and starts pulling

out the baby stuff I found in the kitchen. Bottles, silicone spoons and cups, a couple of bibs.

I freeze, focused on the items on my counter and realizing how out of place they look.

"You've gotta take advantage of the fact these little ones wouldn't know or care if something is new or secondhand. Plus, I like to tell myself it's better for the environment when I keep things from being discarded as waste."

Sophia swings around and catches me staring.

"What?"

I shake my head. "I don't know anything about babies. Not the first thing. What can she eat? What if she wakes up screaming in the middle of the night? How warm should I dress her to go outside? She's so little, what if I do something wrong and mess her up for life?"

"Welcome to motherhood," she proclaims.

"You're not helping," I spit out, trying hard not to let the feeling of panic overtake me.

"Oh, but I am," she disagrees calmly, grabbing me by the shoulders. "Because what you're feeling is what every first-time mom feels. The responsibility is crazy scary when you think about it too hard, so stop doing that. You know what she needs today and you'll figure out what to do tomorrow. That's why they don't grow up overnight, it gives the parents time to figure out the next part."

She gives me a little shake before letting me go. Then she opens my cupboard and starts rearranging things so the baby stuff fits on the bottom shelf.

"This is stuff you don't wanna be looking for when you need it," she explains. "Oh, and by the way, I've already ordered you a copy of *The Wonder Weeks*, a book every new parent should have in my humble opinion. It'll help you better understand why she might be waking up in the middle of the night screaming. Also, I'm a phone call away, and Lisa, who is like…the mother of all mothers, is a few minutes up the road. You'll be fine."

The casual vote of confidence helps and I focus my attention on the box of pictures and knickknacks I collected from the trailer. There were a few snapshots, a dental appointment card for Malco, and a school certificate of achievement Rhea had hanging in her kitchen. I dig up the magnets I took as well and arrange everything on my own fridge.

By the time the guys walk in, I'm hanging the last of the pictures.

"I like it," Honon volunteers, walking up behind me.

I created a grouping of the mishmash of sizes and frames on the bare wall over the kitchen table. Rhea and Malco lying in the snow, red-cheeked and grinning at the camera. Rhea with newborn Athena. Malco holding the tiny baby in his arms.

In the center, I placed a gorgeous shot of the three of them. It must've been the most recent one she had framed, because it appears to be early spring. It looks like a selfie with Athena in one of those baby carriers on Rhea's chest and Malco beside her, almost coming up to her chin. They appear to be standing next to the Animas River with the mountains behind them.

They look so happy.

"Every morning when they have their breakfast, this is how I want them to remember their mother."

———

*Honon*

"What is this?"

Emme stops on the porch of the clubhouse, carrying the baby in the car seat we recovered from Rhea's vehicle. She eyes the brand-new Jeep Grand Cherokee I picked up earlier with suspicion.

"Investment in the future," I explain as I round the SUV and open the back, which already holds a couple of boxes, and toss in our bags. "Only wheels I ever owned are the two on my bike. The club has a couple of vehicles I've used when needed, but I figured it was time to get one of my own."

I take the car seat from her hand and walk around to open the back door. I click the seat into the base I'd already installed. Malco is already climbing in on the other side but when I notice Emme still standing on the porch, I head back to her.

"You don't like it?"

"It's pretty big."

"Gonna need the room if I'm driving around a family. Maybe a dog."

Her eyes flit to me.

"A dog?"

"Kids need a dog."

"Hmm. Is that so?"

I shrug my shoulders. "Seems to be part of the family package."

"I never had a dog," she admits, her eyes getting a dreamy look.

"Then I'd say it's high time."

I grab her hand and pull her toward the Jeep, opening the door for her.

"Cool car," Malco pipes up from the back seat. "Is this ours?"

"Sure is, kiddo."

"Sweet."

Once Emme is buckled in, she immediately glances back to check on the kids while I climb behind the wheel.

"Those boxes yours?" she asks in a low voice, when I start the engine.

"Yup. Aside from my bike, which I'll pick up later, that's the extent of my earthly belongings."

When she stays silent, I glance over and pick up her hand.

"That okay with you?"

She turns those large blue eyes to me and nods.

"But we can't mess this up, Honon."

I bring her hand to my mouth and press a kiss on her knuckles.

"We won't. We've got this."

It takes Malco no time at all to notice the collage Emme made on the wall when we walk into the house. The kid had been excited to discover how close we are to the compound.

"You put up our pictures."

"Emme did," I tell him. "This is your house now, so I guess she figured those pictures belong here too."

Emme took a cranky Athena to the bedroom to change her diaper, but catches my last words when she walks back in.

"They absolutely belong. I put one on your nightstand as well, why don't I give you a tour?"

While she's off with the kids, I quickly haul the rest of the stuff out of the Jeep. Then I grab a beer and walk out on the back deck, which is going to need a better barrier to make it safe for Athena.

I grab a seat on the steps and take in the view. Living here is not going to be a hardship whatsoever. Behind me I hear the sliding door open as Emme steps outside, her own drink in hand.

"Thought I'd join you," she announces as she sits down beside me. "I'm going to have to invest in some proper outdoor furniture."

"We," I correct her, bumping her shoulder.

She lifts her face to smile at me.

"Give me time, I'll get used to it."

Then she snuggles into my side and rests her head on my shoulder.

"Where are the kids?"

"Athena was tired so I put her in her crib. She was out in two seconds. And Malco wanted to putz around in his room."

"I'm sure it's a lot to take in for the kid," I observe.

"Yeah."

"I'm thinking of getting an ATV. Trails up and down this mountain. When the boy's arm is better, I can teach him to drive."

"Slow your roll, Papa. The kid's got two feet that work pretty well, maybe take him for hikes first. An SUV, a dog, an ATV, next thing I know you'll come home with a pony for Athena."

I grin, already imagining the little girl she'll be soon enough, sitting on the back of a cute pony.

"Now, why didn't I think of that?" I tease her, earning me a sharp pointy elbow in the ribs.

From the corner of my eyes, I see movement and snap my head around.

An imposing bull elk steps out of the trees, staying at the edge of the property as he appears to look at us.

"Beautiful, isn't he?" Emme whispers.

I nod.

"He visits every so often to remind me to breathe," she explains.

With a last look in our direction, the animal unhurriedly disappears back into the trees.

Then I turn to Emme and bend down to kiss her.

"I'll do everything to give those kids a good life, Emme."

She lifts a hand to my cheek.

"I think you mean *we*."

# EPILOGUE

*Emme*

"What's with those two?"

Honon turns his head to where I caught sight of Wapi and Lindsey, Mel's daughter, standing off to the side, appearing to be in the middle of an argument. Wapi has his arms crossed over his chest while Lindsey wildly gestures with her hands and clearly has a lot to say.

"Water and oil," Honon comments. "Been like that since they first met years ago. Guess Wapi's years away haven't changed a thing. They hate each other's guts."

I observe them closely for a few moments.

"It may look that way, but don't think so," I muse as I watch the younger woman stalk off, Wapi's eyes following her all the way inside.

"Meat's done!" Paco yells.

We're at Mel and Paco's place for an end of summer cookout. I'm learning every excuse is a good one for the Arrow's Edge MC to throw a barbecue. It has to be number six or seven this summer.

This should be the last one before the kids go back to school on Monday.

"Da-da!"

Athena, who's been playing on a blanket at our feet, pulls herself up on Honon's pant leg. Standing is her latest party trick and dada is her new favorite word. It's cute to see how the man beams when she happens to say it with him around. I don't want to point out she says dada to me when I get her up from her nap, or at her toys when she's playing by herself. Let him think it's reserved for him. Eventually, it will be.

The past almost two and a half months have been interesting, to say the least. Mostly good, but we've also hit a few bumps, especially when Malco started acting out. That took us both by surprise since he'd been such a good kid before. We didn't quite know how to handle the change, and it was Sophia who suggested getting Trunk involved.

He sees Trunk once a week now. He comes to our house and the two of them usually take the ATV out—yes, I caved—and find a rock to sit on and talk. At first it was hard for me not to know everything Malco confided, but Honon said to trust Trunk would tell us if there was anything we needed to know.

Trust. It can still be a bit of an issue for me, but I'm learning. I even added my real name and a snapshot Honon took of me working on a piece to the Twisted Rod website.

Living with Honon and two kids—and since last month a hairy beast named Grunt—has been a steep learning curve. I think for Honon as well, but he is better at taking things in stride with a quick smile and a flash of those dimples. I'm the one who gets in her head and needs time to process things, but the beautiful thing is, I get time to do that.

For all the little ripples, the truth is, I can't imagine my life without him or the kids. It was a lot at once, my heart adjusting to fit them all inside almost painful at times, but now it feels good—full—and is more flexible than ever before.

"Emme!"

I twist my neck to see Malco jump down from one of the suspended bridges running between the trees. It's on my lips to tell him to be careful—after all, he only just got his cast removed a couple of weeks ago—but he's already running toward us with a big grin on his face.

"I'm hungry," he announces.

"You're always hungry," Honon points out.

Malco slaps his hands on his stomach. "I'm a growing boy."

"You'd eat the nuts off a rhino."

Malco grins at him. "No, but I could eat the ass end out of a billy goat."

"All right, you guys," I stop their newfound game which—as I know from experience—can only go further downhill from here.

I get up, detach Athena from Honon's jeans, and set her on my hip, "Let's get some food."

The boy is off like a shot, but Honon falls into step beside me. He hooks an arm around my neck and bends down to press a kiss to the side of my head.

"Happy?"

"Yeah," I admit with a smile.

"Good. Hang on to that feeling, because I have a lead on a Shetland po—"

I elbow him sharply in the ribs.

"No. Over my dead body." I shoot him the most menacing look I can muster. "I mean it."

"I know you do, Wildcat," he mutters, a spark of humor in his eyes and a mischievous grin on his lips.

*Damn that man.*

# ALSO BY FREYA BARKER

**High Mountain Trackers:**

HIGH MEADOW

HIGH STAKES

HIGH GROUND

HIGH IMPACT

**Arrow's Edge MC Series:**

EDGE OF REASON

EDGE OF DARKNESS

EDGE OF TOMORROW

EDGE OF FEAR

EDGE OF REALITY

EDGE OF TRUST

**PASS Series:**

HIT & RUN

LIFE & LIMB

LOCK & LOAD

LOST & FOUND

**On Call Series:**

BURNING FOR AUTUMN

COVERING OLLIE

TRACKING TAHLULA

ABSOLVING BLUE

REVEALING ANNIE

DISSECTING MEREDITH

WATCHING TRIN

IGNITING VIC

**Rock Point Series:**

KEEPING 6

CABIN 12

HWY 550

10-CODE

**Northern Lights Collection:**

A CHANGE OF TIDE

A CHANGE OF VIEW

A CHANGE OF PACE

**SnapShot Series:**

SHUTTER SPEED

FREEZE FRAME

IDEAL IMAGE

**Portland, ME, Series:**

FROM DUST

CRUEL WATER

THROUGH FIRE

STILL AIR

LuLLaY (a Christmas novella)

**Cedar Tree Series:**

SLIM TO NONE

HUNDRED TO ONE

AGAINST ME

CLEAN LINES

UPPER HAND

LIKE ARROWS

HEAD START

**Standalones:**

WHEN HOPE ENDS

VICTIM OF CIRCUMSTANCE

BONUS KISSES

SECONDS

# ABOUT THE AUTHOR

USA Today bestselling author Freya Barker loves writing about ordinary people with extraordinary stories.

Driven to make her books about 'real' people; she creates characters who are perhaps less than perfect, each struggling to find their own slice of happy, but just as deserving of romance, thrills and chills in their lives.

Recipient of the ReadFREE.ly 2019 Best Book We've Read All Year Award for "Covering Ollie, the 2015 RomCon "Reader's Choice" Award for Best First Book, "Slim To None", Finalist for the 2017 Kindle Book Award with "From Dust", and Finalist for the 2020 Kindle Book Award with "When Hope Ends", Freya spins story after story with an endless supply of bruised and dented characters, vying for attention!

www.freyabarker.com

Ingram Content Group UK Ltd.
Milton Keynes UK
UKHW020746280323
419292UK00015B/555